Blood, Ash, and Bone

Books by Tina Whittle

The Dangerous Edge of Things
Darker Than Any Shadow
Blood, Ash, and Bone

Blood, Ash, and Bone

A Tai Randolph Mystery

Tina Whittle

Poisoned Pen Press

Copyright © 2013 by Tina Whittle

First Edition 2013

10 9 8 7 6 5 4 3 2 1

Library of Congress Catalog Card Number: 2012910492

ISBN: 9781464200939   Hardcover
       9781464200953   Trade Paperback

Poisoned Pen Press
6962 E. First Ave., Ste. 103
Scottsdale, AZ 85251
www.poisonedpenpress.com
info@poisonedpenpress.com

Printed in the United States of America

To Archie and Dinah Floyd—my dear parents—who taught me the power of stories and the importance of family, and who always believed in me, and encouraged me, and loved me.

Acknowledgments

A writer is only as good as her support group, and mine is made of stars and magic and solid gold. Special thanks to three ladies of The Mojito Literary Society—Annie Hodgsett, Susan Newman, and Laura Valeri—who are always there to share their brilliance, encouragement, and enthusiasm. Fine writers in their own right, they are fine friends and human beings too. In addition, Amber Grey lent her editorial expertise and wholehearted encouragement. I owe them all buckets of gratitude.

Big thanks go to historian and fellow mystery writer Jon Bryant, who not only helped me piece together this tangled web, he also provided the essential story seed from which the book blossomed. In addition, he lent wordsmithing, research acumen, and general rah-rah support to this effort. Special thanks also to Pam Wynne, who shared her expertise on private detective licensure in the state of Georgia, and Girish Patel, who finally learned to hold on to his peanuts.

My loved ones deserve special kudos, especially my parents, Dinah and Archie; my parents-in-law Yvonne and Gene; my sibling and siblings-in-law, Tim and Lisa, and Patty and Rich, plus my wonderful niece and nephews. And, as always, much gratitude to the fine folks at Poisoned Pen Press—especially Barbara Peters, Annette Rogers, Jessica Tribble, Rob Rosenwald, and Suzan Baroni— a writer's dream team that serves both writers and writing in exemplary fashion. Sincere thanks to the creative team of Nan Beams and the folks who lent their artistic genius to the design and cover art. I am also grateful to my fellow PPPers—the Posse—for their unwavering good cheer, good advice, and good faith.

And, last but never least, XXX and OOO to James and Kaley, who have my love forever and always.

Chapter One

"Do it again," he said.

I wiped the sweat from my forehead, my legs shaking. "You're kidding."

"No. One more time."

"I need to catch my breath first."

He moved behind me and ran his hands down my ribcage to the small of my back, palms flat. He toed my feet two inches further apart and tucked my hips under. "One more time. Shoulders down and back. Keep your feet in neutral."

"Can't we move to side kicks?"

"Round kicks."

"Trey—"

"One more set." He stood in front of me again and picked up the kick pad. "Keep it sequential."

I gave up arguing and straightened my stance. We were alone in the workout room at the gym, his students long gone. No way to avoid his laser-lock attention. I took a deep breath and kicked one more time, channeling my annoyance into the kinetic chain of hip-thigh-ankle. To my astonishment, I landed it solid, all of my mass and energy converging in a blow so powerful it knocked Trey back a step.

I bounced on the balls of my feet. "I nailed that!"

He didn't smile, but I did detect satisfaction. He always looked so boyish with a light sheen of sweat on his forehead, his black hair mussed.

"Good," he said. "Stop bouncing and finish the set."

I squared my stance as he put the kick pad up again, then launched into the rest of the set, seven more kicks in rapid succession. I felt like a ninja, a starburst, a firework.

I put my hands up in a fighting stance. "Come on, let's do some sparring."

"Not today."

"You always say that."

He lowered the kick pad and started untying his handwraps, eyes down. I put my hands on my hips.

"Trey. We have talked about this."

He shook his head, not looking at me. "Nonetheless."

I exhaled in frustration. Three months previously, in the heat of a bitter argument, I'd grabbed his elbow. He'd popped my hand away in a Krav block, a move as precise and sudden as a lightning strike. It hadn't hurt, but it had certainly shocked me. Trey too. He'd stared at his hands like they were alien things, then babbled an apology. And we hadn't sparred since.

"You still spar with your other students. Why not with me?"

He didn't deny the charge. His attention remained on the neat unwrapping of his hands.

I spread my arms. "Look at me. Shin pads, combat vest, gloves. I've even got the damn helmet on. You're wearing a t-shirt and shorts, barefoot. I'm a virtual tank, and you're one layer from naked."

He folded his arms. I recognized the gesture—full defensive lockdown—which meant I wasn't breaching his perimeter with a direct assault.

I took two steps closer, and he narrowed his eyes, wary. Up close, he smelled like sweat and bleached cotton. I imagined how he would taste, the salt sting of bare skin against my tongue. I ran one hand up his arm, from wrist to elbow. He didn't visibly react, but I knew he craved the flare and ignition as much as I did, even if he was better at tamping it down.

I smiled at him. "We'll take it slow and easy. No sudden moves, no surprises."

He didn't budge. I ran one finger down his breastbone, feeling the contraction of each muscle group—first the pecs, then the diaphragm, then the abs. He could make a fortress of his body. He was doing it right in front of me.

He cocked his head. "Tai? What are you doing?"

"Sparring."

"This isn't sparring."

"You sure?"

And then I yanked my knee up within a millimeter of his groin. He froze, and his eyes went ice-blue. And he got calm. Real calm.

I looked him in the eye. "So drop the over-protective routine, Mr. Seaver. I may not be the Krav Maga god that you are, but I can take care of myself."

He hadn't moved an inch. "A point."

I smiled bigger. "In my favor, I do believe."

And then it happened. Suddenly the world somersaulted—wheel and whirl and reel and tumble—and the back of my skull slammed against the cushioned mat with a thud. I blinked into the overhead fluorescents, flat on my back.

Trey stood at my feet, hands on hips, not even breathing hard. He hadn't broken eye contact, had simply grabbed my arm and flipped me, one deft move. Close the space, vault, and release.

I squinted up at him. "Omigod, you have to teach me that."

"What?"

"Seriously. That was awesome." I held a hand in his direction and wiggled my fingers. "Help me up."

His natural courtesy almost undid him, and he reached out to take my hand. Fortunately for him, his training kicked in a millisecond later, and he snatched his hand back before I could grab it.

I grinned. "You almost fell for that."

He glared at me, then headed for the door.

I rolled to my stomach. "And where do you think you're going, you sneaky son of a bitch?"

He bent over his gym bag and pulled out his gloves. "To get my sparring gear."

◇◇◇

He drove me back to Kessesaw the back route, avoiding the interstate, keeping the Ferrari right at the speed limit. I watched Atlanta roll by—steel buildings, gray asphalt, tree branches going bare against a gunmetal November sky. My thighs ached from the last thirty minutes on the mat. He'd been relentless. I hadn't been able to get in a single punch, much less block anything he'd sent my way, and he'd sent the whirlwind.

"That still wasn't sparring," I complained. "That was you teaching me a lesson. You dominated the entire time."

He turned onto my street, a narrow lane lined with small mom-and-pop stores, of which my gun shop was one. It was fully dark now, the streetlights blooming in the night like nocturnal flowers.

"Of course I dominated. I'm better than you are."

"That doesn't mean you need to go full bad ass on me! What happened to the zone of proximal learning, keeping students at the edge of their comfort zone?"

He didn't reply.

"You used to give me a fighting chance. But tonight, all you did was knock me down over and over. I didn't learn a damn thing."

He glanced my way. "Nothing at all?"

"No."

"Are you sure?"

I frowned. "Is this you being cryptic? Because I'm not used to that."

He considered his words. "Every offensive move exposes a defensive vulnerability. The same move that put you close enough to attack also put you too close to defend."

"I couldn't have defended against a front takedown, you haven't taught me how!"

"I keep explaining this, and you keep ignoring me—don't move outside your training. Stick with what you can execute cleanly and effectively."

"Or get knocked on your ass, I get it."

"I'm serious."

"I am too."

"I'm more serious."

I laughed at that. "Don't worry, coach, the next time I seduce you, it will be for real. And then you'll be in big trouble."

His mouth quirked in an almost-smile, and I felt a current of relief. Usually I spent post-workout nights at his place in Buckhead, but since I had an appointment with my friendly neighborhood ATF agent in the morning—plus a ton of packing for the upcoming Civil War Expo—we were headed to Kennesaw instead, to drop me off at my apartment above Dexter's Guns and More.

"Seduction is not the point," he said.

"What is the point?"

"That one move won't save you, not in a real fight. Not with a trained fighter."

"If you'd been a real bad guy, I would have shot you."

"If I'd been a real bad guy, you wouldn't have gotten that chance."

Another valid point. But I wasn't interested in the finer instruction of hand to hand combat. At least not the combat part.

I leaned over and nuzzled behind his ear. "Come up with me. The place is chaos, but no more pizza on the floor, I promise."

He raised one dubious eyebrow.

"Come on, I told you I'd replace the shoes."

"You can't afford Prada."

"I was thinking Hushpuppies."

But he wasn't listening anymore. His eyes were focused instead on the front door of my shop. "Tai? Who is that?"

I squinted through the windshield and saw the figure waiting next to the motorcycle, his features shadowed in the amber haze of the streetlight, blurred by cigarette smoke. My stomach clenched.

"Aw hell, not tonight."

Trey pulled the Ferrari into the space next to the door, the tires crunching gravel. His shoulders dropped, and his expression went cool and questioning. His ex-cop face.

The man beside the bike was tall and husky, with broad shoulders under a road-fatigued leather jacket, his Levis and black leather boots dusty from the road. His salt-and-pepper beard was neatly trimmed, but the hair was a shoulder-length tangle of curls. He'd been riding without a helmet again, which meant he'd come through some state besides Georgia on his way into town. I couldn't see his eyes, but I knew they were blue. Not blue like Trey's, which were a crystalline sapphire blue. Blue like the edge of a thunderhead, a tumbling gray-blue.

I exhaled sharply. "That would be John, my ex. So you should probably stay in the car—"

Trey got out of the car. "Is he the one who left you for your roommate?"

"Yes, Trey, thank you for that succinct reminder." I snatched my workout bag from behind the seat. "Which is why I'd like to handle this myself, if you don't mind."

"I don't think—"

"He's harmless. Gritty on the surface, marshmallow underneath."

Trey ran his eyes down my face and across my mouth. I didn't complain; I was used to having my veracity verified on a regular basis. It wasn't even insulting anymore, just another quirk in a Smithsonian-worthy collection of quirks. But I was telling the truth, so I let Trey see it.

"You're doing it again," I said. "That over-protective thing."

"But—"

"Go home. I'll call you tomorrow."

He eyed my visitor, then nodded reluctantly. I kissed him goodbye, with perhaps a little more display than necessary.

Afterward, he put his mouth to my ear. "Tonight. Call me tonight."

"I will. Now go."

He climbed back into the Ferrari, eyes still on the guy standing at my door. He revved the engine and pulled a tight arc in the parking lot, kicking up gravel.

I went up to my visitor. I could hear the tick-tick-tick of the Harley engine cooling. So he hadn't been there long.

I stuffed my hands in my pockets. "John Wilde."

"Tai Randolph." He smiled, his eyes sparkling. "That's the kind of guy you're seeing now? Some uptown yuppie?"

I looked over my shoulder to see the taillights rip around the corner, the F430 coupe taking the turn at an almost ninety degree angle.

"Uptown, yes. Yuppie, no. Trust me on that one."

John laughed. He had a really good laugh, and it came from deep in his chest. His voice was still pure Alabama, slow and rich, like a deep river.

"A Ferrari." He shook his head. "Your taste in men certainly has changed."

"Not as much as you might think." I unlocked the door and bumped it open with my hip. "Come on in. Then you can explain why out of all the gun shops in the greater metro area, you ended up at mine."

Chapter Two

He plunked his helmet down on my counter. It had been almost two years since I'd seen him, but he'd changed little. A smattering more gray perhaps, and a new tattoo, an intricate piece of Celtic knot work winding around his left wrist. His body was a map of ink, a walking gallery.

He looked around the shop. The display cases were mostly empty—I'd stored the expensive firearms in the gun safe—but the shelves of bullets and shot cartridges made no bones about my profession. Neither did the wool kepis on the hat rack, or the Confederate belt buckles on the counter. There were boxes everywhere—some taped shut, some spilling Civil War collectible manuals, some still empty. In the corner, my failed experiment with rolling my own black powder charges leaked gritty soot all over spread-out newspaper.

"Nice place," John said. "Kind of a mess, though."

"I'm packing for the Southeastern Civil War Expo next week. This is my first time as a vendor, so I'm a little disorganized."

His face went solemn. "I sure was sorry to hear about your Uncle Dexter passing. He was good people. To lose him so quick after your mama…"

We stood a few seconds in awkward silence. John had left me three months after my mother's funeral. I waited for some anger to wash up, but felt only an edged curiosity.

"You want something to drink?" I said.

"Got a beer?"

I went upstairs and grabbed a Guinness for him, a Pellegrino for me. Back in the shop, I sat at the counter and sent the beer sliding his way. "So what brings you to the ATL?"

"Looking for you."

"Why?"

He popped the top off the beer with his thumb. "Been reading about you."

"And?"

"You're quite the celebrity. Got yourself mixed up in some murders. Handled yourself real well from what I read."

I remembered the article in the Atlanta paper. *Feisty if somewhat foolhardy*, the reporter had said of me. And then she'd slobbered love all over Trey. *The enigmatic and intriguing corporate security agent.* The cops hadn't been happy with either of us, however.

I took a cold sharp sip of Pellegrino. "You still haven't explained why you're here."

"You remember Hope?"

I tried to keep my expression neutral. Hope. My former roommate, former co-worker, former friend. Until she and John had run off together, of course, leaving me with a cracked heart and an avalanche of back rent.

"What's Hope got to do with anything?"

He pulled out a pack of Marlboros and held them my way. I shook my head firmly. He stuck one between his lips, dug a lighter from his jacket. "We got married last month."

"Congratulations."

"Not really. She left me a week ago, and she took something with her that's mine. I want it back."

"And you're talking to me because…?"

"Because you seem to know your way around a tricky situation."

"Meaning?"

"Meaning I need you to find an artifact for me."

"You know I charge a finder's fee."

"I expected as much."

"Ten percent of the appraised value upon delivery." I tipped my Pellegrino at him. "For you, though, let's call it fifteen percent."

He laughed. "Fair enough."

And then he pulled a checkbook from his pocket, snagged a pen from the counter. A few squiggles and flourishes, and he sent the check my way.

"That should cover things."

I stared at it. John didn't say anything. He let the numbers speak for themselves.

I dragged my eyes from the check. "Is this for real?"

"Real as rain."

I examined it closer, then shoved it back. "It's post-dated."

He shoved it my way again. "I don't have the money right this second. But I will soon, if you help me."

"You'd better start at the beginning."

And so he did.

"Hope and I run a pawn shop down in Jacksonville. We sell the usual stuff, TVs and guns and video games, but we do some antique trade too. One day we hit this estate sale. The woman running it was an out-of-towner—from Des Moines, I think—and she offered me this roll-top desk filled with papers, pen, books, old stuff. The price was cheap, and it was solid walnut, so I bought it." He smiled his gotcha smile. "Turns out, she hadn't even looked through the drawers. Because if she had, she'd have found it."

"Found what?"

"The Bible." He leaned forward, eyes blazing. "An 1859 Oxford King James. It was covered in burgundy-colored velvet, crushed and stained, but in good condition overall."

"And?"

John savored his words. "It belonged to General William Tecumseh Sherman. A gift from President Abraham Lincoln, signed and inscribed."

"Dated?"

John smiled wider. "December 21st 1864."

I tried to hide my excitement. I knew this story. I used to tell it every day during my days as a tour guide in Savannah, parking my herd of tourists in front of the Green-Meldrim House and explaining how, on that very soil one hundred and fifty years before, the mayor of Savannah surrendered his city to General Sherman, who had previously burned Atlanta to ash and then marched a swath of destruction to the sea. How Sherman had then offered the city of Savannah, along with some cotton and ammunition, as a Christmas present to the president.

"You found this Bible in the desk?"

"Hope did."

"And now she's run off with it?"

"Not just the Bible. Everything from the desk is gone—papers and pens and inks and books. She said she was taking it to an expert up here. But a friend of a friend called me and said they spotted her in Savannah."

I sat back in my chair, fiddling with the check. "So call the cops."

"I don't want the cops on this, I want you."

"Why me?"

"Because it's personal."

"Find her yourself then."

"I can't."

"Why not?"

"Because she's in Savannah. And I can't go back there."

"Why not?"

"You know why."

Suddenly things were starting to make a whole lot of sense. "Don't tell me you still owe Boone money?"

He sucked in a long drag on the cigarette. "Yeah."

"Then you shouldn't be in Georgia, much less Savannah, especially now that he's out of prison. He'll—"

"I know what he'll do. But I also know that if you find that Bible for me, I'll have more than enough money to pay him back, interest and all."

"How much are you in for?"

"Twenty grand."

I was stupefied. Beauregard Forrest Boone—gunrunner, moonshiner, smuggler, and former KKK Grand Dragon—was one of the most dangerous men in Chatham County. The second John stepped across the county line, Boone would find him. And John could very likely end up as crab snacks in one of the salt marshes.

I shook my head emphatically. "Forget it. No way I'm pissing off Boone for you."

"Boone always had a soft spot for you."

"Doesn't mean I can't piss him off."

John spread his hands. "Come on, Tai, there ain't nobody that can work that territory like you. And now that Hope's hooked up with Winston again—"

"Winston who runs the tour shop?"

"The same." John's mouth pursed. "Goddamn Hawaiian-shirt-wearing, Yankee son of a bitch."

I turned the bottle up and took a long swallow. What an incestuous little knot Hope was tying. Winston Cargill of the brightly flowered shirts had been my boss, and Hope's, when the two of us worked as tour guides. A former history professor, he'd ditched that career when he discovered that selling history was more profitable than teaching it.

I started connecting the dots. "You think she's hitting the Expo?"

"Of course she is! Every Civil War nut south of the Mason-Dixon line will be at the Expo. And I know how Hope thinks. She's looking to find one of those big-money, under-the-table collectors. And if she makes that sale, she can disappear, and there won't be any way in hell I can prove a thing against her."

He was right. And since he couldn't work the event, he needed someone who could. Someone already planning to be there for reasons that had nothing to do with Hope. Someone with connections and smarts in the Civil War trade. Someone exactly like me.

"What'd you do to her?"

"Nothing!"

I rolled my eyes. "Come on."

He picked at the beer label with his thumbnail. "She thinks I'm having an affair."

"Are you?"

"No. But I bet she is, probably with Winston. She could always wrap him around her little finger."

"So what if she is? I still haven't heard a good reason to help you."

He leaned across the counter. "It's a lot of money, Tai. My best guess? If that Bible goes to auction, it'll pull mid-to-high six figures minimum. But if it disappears into the underground…" He spread his hands. "Nothing. For nobody. And the world loses a piece of history to boot."

History, yes. Irreplaceable. But it was the money I couldn't stop thinking about. I'd redone the flooring, but my cabinets and display cases were in bad shape. The inventory needed expansion, especially in the long gun department, and Trey was making noises that the security system needed upgrading. My apartment was a bare-bones studio with a sofabed and a decrepit shower stall, and I owed Trey new shoes, Prada apparently.

But it was more complicated than money. This had been explained to me in painstaking detail by the Atlanta Police Department after my last foray into private detecting. The fact that I hadn't received any monetary compensation had been the only thing keeping me on the good side of the law.

I drummed my fingers on the counter. "This isn't an ordinary runner's job. There's a crime."

"Not if you find her before she sells it."

"John—"

"I'm willing to make a deal. If she'll give you the Bible to sell, I'll split the profits with her fifty-fifty. I won't press charges, and she and Winston can sail over the damn sunset for all I care."

I thought hard. The Expo was already on my agenda—how hard would a little extra relic hunting be? Plus, if I managed to track down the Bible, the Expo would provide an excellent opportunity to find a buyer, maybe even get some good publicity for the shop. On the other hand, this was John, a complication magnet.

"I need to think about it," I said.

He waved a hand at me. "Forget it. I should have known you'd still have hurt feelings. After what I did—"

"Oh please, I got over that a long time ago."

I said it too emphatically, and John caught it. He didn't challenge me, though, simply stood and sent the check my way one more time. "Whatever. You think about it and let me know tomorrow. I'll be at Last Chance Tattoo until noon. If I haven't heard from you by then, I'll hit the road."

He got his helmet and walked out, the door bell jangling in his wake. I heard the rumble of the Harley, then silence. I stood at my counter and stared at the check. I didn't touch it.

But I didn't shove it away either.

Chapter Three

Trey's voice held a tone of disbelief. "That's what he wanted? To hire you?"

I tucked the phone against my shoulder and unfolded the sofa bed. "So he says."

I climbed into bed. The mattress smelled like stale popcorn and gun oil, but thanks to Trey, it had 400-thread-count Italian sheets.

I curled around a pillow. "I don't suppose you know anybody with expertise in that area?"

"I do. Audrina Harrington."

"You're kidding."

"No. She hired Phoenix to create a safe room for her collection. I designed the security system."

Audrina Harrington, Atlanta's most famous doyenne of all things related to the War of Northern Aggression. Her family traced their ancestry back to Mary Rose, one of the Confederacy's most notorious spies, and she still maintained a certain aristocratic hauteur, like an exiled countess. She was also, as John put it, one of those big-money, under-the-table collectors. Unlike my customers, she didn't run around in green fields waving her bayonet. Instead, she accumulated Civil War artifacts with a hoarder's zeal, her specialty being ephemera—books, letters, papers, documents.

I pulled my computer from under the bed and typed her name in the search box. Sure enough, the *Journal-Constitution* had done a full color spread, featuring the diminutive Harrington surrounded by her faded brittle treasures. She stared straight at the camera, a tiny birdlike creature, her vivid clothes like plumage, her steel gray hair like a cap of feathers.

"Wow. Lots of photographs."

Trey made a noise of annoyance. "She wasn't supposed to show anyone that room. That completely defeats its purpose."

"Y'all should have told her that before she brought in the *AJC.*"

"I did tell her. It's an environmentally-regulated storage room now, not a true safe room. But her brother convinced her the publicity would be good for their foundation."

His voice held disapproval. Trey did not like people hiring him to make rules and then ignoring the rules he made.

"Is that the man standing next to her in the photo?"

"Describe him."

"Short, stout, silver-haired?"

"Yes. That's Reynolds Harrington. He's responsible for bringing in the external funding, mostly corporate, some private donors. Miss Harrington manages the family assets."

I clicked on a link for the Harrington Foundation. A quick scan of the website revealed two things—a serious commitment to curating the largest museum-caliber collection of Civil War antiquities outside of a museum, and an equally serious bankroll to fund it.

"You think she'd talk to me?"

"I could get in touch, if you'd like."

"I would. Thank you." I stretched out under the sheets. "Not that I've decided to take the case or anything."

"Case?"

"Situation. Whatever. I haven't given John an answer yet."

A pause. "Has there been foul play?"

"Beyond Hope running off with his possessions? No. I mean, there's lots of hypothetical hinkiness, but nothing obvious."

Trey waited, but I had no further explanation. The memory of the check still loomed crisp in my mind. So did John's face.

And Hope's. And the humiliation I'd felt at their hands. It had been over a year, and the fire of anger had diminished. Time helped. So had acquiring a top-of-the-line boyfriend. But the scars remained, thick ropy ones.

"I'll do a little poking about and let you know more at dinner tomorrow night. We're still on for dinner, right?"

"Right."

"And you're helping me pack on Sunday?"

"Yes."

"And you finalized the paperwork to get the week of the Expo off?"

"Yes."

Our first getaway. Not exactly a vacation—the Expo and related events would keep me busy for several days—but a first of some kind. Almost portentous.

"Are you ready for the interview tomorrow?" he said.

"I hope so. The ATF guy is showing up at eight sharp, ready to talk federal firearms license renewal."

"You're wearing your suit, right?"

I looked over to where my only suit, a purple pants-and-blazer set, hung on the bathroom door. The ATF's letter called the meeting "informal." Trey insisted I wear the suit anyway.

"Ready to go. I even ironed the thing."

"Good. If you need anything—"

"—I'll holler, I promise." I reached over and turned out the light. "I miss you."

"You could have come back with me."

"I've discovered that nights at your place do not make for productive mornings."

A soft exhale at his end, almost like a laugh. "I've discovered the same thing." A pause. "I miss you too."

He'd once explained what that felt like to him—a hard knot in the diaphragm, surrounded by an achy spreading warmth. I put my own hand in the same spot on my own body and felt the same tenderness. I wasn't someone people usually missed, especially not people like Trey. Usually people like Trey sighed with relief and straightened the slipcovers when I left.

"Tai?"

"Yeah?"

"This may sound overprotective, but—"

"It's a runner's job, that's all. No bodies, no fires, no stalkers, no drug cartels. I do this all the time."

Silence at his end.

"Trey, listen to me. I learn from my mistakes. I know to back off if things get dangerous."

He listened. His exquisitely fine-tuned ability to detect other people's deception did not extend to phone conversations, which was a relief. But I was telling him the truth this time. I didn't need any drama on my plate.

"Okay," he finally said. "But if the situation changes—"

"Then I drop it."

He hesitated, then acquiesced. "Okay."

◇◇◇

I tried to sleep. Eventually I got up and dug the box out of the closet. I found the photograph quickly—me, reclining on the hood of my cherry-red Camaro Z-28, the late summer sun flaring off the chrome. Tybee Beach glowed in a sandy blur behind me, the sky a milky blue. I wore a halter top and jean shorts, a two-week-old tattoo hidden beneath the denim. My first ink, a gift from John's talented hands, a red fox with vixen eyes.

Only two men had seen that fox—and they'd been standing face to face in my parking lot one hour ago.

I touched the image, half-expecting it to be warm beneath my fingers. I was alone in the shot, but I could see John in the gleam of my eyes. He was behind the camera, and I stretched in the heat of his gaze, grinning, one hand shading my face from the noonday glare.

I tried to inhabit the photograph—the sun-baked metal, the sand gritty between my toes. The girl I was then had been perched on a slice of between-time. Within a month, my mother would be diagnosed with breast cancer. I'd sell my wild red car and drive her more sensible four-door back and forth to chemo. In less than a year, she'd be dead, and I would be the one at her bedside when she took her last breath. And soon after that, John and Hope would sneak off in the night.

I placed the glossy 3X5 back in the box and turned out the light. I'd known my past was waiting for me down in Savannah. I'd been preparing. But I hadn't been prepared for it to show up on my doorstep in Atlanta, unannounced, with eyes that still looked like a storm about to erupt.

Chapter Four

As it turned out, my interview with the ATF was not a formality. The inspector, a newly-minted devotee of all things bureaucratic, kept using the word "irregularities" to describe Dexter's previous application. He kept quoting Statute 478.44 at me. It took all my self-control not to bean him with the ledger book, especially when he used the dreaded A-word—audit. In four weeks.

After he'd gone, I looked at the list of upgrades I needed to reach even minimum compliance, and the list of penalties waiting for me if I didn't. The words "possible jail time" floated amongst the dollar signs. I took a deep breath. Then I poured a quart of dark roast into my travel mug, slapped on a new nicotine patch, and made my way to Last Chance Tattoos and Cigar Emporium. There I found John getting a fill-in on his upper shoulder, sitting shirtless while the artist worked behind him, squinting in concentration, her spiked purple hair luminous in the smoky light. The air buzzed with the sound of needles.

I pulled over a stool and sat in front of him. He eyed my pantsuit.

"What's with the get-up?"

"Interview with the ATF."

John put a beat-up coffee mug to his lips. "Bummer. Those guys can ream you from every direction."

"I know. So don't start with me this morning." I pulled a pen from my tote bag and used it to fasten my hair into a knot at the nape of my neck. "I decided to take your job."

"Good to hear."

"On one condition."

"Shoot."

"You are hiring me to locate a particular artifact, nothing more. My job is to find your Bible and present whoever has it with your terms for its return."

"That sounds fair."

"And if said person refuses, the ball's in your court. Call the police, come get it, whatever. Plus you'll owe me any expenses."

"Also fair." He stuck his hand out. "Shake on it."

I shook. "So we start with backstory. Tell me about the box of stuff Hope took."

"What's to tell? It was mostly junk—old books, pens, pencils. Scraps of paper. Dusty, like the guy hadn't cleaned out his desk since the fifties."

"What guy?"

"The uncle."

"What uncle?"

"The one who died."

I stared at him, a chill creeping down my spine. "What do you mean, died?"

John chuckled and sipped his coffee. "Damn, Tai, why else do you think his niece was having an estate sale?"

I smelled bourbon in his coffee. The tattoo artist eyed me, the sunlight setting her piercings aflame.

I stood up. "Sorry. I don't do dead people."

John's jaw dropped. "But this isn't about the dead guy!"

I shook my head more firmly.

"Come on, Tai! It's not like he was murdered. He had a heart attack or something."

"Or something."

He glared at me. "So you're going back on the deal, that it?"

"It wasn't a fair deal. You didn't mention the corpse."

"Corpse!"

"That's what you call a dead person!"

He took a drag on his cigarette. I massaged my bicep, willing the nicotine patch to kick in before I snatched the butt out of his hand and sucked it dry.

"Fine," he said. "I knew it was too much to ask. Considering."

"Don't try that. This has nothing to do with me and you."

"Of course not. There is no me and you." He blew out a thin line of smoke. "Unless you want there to be."

"I don't."

"You sure?"

"Dead sure."

He grinned. I glared. The needles whined. And I was two seconds from turning my back on him when I remembered the upcoming audit and all the expensive upgrades I'd need to implement. But I also I remembered my promise to Trey, to drop it if it got complicated. And then I remembered Garrity, who was two blocks down in his office at Atlanta PD headquarters. With any luck, he was at his desk and looking for lunch.

I did a quick calculation. "Here's the deal. I've got a source at the police station. I'm gonna ask him to make some calls. And if I learn there was the slightest hint of suspicion about that old man's death, I'm done. No deal. Got it?"

"Got it."

"Now here." I shoved a yellow pad at him. "Write down everything you know about the old man, his relatives, what was in that desk. I'll get back to you tomorrow."

He took the notepad. "You want to take the chair? Stevie here would be glad to let me borrow her equipment, touch up that critter of yours, isn't that right, Stevie?"

Stevie grinned. She had red lips and a single gold incisor with a rhinestone.

"My critter is fine." I handed him a pen. "Now write."

◇◇◇

Inside the APD headquarters, chaos reigned—phones ringing, uniforms huddling, the smell of burnt coffee. I saw Garrity at his desk, phone to his ear. He was a kinetic knot of energy, red-headed and sharp-featured. The laugh lines at his eyes and the corners of his mouth told me he used to smile a lot, once upon a time.

"No comment," he said into the phone.

He spotted me and waved me over. I dropped into the chair in front of his desk, the only horizontal space not sporting a skyscraper of paperwork. He kept the phone to his ear. *Reporter,* he mouthed.

I placed the take-out bag on his desk. Thai-German fusion—pad thai schnitzel for him, bratwurst curry for me—and two sweet teas. Garrity responded well to bribes, and I needed all the leverage I could muster.

He slammed the receiver down. "Would you believe we're having a rash of hair weave thefts? Seriously." He scrunched his eyes at me. "What's with the purple?"

"Long story involving the ATF and Dexter's lack of organizational skills."

"You're not getting audited, are you?"

I nodded.

Garrity winced. "Crap. You got a lawyer?"

I felt that rippled of apprehension again. "I need a lawyer?"

"Hell yes. Get Trey to recommend somebody from work. Phoenix is lousy with lawyers."

"I can't afford a lawyer."

"That doesn't matter. Get one."

I tried to cross my legs and accidentally kicked an empty soda cup under the desk. Across the room, a woman in a nun's habit lay on the floor, refusing to budge, while two detectives stood at her feet, pleading with her to get up.

"Is it always this bad?" I said.

"Full moon coming. Usually starts three days before the peak then tapers. This is worse than usual." He sat back, tapping his pen on his coffee mug. "So I got your message. Another suspicious dead guy?"

"Actually, not suspicious at all."

"Then why are you asking me to chat up the authorities down in…where was this again?"

"Jacksonville."

"Uh huh." He reached inside the takeout bag and removed a Styrofoam container. "Explain."

I explained. Garrity forked up a mouthful of noodles and shoved them into one cheek, like a chipmunk. "So this guy just dropped dead?"

"Apparently. I'm trying to decide if there's a crime involving said dead guy, because if there is, I'm dumping it. I don't want any part of any adventure that begins with a body. Been there, done that, got the official warning."

"So you want me to call some stranger—"

"Fellow law enforcement officer."

"—to ask if there was anything suspicious about this old guy's death, so that you can then decide whether or not to chase one of his possessions all over Savannah?"

"That's about it."

A long uncomfortable pause followed. "Let me get back to you on that."

"Please do. Trey and I are leaving for the Expo Monday morning, and I'd like to be able to reassure him one more time that I'm being sensible."

"Uh huh." More chewing. "So what's he have to say about this?"

The question was casual on the surface, but heavy with subtext. Trey and Garrity had been partners during their uniformed days on the APD, friends afterwards. Trey's car accident and subsequent brain injury changed all that, fraying and twisting those bonds—Garrity rejected and angry, Trey confused and distant, neither of them knowing what to do about it. I didn't have a clue either.

"So far, Trey has no complaints." I pulled the lid off my tea, fished around for the lemon. "Which is strange. Usually he has very logical points to make about why I'm being an idiot. Usually you do too."

"Yeah, but this is the kind of thing you deal with all the time, right? Finding specific antiques for specific people, usually with a dead relative attached?"

He was right. I was no stranger to runner work. Most of my reenactor clients had wish lists as long as their forearms, plus customers were forever bringing in relics for me to identify or sell, usually from some long-dead ancestor's attic. Of course none of those people were my ex-boyfriend.

"Yeah, but I'm feeling extra-cautious on this job. So will you call the nice policeman down in Duval County for me?"

He went back to his noodles. "Leave me the info."

A voice came from across the room. "Hey, Garrity, call coming through."

"Send it to Hawkins."

"It's the FBI."

Garrity paled. "Shit. I didn't expect it to be that fast."

He started cleaning up his desk, as if the mysterious caller could see the clutter through the phone line.

"Expect what?" I said.

"Nothing. Now go, I have to take this."

"Since when does the FBI concern itself with hair thieves?"

"It doesn't. Go."

He grabbed my elbow and propelled me out of the room, barely giving me enough time to grab my food before he shut the door behind me. I leaned my ear against it and heard him pick up the phone, his voice deliberately casual. "Garrity here."

I scooched closer. The officer in an adjoining cubicle cleared his throat. When I looked his way, he pointed toward the exit. Pointedly. I took the hint.

Back in the car, my phone chirped at me. It was a text from Trey—his connection to Audrina Harrington had paid off, in spades. She was inviting me for tea at her estate. In thirty minutes.

I pulled down the rearview mirror and checked my reflection. My makeshift hairpin wasn't working to contain the blond frizzle, but the make-up was acceptable. I removed a splotch of basil from between my front teeth and twisted the key in the ignition.

My purple pantsuit and I had one more assignment.

Chapter Five

Audrina Harrington's mansion, a three-story Greek Revival on Tuxedo Road, reclined on an eighteen-acre swath of manicured fescue. Neighbored by blocky Tudors and rectangular Georgians, it disguised its years behind wrought iron gates and tangled sweet pea vines, as artfully coy as an aging concubine.

I parked, aware of the swivel of security cameras as I walked to the front door. Doric columns stood sentinel, six of them, regular and fastidious. No noise from the street intruded in that insulated space, only the whispery rasp of fallen leaves and dry wind. I clutched my tote bag and rang the bell.

The door opened immediately, revealing a man with a clipboard in hand. He frowned. "Tai Randolph?"

I nodded, trying not to stare. He was six feet tall, with black hair and blue eyes, and he wore a tailored black suit, white shirt, and tiny discreet earpiece. Beefier than Trey, without the elegant cheekbones and tiny silver scars at the chin and temple, but definitely the same species.

"Umm," I stammered.

The man's eyes were stern and bored. "Miss Harrington was expecting two."

"Mr. Seaver couldn't make it. Which is a shame, really."

I thought for a second he'd turn me away, but he made a note on his clipboard and waved me in. "Miss Harrington will see you in the gazebo. Straight down the hall, then through the doors."

I could feel his eyes on my back as I followed his instructions, my footfalls silent on the inch-thick carpeting. The drawing room lay to my left, with pale blue walls and watered silk drapes, the dining room to my right. I caught a glimpse of a mahogany accordion table underneath a Waterford crystal chandelier. The furniture reeked of lacquer—even the air felt heavy and pre-served—but I saw no sign of the fabled Harrington collection.

I saw the woman herself, however, on the patio. She waited in her gazebo underneath the spreading arms of an ancient magnolia, a tiny woman in white palazzo pants and a jeweled navy top. Even from a distance, she displayed the brittle authority of someone so accustomed to command that it came as naturally as breath.

I approached the linen-covered table. Her eyes were ice gray, her soft thin skin like parchment. She had at least seven decades on her, possibly eight, and she wore them as well as her clothes, definitely a woman who understood the necessity of maintenance.

Before I could speak, she arched a precisely penciled eyebrow in my direction. "Where's Trey?"

I noticed then that the snowy tabletop had been set for three. "He couldn't make it, unfortunately, but—"

"Tell me who you are again."

"Tai Randolph. Pleased to meet you, Ms. Harrington."

"*Miss* Harrington. Never married, never wanted to be, never cared to leave anybody guessing about that."

"Sorry about that. *Miss* Harrington."

She threw a suspicious glare my way, her eyes raking me up and down. There was a bite of winter-sharpened autumn in her garden. I imagined it was so even in the summer, that it was always cool under that gazebo.

I kept smiling. "Trey sends his regrets. He really wanted to come."

That was a flat-out lie, but it pleased her. She waved at one of the empty chairs. "Sit."

The delicate rattle of china cups in saucers announced the delivery of our tea. I smelled oolong. Trey's favorite.

"Thank you." I smiled up at the server.

He placed the teapot in the center of the table and returned the smile. "You're welcome."

I blinked at him. Another six-foot creature with black hair and blue eyes. This specimen was slim and vivacious, with a tanned complexion and a slashing white grin like a Jolly Roger.

I bit my lip to keep from laughing. "Three sugars and lots of cream, please."

He obliged me. Miss Harrington ignored the tea tray, folding her hands in her lap. "Trey says you've found something remarkable, a Bible with connections to both Lincoln and Sherman. Is that so?"

"It is."

"Tell me more."

I dabbed at my mouth and did just that. She listened. The waiter delivered a three-tiered silver tray to the table, stacked with scones and clotted cream and cheese straws. At the end of my tale, Audrina sniffed loudly.

"Poppycock. Have you seen this Bible?"

"No."

"Then it doesn't exist."

"What if it does?"

"Then it's a forgery. My authenticator tells me there's not a single clue supporting such a document's existence."

I folded my napkin in my lap. "Sometimes things hide in plain sight. You know this better than anyone."

I saw the spark of pride flare in her watery eyes. My preservation-minded customers spoke of her with bitterness. She didn't let her things out to play. Once they were in her possession, they rarely saw the light of day, existing under glass in her hermetically-sealed safe room.

"It could exist," she admitted. "Flying monkeys could exist. But in the tales associated with Sherman's March to the Sea and his subsequent takeover of Savannah, in the multiple and long-winded accounts of what transpired, there is no mention of such a Bible. In that hugely self-congratulatory moment, can you think of any reason such a thing would have escaped notice?"

I took a sip of tea. "There was the tragedy, of course."

"What tragedy?"

"The general's infant son, Charles Celestine, died during the Savannah Campaign. Sherman had never even seen the child." I dabbed my lips. "He learned of the death from the newspaper."

Miss Harrington stared at me. "Go on."

"I'm sure you know that Sherman was plagued with fits of melancholy his whole life—what we'd diagnose as major depressive episodes today—so it's possible that during this sad time, his affairs weren't as meticulously arranged as usual."

Her manicured nails drummed the tablecloth. My recitation appeared to surprise her, which surprised me. I'd gotten it in my head that she was an expert on such matters. Apparently, however, her fascination lay in the collection, not in the history behind it.

"And so?" she prompted.

"And so the Bible could have been stolen, hidden, accidentally left behind. One tiny margin of error, a thousand possibilities."

She tossed her napkin on the table. The server pulled her chair back, and she stood. The top of her head barely reached my clavicle.

"This way," she said. "And don't dilly dally. I haven't got all day."

◇◇◇

Her library felt like a set piece for *Masterpiece Theatre*—walls paneled in polished butternut, nail-backed reading chairs paired next to the fireplace, floor lamps oozing honey-thick light. It was mysterious and cloistered, a place where illicit lovers groped and high class matrons hissed threats as deadly and fine as powdered poison. And its bookshelves held the stories of the doomed glorious South—leather-bound editions of Robert E. Lee's memoirs, Stonewall Jackson's letters, Matthew Brady's collected photographs—all of them pristine, as if their pages had yet to be cracked.

"It's lovely," I said.

She harrumphed. "This isn't it. Turn around. And close your eyes."

I did as she asked. Behind me, I heard the beeping of a keyless entry system, then a click. Cool odorless air flowed from deep within...somewhere.

"You can turn around now." She gave me that look again, like a pissed off egret. "Now be quick. Like I said, I don't have all day."

I stepped across the threshold into a low-lit room, rectangular and sterile. I remembered the specs from the *AJC* article—constant temperature of sixty-five degrees, constant humidity of thirty-five percent. The serviceable wood tables and chairs were plain, every square inch of wall and table space devoted to display cases. I saw swords and scabbards, full Confederate uniforms, derringers and Sharps carbines and bullets, even a saddle, all of them behind glass, protected and preserved.

The real glory, however, was the papers. The ephemera, as it was called in the trade. Books, certificates, photographs, letters, more pieces than I could count. If some apocalypse ever did strike Atlanta, future generations would find Audrina Harrington in this cloistered space, surrounded by her treasures like an entombed pharaoh.

A man rose from behind one of the tables as we entered, a grid of beige papers and magnifying glasses before him. I'd been so overwhelmed by the sheer volume of the room, I hadn't noticed him, but when he stood, I recognized him instantly—six-four, dark shiny hair, every inch the suave professional in his navy suit and blood-red tie.

He came around the table. "Ms. Randolph, I presume? My name is—"

"David Fitzhugh. I know. I've seen you on *Antiques Roadshow*."

"Really?" He flashed a full white smile. "Which episode?"

"The one with the McElroy saber."

The smile widened. Fitzhugh Appraisals and Authentications was the Southeast's leading consignment shop for Civil War artifacts. Fitzhugh himself struck me as more used car salesman than scholar, but his record spoke for itself. In a crowded field, his company moved more historical collectibles than his top ten competitors combined. My dinky shop pulled in peanuts compared to his operation.

He maintained the full wattage grin. "Miss Harrington told me we'd be having a visitor. She said you'd found something extraordinary."

"All I have so far is a tantalizing story."

"Then let's hear it."

As I repeated the tale, Audrina kept her mouth compressed in a severe line, her thin arms crossed. But her eyes flashed with avid curiosity.

When I was finished, Fitzhugh clucked his tongue. "I'm sorry, Ms. Randolph, but I'll tell you what I told Miss Harrington— that sounds like a fantasy to me."

"Why do you say that?"

"Because history is silent on this Bible, and history is never silent."

"Ah, but you're wrong. History often keeps her mouth shut, and for good reason."

He looked at me with the patience that experts reserved for impertinent amateurs. "Trust me, I've been doing this for thirty years. A Bible like that doesn't suddenly appear. The rumors come first, then the false leads, then the fakes."

"What if we're at the 'rumor' stage?"

He gestured at the manuscripts before him. Flesh-colored cotton gloves gave his hands an odd mannequin-like appearance. He pointed to an old book, its pages yellowed, crisp with age.

"Do you know what this is?"

"It looks like a diary."

"It is. It belonged to Confederate Lieutenant James H. Polk. That's him, here."

He pointed to a tintype photograph. A fresh-faced young man stared at me from one hundred and fifty years in the past.

"He signed the diary, dated it too. It's filled with the usual stuff of the soldiering life—politics, complaints about the food, letters from other soldiers."

"In other words, you have supporting provenance."

He smiled. "And that's why Miss Harrington authorized me to pay almost four thousand dollars for this grouping. So please understand, we're not interested in funding a wild goose chase."

I blinked at him. "Funding?"

Fitzhugh's smile thinned. "I've done my research too, Ms. Randolph. You inherited a ramshackle gun shop with an equally ramshackle clientele. You are in no position to run across a historical artifact worth a few hundred thousand dollars. And you have no money to go chasing one."

I kept my voice steady. "I came here for information, not money."

"Then I'm sorry if I offended you. But Miss Harrington is approached relentlessly with relics for sale. Ninety-five percent are either deliberately forged or misidentified by overenthusiastic amateurs. The other five percent are sentimental slop with no historic value whatsoever." His tone was magnanimous. "But go ahead. Chase your Bible. And should you actually find it, here's my card. I'll offer you my ten dollar special."

I took his card. "Which is?"

"I look at your item for two minutes and tell you it's worthless."

I was surrounded by the authentic and documented and preserved in that library. The cataloged and categorized and recorded. There was no room to be surprised, no room for a single story to breathe its way to life. I suddenly developed an irresistible craving to prove this smug gentleman wrong.

"What if my Bible turns out to be real?"

He smiled again, showing his big teeth. "You show me that Bible, and I will eat one of your Confederate hats."

I smiled back. "If I were you, I'd keep some ketchup handy."

◇◇◇

A third version of Trey escorted me back to my car, this time a lithe Asian with a dancer's carriage and eyes like Swarovski sapphires.

I shook my head. "This gig must pay ridiculously well."

"You wouldn't believe." He grinned. "Of course you have to put up with a little ass-grabbing every now and then, but the dental is amazing."

Chapter Six

When I got back to the shop, I was surprised to see the Ferrari parked out front, Trey standing next to it. He was in full Armani mode—black suit, white shirt, black tie—and he had that squinched annoyed expression on his face.

"Oh god," I said, hurrying to unlock the door. "I'm sorry I'm late. But apparently Dexter wasn't much on the record keeping, so now I'm being audited by Agent Cranky Pants."

"He's not an agent. He's an ATF-compliant industry operations officer."

"Oh. Does that mean I can stop worrying?"

"No. An unfavorable audit could result in fines, imprisonment—"

"I know, I know. Don't remind me." I bumped the door open with my hip. "Wait a second, I thought we were meeting at your place."

"We were."

"Were?"

He folded his arms. "I have to work tonight."

"What? Why?"

"An important client asked for me specifically. Marisa said that my participation is nonnegotiable."

He hated it when his boss offered him up on a silver platter, like a haute couture hors d'oeuvre. Trey was a premises liability genius, but some clients wanted him more for his intriguing presence than his skills. He knew this. It bothered him.

I went inside, and he followed. He picked up a handful of loose coins from the counter and poured them into my spare change cup.

"How was your meeting with Audrina Harrington?" he said.

"It was going great, until her lackey accused me of money-grubbing." I threw my jacket on the counter. "By the way, you're not allowed to go over there by yourself anymore. I'm afraid you won't make it back out one day."

He ignored the comment, preferring to sift through the jumbled pens lying around the cash register. "Did she have any information about the Bible?"

"No. She seemed interested, but her authenticator convinced her it was a wild goose chase. So I'm back where I started."

Trey kept his eyes on the counter. He'd put the black pens into one pile, the red ones in another. Now he had my receipts and was sorting them into chronological order.

"Okay, that's enough." I gently extracted the papers from his hands. "Spill it."

"Spill what?"

"Why you drove all the way out here to tell me you're heading into work when you could have called."

He looked me in the eye for the first time since he'd come in the shop. "I can't go to the Expo next week. Marisa cancelled my leave."

"What?"

"I know. I'm sorry."

"Let me guess—it's because of the same important client that's ruining our dinner."

"I don't know yet."

He delivered the news with stoic grumpiness, shifting his gaze to the wall behind my shoulder. Something deeper was bothering him. I could read it in the wrinkle between his eyes.

"Are you okay?"

"What?"

"You seem—" My cell phone interrupted my question. I gave it a quick look. "Hang on, I have to take this. It's Garrity calling about the dead guy."

Trey was suddenly alert. "What dead guy?"

"I'll explain in a second." I put the phone to my ear. "You find anything?"

"I talked to the coroner in Jacksonville. Your guy died of a massive heart attack. I'm looking at the file now." I heard the sound of pages turning. "Arteriosclerosis leading to total blockage of the left anterior descending artery. No foul play whatsoever."

The tension in my chest eased. "So it happened like John said."

"Apparently so."

"So this isn't a murder?"

"Apparently not. I made you a copy of the police report. I'll fax it over."

"That's it? No lecture?"

"I'm not in the mood. Besides, there's nothing in this file that makes my cop nerve twitch."

"Nothing?"

"Nothing. Nice mild-mannered retiree, lived alone, heart exploded. His distant relative buried him and cleaned house quick—a niece, it says. No drama, no contested will, no massive inheritance to start a catfight. End of story."

"Huh."

"You sound disappointed."

"Only surprised. Things never turn out this way for me."

I looked at Trey. He was scrutinizing me with increasing impatience, arms crossed, on the verge of pacing back and forth across my floor. I held up a finger. *One more second.*

"Go chase your antique," Garrity pronounced. "I gotta run."

"More FBI stuff?"

Trey's ears pricked up at this. Garrity wasn't biting, however. "Don't go throwing that around, you hear me?"

"You know me, soul of discretion."

"Seriously, Tai."

"I am serious. Thanks for the information."

I heard a grunt that could have been "you're welcome" as I hung up. I slipped the phone in my pocket and folded my arms to match Trey's.

He glared. "You have Garrity doing research for you. On a suspicious death."

"Not suspicious anymore. And I was going to explain at dinner, except that not only are we not having dinner, we're not having a vacation either, so don't give me that look."

The look intensified.

"Don't even start. I found out about the dead guy this morning because John, being John, neglected to mention that part of the story. But I wasn't hiding it from you."

His eyes dipped briefly to my mouth—reading me again—and I felt the first twinge of annoyance. "Cut it out, Trey. Trust me or don't trust me, but kill the lie detector routine."

I watched the transformation happen right in front of me. He closed his eyes, counted to three, then opened them, and the fired-up was all gone. His expression was flat and iceberg frosty.

He turned on his heel and headed for the door. "I have to go."

I scrambled to stand in front of him. "Oh no, you don't. We're in the middle of something, and it's important. You can't—"

"Yes, I can."

And he did. He straightened his jacket and left without looking back. I stared at where he'd been standing, at the wreckage of boxes and tape and packing peanuts, the empty shop echoing with the sounds of the slamming door and the obscenely cheerful jingle of the chimes.

I kicked a piece of cardboard. "Damn it all to hell." And then I got to work packing.

◇◇◇

My brother showed up fifteen minutes later. He found me sitting with a lap full of long underwear hand-stitched by a cousin of mine in Alabama. My hard-core clients wouldn't wear anything else—stitch Nazis, they were called behind their backs—but even my more progressive clientele liked being authentic right down to their skivvies.

"I passed the Ferrari on the way in," Eric said.

"Probably."

"Headed back to Buckhead."

"That's what it does. It goes very specifically in one direction, and then it reaches the point beyond which it will go no further, so it stops. It does not veer, it does not backtrack, and it does not listen."

Eric had come to get his stack of forms for the ATF audit. Since he was technically co-owner of the shop, he was required to read and sign all the paperwork too. But that wasn't why he had his psychologist face on.

"Argument?" he said.

"No. He didn't hang around long enough." I yanked a length of tape from the dispenser and slapped it on a box. "Tell me, how much of that stubbornness is frontal lobe damage and how much is him being a first-class jerk?"

Eric stayed calm. Even in jeans and a t-shirt, glasses shoved up in his dark blond hair, he exuded professional concern.

"What happened?"

I gave him the short version. He listened without interrupting. He seemed older, grayer at the temples, and I realized I hadn't seen him in almost a month. His industrial psychology practice kept him out of town a lot—expert witness gigs, conference presentations. He thrived on the energy of an ever-revolving life, but now he looked patient and thoughtful.

"So you're going to the Expo on your own?"

"Sure. Unless you want to come."

He made a pained face. Neither of us had been to Savannah in a long time, Eric not since Mom's funeral, me not since I'd moved to Atlanta. The Lowcountry lay to our south, deep with our history.

"I'd rather talk about what happened here," he said.

"I thought you couldn't talk about Trey. Former client confidentiality and all that?"

"I don't want to talk about Trey, I want to talk about *you* and Trey."

"Oh Lord, not again." I brushed my hair from my forehead and picked up another packing box. "I know he's a walking conundrum, I get that, but sometimes I can't tell what's him and what's the brain rearrangement."

"They're the same."

"You know what I mean."

Eric pulled his glasses from his hair and perched them on his nose. Suddenly, he was one hundred percent PhD again. "It's a convoluted process coming back from an injury like his. Lots of personality upheaval, lots of breaking down and building up."

"But I'm the one doing all the breaking down, and then he refuses to hang around to do any building up!"

"I'm not surprised."

I slammed open another box. "Jeez, people pay you for this kind of talk? Seriously?"

"You're a classic catalytic personality, Tai. Situations tend to blow up around you. Trey, however, inclines toward the rigid and controlling. It's his primary coping strategy, and considering the blow his executive function took, it makes perfect sense."

"You're not seriously suggesting Trey is typical?"

Eric shook his head. "No, no. His methods of compensation have been…unusual. The Armani and Ferrari especially. But they're all part of a larger recovery context."

"That's what I'm trying to tell you! I know he's not…But I can't help thinking…" I dumped a stack of long johns into the box, not even bothering to fold them. "What if I'm just another piece of weirdness in his recovery complex? What if he's only with me because the part of his brain that should know better is broken?"

Eric didn't say anything for a few seconds. Then he crouched in front of me, face to face. "You know you're impossible. You're aggressive and stubborn, quick-tempered and impulsive. You take everything personally whether it's meant that way or not. And you're convinced you're right, all the time."

"Thanks, bro."

"You're also generous and smart and open-hearted and brave. Trey needs someone like that, like you, and he's lucky to have you. But you're angry right now, and that's making you defensive and selfish."

I pointed at the door. "He's the one—"

"No, you're the one jumping headfirst into another problematic situation all by yourself, which, may I add, is a tendency you should start examining with professional help."

"You may not add that."

He ignored me. "Trey's got every right to be confused, worried, and angry. He may not have the neuronal connections to articulate it clearly, but his emotional response is—in this case anyway—utterly normal."

"But—"

"No buts. You know why he walked out that door. But what you need to ask yourself is why he bothered to drive all the way up here in the first place."

My brother stood and offered me a hand. I took it, and he pulled me to standing. I remembered Trey's words from that night during the summer, both of us sitting on the edge of the bed, the rain driving hard outside. *I will always show up, for as long as you want me to. I promise.*

I checked the clock on the wall. If I really dug into the packing, I could be in Buckhead by eight. Trey probably wouldn't be back by then, but that was okay. I could use some time to prepare.

I managed a half-smile. "You occasionally make sense, you know that?"

Eric laughed, the corners of his eyes crinkling. "Thanks, sis. Good thing to know all those years at Yale weren't wasted."

Chapter Seven

I sat on the floor of Trey's apartment and studied the papers I'd spread in a semicircle. They made a nice white arc on the black hardwood, as perfectly bichromatic as the rest of the place. I had a glass of wine in one hand, and my cell phone in the other, but the conversation with the dead man's niece was not going well.

"So you didn't have much to do with your uncle?" I said.

"I met him twice, twenty years ago. What do you think?"

I studied the dead man's photograph. Slight, balding. A round bulb of a nose, twinkly eyes behind old-fashioned horn-rimmed glasses. I finally had a name—Vincent DiSilva—and other basic information. I wondered what his niece looked like. All I had of her was her voice, which was paranoid laced with cynical. She'd been listed as his next-of-kin, his sole heir. Not that her inheritance had amounted to much—a tiny cinder-block ranch house from the fifties, like a million others in Florida, and its meager contents.

"Did he do any collecting? Antiques maybe?"

"His house was wall-to-wall junk, like on that reality show about hoarders. Paper, furniture, boxes of books. Dusty old shit. Does that count?"

I rolled wine around in my mouth to keep from saying the first words that rose to my lips. "Did you keep any of his things?"

"Why would I? What didn't sell went to Goodwill, and the rest went to the dump."

"I thought maybe—"

"Why are you asking all these questions? You aren't trying to get your money back, are you?"

"No."

"Good. Because I sold everything 'as is,' like it or lump it. You aren't trying to hit me up for any bills, are you?"

I kept my voice patient. "I'm looking for information, that's all. His obituary says he was a drafter with Lockheed Martin for thirty years. Do you know—"

"I told you everything I know. I did my duty. I went down there, I buried him. I didn't know him, so I don't miss him, but he seemed to be an all right guy. Not many of them in the world."

And now one less, I thought.

The niece kept talking. "But he's dead. And I gotta get back to work."

She hung up on me. I put down the phone and stared into my chardonnay. Another dead end. Which should have been a relief. Not a hint of foul play. A nice mild-mannered senior dies at home. As inciting incidents went, it was hardly front-page.

And yet...

I left the materials spread out and went onto the terrace. Far below me, the serpentine glitter of traffic wound its way between the high rises. Saturday night in Buckhead in all its techno-funk and Jello shot glory. Up on the thirty-fifth floor, the breeze had bite; it slithered up my bare legs and underneath the dress shirt I'd borrowed from Trey's closet.

I swirled the wine. John's story was missing one of its bones, whatever it was that connected a quiet unassuming retiree with a Bible worth a couple of hundred thousand dollars, a Bible not mentioned in his will. But I could not figure out what that mysterious link might be.

My phone rang, and I fished it out of the shirt pocket. "Rico! You're actually calling me back! Or did you mean to dial Kim Kardashian?"

His rich laugh echoed through the phone line. I could picture him at the other end—six-foot-two and two hundred and fifty pounds, probably wearing unlaced Converse, black eyes hidden behind sunglasses.

"I think I saw her, for real. Hard to tell. There's a surplus of loud busty chicks in Hollywood."

Back inside the apartment, the front door opened, and Trey came in. He didn't see me, busy as he was locking the door behind him. Three locks, including an industrial deadbolt.

"It's not the same around here without you," I said.

"No doubt. How's Mr. Tall, Dark, and Heterosexual?"

Trey went to his desk and put down his briefcase. There he pulled off his jacket and hung it precisely on the back of the chair, exposing the dark leather of his shoulder holster. He removed his Heckler and Koch P7M8, unloaded it, then stored it in the lockbox in his desk drawer. The ammo went into its own box, also locked.

"Same as always," I said. "He misses you too. In his own way."

I tapped on the glass, and Trey turned. I waved. He cocked his head, one eyebrow raised in puzzlement. Of course I *was* standing on his terrace wearing nothing but a button-down shirt that barely covered my butt.

Rico laughed. "I'm sure he does." He whispered something to someone nearby, probably one of his entourage. "I gotta go. My limo's here."

I snorted.

"Don't hate, baby girl. Tell me what you wanted and make it quick."

I told him. He got annoyed instantly.

"You can do your own background searches, you know."

"I did, the basics anyway. But accessing the deep web databases either costs money or takes talent, and I have neither."

"I've got two shows, back to back—"

"It'll take you twenty minutes."

A huff of resignation. "Fine. But I won't get to the computer until tomorrow night at the earliest." He paused. "You're not getting into trouble, are you?"

"Trying to avoid it actually."

"Good. Send me whatever you got. I'll call you when I'm done."

"You're the best. Now go catch your limo. I gotta seduce my boyfriend."

He laughed and hung up. I slid open the glass door and stepped inside, shutting it behind me. Trey was examining the papers on the floor. His eyes flicked up to mine.

"What's this?"

"Background research, plus the stuff Garrity sent on the recently deceased old guy in Jacksonville. He says everything seems on the up-and-up to him. But I left it there for you to see too."

Trey circled the paperwork like a hawk, tight slow spirals. "This says he died of natural causes. A heart attack."

"He did."

He studied the pages for another three minutes. I waited. Finally he looked up, still wary, but curious.

"You didn't tell me you were coming."

"No. But we need to talk."

His eyes dipped to my chest, then to the top of my thighs. "You're here to talk?"

"Among other things. I figure once we're done talking, there will be making up to do." I moved closer and slipped my arms around his neck. "And then goodbye-saying."

He tilted his head. "About that."

"About what?"

"About goodbye. As it turns out, I'll be able to come with you after all."

"You don't have to work anymore?"

"I still have to work. I'm working in Savannah, however."

"You are? Really? That's very…coincidental." I pulled back and examined his face. "You don't seem thrilled."

"No, I'm thrilled." His expression remained deadpan. "But I'm also confused."

"About what?"

"I can't tell you."

"Ah."

I took his hand and led him to the sofa, where we sat side by side. He stared out the window at the city-spangled nightline, forehead wrinkled, his index finger tap-tap-tapping against his thigh.

"I'm flying down Monday morning." He looked at me directly for the first time. "You can too. If you want. At Phoenix expense."

"I can't see Marisa going for that."

"It was her idea."

Now I was confused. "Boss Lady offered to buy me a plane ticket?"

"We're taking the client's Gulfstream. You don't need a ticket."

I tried to make sense of this, got nowhere. "Marisa hates me."

"She doesn't hate you, she just doesn't like you. Or trust you. Or—"

"What about all my merchandise? I've got a trunk full of t-shirts and handmade underwear that needs to get to Savannah too."

"There's room in the cargo hold for all of that."

I was growing more and more suspicious. Marisa did not play nice. We both knew this. But I also knew that Trey deeply resented being sent on certain types of fieldwork assignments. Part of his agreement to work at Phoenix was that he got to stay behind the desk most of the time. He was a paperwork junkie, my boyfriend. He mainlined tedium like it was heroin.

But he was also good in the field, even if it sometimes took him to the edge of his comfort zone. I wondered if perhaps that was my role in this turn of events, a bribe to keep him mollified. But truth be told, I was one of the hazards that made him somewhat dangerous in the field. He didn't deal well with distraction. Distraction was what I did best.

"Trey? Did you tell Marisa about my booth at the Expo?"

He nodded. "When I filled out the request for leave."

"Did you tell her about the Bible?"

"No."

"You sure?"

"Yes."

I wasn't convinced. His sudden assignment to Savannah, Marisa's sudden generosity. All of it smacked of behind-the-scenes maneuvering.

"Tell me this then." I straddled him, looping my arms around his neck. "Does this new assignment involve the same mysterious client who disrupted our dinner plans?"

"Yes. But—"

"I know, I know. You can't tell me who it is."

"Correct."

I unknotted his tie and pulled it loose. Then I reached down and untucked his shirt. I saw the first flare of arousal in his face—pupils dilated slightly, a flush along those gorgeous cheekbones.

I leaned closer. "It's Audrina Harrington, isn't it?"

Trey froze. "I can't tell you that."

"You just did."

He exhaled in frustration. I started on the buttons, his skin warm beneath the pads of my fingers, then slid my hands under his collar. Such exquisite shoulders—broad, lean, the kind of shoulders a girl could really hang onto.

"Audrina and Fitzhugh pretended they didn't believe my story, but they did. And now she's hired you so that you can keep an eye on me so that when I find the Bible, they can snatch it."

"That's not the reason I'm going."

"That's not what they told you, but trust me, that's why you're going." I moved my hands over his chest and then downward, over the flat plane of his abs to his belt buckle. "They're devious, Trey, underhanded and scheming. And they'll make pawns out of us in a heartbeat."

"I'm still not...ahhh." He closed his eyes, then opened them. "I thought we were going to talk first and then make up?"

"I changed my mind. We're going to talk and make up simultaneously."

"I'm not sure I'll be good at that."

I kissed him good and deep, slow. He kept his hands to himself, waiting, but I could feel his resistance crumbling, and knew I had precious little time to make my case.

I moved my mouth to his ear. "I've decided to take John up on his request."

Trey pulled his head back. "You have?"

"I have." I shifted my hips, and he inhaled sharply. "I've spent all afternoon gathering the evidence to prove that it's safe to do so. But in the end, it's not about proof. It's about trust."

"Is it?"

"It is. I can't afford to be picky about my clients, especially not with an ATF audit coming hard and fast. I need this money, I need this job, and I need you to drop the over-protective routine so that I can do it."

His eyes narrowed. I saw the flash, the sapphire-blue melting and recrystallizing, and I knew the scales had tipped. His hands moved to my waist, and he lowered me backward—inexorable, irresistible, a force of nature—until I was on my back with my legs wrapped against his hips. He tangled one hand in my hair and pulled my head back, passive no longer.

"And I need you to be sensible," he said.

His other hand moved up my thigh, his touch both tender and treacherous. I was losing the advantage, and fast.

"Trey? Do we have a deal? I play things sensible, you let me play them my way?"

He pressed a kiss to my throat, lingering in the hollow, then moved up my neck. Not paying my words a bit of attention now that he had an entirely different target in the crosshairs.

I closed my eyes. "I need…oh damn…I need to hear a yes, Trey."

His hand moved under the shirt, and then I felt—oh yes, I certainly did—and then there was thrumming in my head, and it spread like fever with every red beat of my traitorous heart. His mouth moved to my ear, and the rest of him—omigod, the rest of him—and my vision fluttered and blurred.

"Yes," he said.

Chapter Eight

The Gulfstream 280 was certainly impressive on the outside, all pointy-nose and sleek angles, like a raptor at rest. It was the interior, however, that spoiled me forever for commercial travel.

The cabin smelled good, for one thing, not like sweat and stale pretzels. The cool air was pristine and faintly lemon-scented, like someone had opened a can of fresh oxygen. Sunlight poured in through twin rows of oval windows, firing the burled wood trim to liquid gold. Everywhere I looked, I saw the burnished sheen of lots and lots of money.

I threw myself on the loveseat, a fat chunk of white-chocolate leather. "Dibs."

Trey shook his head. "Don't sit there. It's very uncomfortable during take-off." He indicated the back. "Follow me."

He walked past me to paired seats in the rear corner. I should have known. He wanted his back to the wall and a view of the entire sitting area. From this vantage point, he could even see the cockpit controls, the flashing array of lights and switches and gauges, bewildering and impenetrable.

Marisa entered behind us, in full boss lady mode, her platinum hair pulled tight, her ivory suit the same color as the leather. She frowned when she saw us, then strode down the aisle like a Lord and Taylor Valkyrie.

She directed the full force of her high-caliber annoyance at Trey. "Those are the VIP seats."

He fastened his seatbelt. "I know."

"You can't sit there."

"Yes, I can."

She looked aghast. "Please tell me you didn't ask Mr. Harrington if you could have his spot."

Before Trey could reply, a booming baritone interrupted the conversation. "It's okay, Marisa. I offered."

The man behind the voice was short and round, with silver hair slashing across his forehead in an Errol Flynn wave. He had a neatly-trimmed goatee and eyes like a satyr and was already brandishing both a martini, half-gone, and a cigar, unlit. I recognized him from the *AJC* article—Reynolds Harrington, Audrina's brother.

He stood beside Marisa. "My sister said to make sure Trey here was comfortable." He turned to me and stuck out his hand. "Reynolds Harrington. You must be Tai."

I smiled and took his hand. "I guess I must."

He had a playboy's grip—firm but gentle, with soft friction against my skin as I pulled my fingers back.

He returned his attention to Trey. "Glad you could make it at the last minute. Frankly, I never thought Audrina would go for this, but the old gal's finally coming into the twenty-first century."

Trey didn't reply. He shot a glance at Marisa, then Reynolds. When he didn't know how much to reveal about a subject, he usually said nothing. But his nothings were as telling as his somethings.

I kept the smile on Reynolds. "Big plans?"

"A golf tournament, if Trey and Marisa say it's feasible."

"Oh wow, it's up to these two, huh?"

Trey said absolutely nothing. Neither did Marisa. At the front of the plane, the flight attendant welcomed two more passengers on board. One of them carried a magnum of champagne, the other a bag of golf clubs. The latter belonged to Reynolds, I was guessing, since he already wore the attire—white pants, a yellow collared shirt, a single glove stuck in his pocket.

"I've been telling Audrina for some time now that she shouldn't keep the family collection locked up in that house. History belongs to the people. It needs to be shared."

"Admirable sentiment," I said. "But how does that involve a golf tournament?"

"Sharing means a museum, and a museum means fundraisers. I have a week to put together a plan, within budget, so I called in the best. According to Audrina anyway." He looked me up and down. "Do you golf, Ms. Randolph?"

"I do indeed, Mr. Harrington."

"Then come out tomorrow morning, and I'll tell you all about it. Marisa and I are trying out the resort course. We'd love for you to join us."

Marisa shook her head. "Unfortunately, Tai's working tomorrow, aren't you, Tai?"

"I can always fit in a round of golf."

She looked as if she wanted to strangle me, then jabbed her chin at Trey. "You come too."

Trey stiffened. "I don't golf."

"All the more reason to come. You'll need a feel for the game if you're going to design the security plan."

"But—"

"I'll help you with the paperwork afterward. Take a break. Enjoy the morning."

Trey glared at her. Reynolds smiled. I settled into my sumptuous seat and fastened my seatbelt. I remembered Audrina's pretend disdain, paired it with Reynolds' effusive inclusion and Marisa's steely machinations. Wars within wars going on here.

I widened the smile. "It's a foursome."

"Spectacular." Reynolds stuck the cigar between his teeth. "See you bright and early at the clubhouse. Eight o'clock tee time."

He wandered back to the front of the plane to greet the new arrivals. When he was out of earshot, Marisa leaned toward Trey, the Charlestonian lilt in her voice suddenly acidic.

"Don't start."

He tapped the folder in front of him. "I was hired to create a premises liability and general assessment prelim. That does not include playing golf."

Marisa picked up the folder and scanned it. It was a neat day-by-day breakdown of Trey's duties and responsibilities, organized chronologically and cross-indexed with a master checklist. She scribbled something in the margin, initialed it, then flipped the pages, crossing out that entire agenda and writing "golf" instead.

She handed it to Trey. "Now it does."

He said nothing. She leaned even closer, and the carefully-constructed package revealed itself for the artifice it was. The heavy make-up, the hair expertly sprayed into immobility, the tightly-girdled figure packed into structured linen.

"Let me remind you," she said. "In every contract you sign, there is an 'as-needed' clause."

"I know that."

"Then you know that if I say something is needed, you provide it. That's how that clause works."

Trey glared some more. Trey could work a glare like no man I'd ever known. This one whizzed inches from my face and caught Marisa right between the eyes.

She didn't blink. "I know you'd rather be behind your desk, up to your elbows in paperwork. But you're my premises liability agent. That means you occasionally have to visit some premises."

More glaring. But no arguing. Someone up front called her name, and she tossed a hand in their direction without taking her eyes from Trey.

"You will reschedule," she said. "You will behave. And you will golf."

She straightened her jacket, turned her back to us, and headed for the front of the plane. Apparently she was playing with the big boys once again, ending Phoenix's short era of downsizing and discretion.

I turned to Trey. "So what now?"

"Now I'm rewriting my agenda so that I can squander five hours of research time tomorrow."

He looked frazzled. I reached over and put a hand on the back of his neck. Tight as the skin of a drum. I rubbed my thumb against the grain of his deltoid.

"Breathe, boyfriend."

He inhaled. Exhaled. The flight attendant came by with snacks and drinks. I got both, a white wine paired with smoked almonds and wasabi-roasted peas in a tiny delicate cup. Trey declined.

"This assignment should be straightforward," he said. "A simple premises assessment. I'm already wasting Saturday night with that dress ball. Wasting an additional morning is—"

"Did you say dress ball?"

"Yes, the Black and White." He frowned. "Aren't you going?"

"Not on your life."

"But it's the culminating event of Expo."

"It's out of my income bracket. Also, there's not an army in the world that could get me in a hoop skirt. You're on your own, Rhett."

Trey blinked at me. "Hoop skirt?"

"It's period dress, Trey, didn't you know?" I smiled. "You'd better hope Armani makes nineteenth-century frock coats."

"This is ridiculous."

"I agree. Have fun."

He looked as if he might choke on his own outrage. "Every item on my schedule is…and I suspect that…I mean, it seems as if there's an agenda that has not yet been shared with me. As if I'm being…I need a word. Multi-syllabic, starts with 'm.'"

"Manipulated?"

"Yes. Exactly. And that you're being manipulated too."

"Probably. Yes."

"But Marisa agreed…we agreed."

For the first time, I heard the betrayal in his voice. Back in the spring, Marisa had authorized all manner of subterfuge to spy on him. Nothing personal, she'd explained, just business. They had reached a tentative tête-à-tête, but he had not forgotten. And while his intuition had several wires sprung, it functioned well enough to flare the occasional red alert. It was flaring red now.

"Don't be fooled by that charade," I said. "Marisa wants me on that golf trip. Because you're right—we're being manipulated, both of us."

"How?"

"The Harringtons are after the Bible, and they're using us to draw a bead on it. Me to find it, and you to inadvertently sell me out."

He looked insulted. "I would never—"

"Not intentionally, of course, but you know as well as I do that sometimes you accidentally reveal exactly what you're trying to conceal. Marisa's counting on some informative pillow talk to fall out of your mouth."

"I assure you, my assignment doesn't include spying on you, in bed or otherwise."

"Of course it does. They just haven't told you so." I regarded him over the rim of my wine glass. "But guess what? Savannah is my own personal briar patch. I've got moves here, boyfriend. Try and keep up."

He narrowed his eyes. "You're enjoying this."

I took a sip of wine. "Oh, yes. Immensely. You might too if you'd loosen up a bit."

He kept his eyes on me as the jet engines roared and the plane swung toward the runway. I knew the look. It was the look I got when I pulled off a Krav move perfectly, or hit a solid kill shot at the range. A surprised but confident look, as if I'd upped the ante when he had four aces in pocket.

The plane rocketed down the runway, the sudden force slamming me backwards in my seat. And before I could figure out what was happening, my snack cup went flying toward the back of the plane. It hit the restroom door with a ballistic smack, scattering nuts and dried peas like BBs.

I looked around the cabin. Every single person—Marisa, Reynolds, the guy with the golf clubs—had a steadying hand on their plastic cups. Trey's expression was bland, practically innocent. He raised his hand for the flight attendant.

"Excuse me," he said, "my girlfriend lost control of her snack mix."

Chapter Nine

The windshield wipers swish-swished as we crossed the Talmadge Bridge, the river a slate-colored twist beneath us. Our rental, a Lincoln Town Car, ferried us over the water in a cushioned bubble, as if its tires weren't even touching the pavement. In the distance, the faux gaslights of downtown Savannah glowed through the patchy fog.

Across the river on Hutchinson Island, the Westin Hotel stood sentinel against the mother-of-pearl sky, a sixteen-story, sandstone-colored rectangle with eighteen holes of golf spreading behind and six hundred feet of deepwater dockage before. Right next door, the Savannah International Convention Center stretched along the water—post-modern, stark white, its curved roofline half-concealed by the shrouding mist.

"Our home away from home," I said. "For the next week anyway."

Trey flexed his fingers and frowned. "This steering is loose. And everything's…soft."

"You're used to the Ferrari, that's all."

I turned back to the window, listening to the clop-clop-clop of the bridge plates underneath us. I'd left Atlanta in cold clear sunshine, but Savannah was warm and misty, in the first stages of a soft ripening autumn. It stirred something deep inside me, something tidal.

"The whole city's cursed, you know. By a frustrated journalist, shaking his fist on his way out of town: 'I leave you, Savannah, a curse that is the far worst of all curses—to remain as you are!' And it has, in many ways. Exactly the same."

Trey kept his eyes on the road. Marisa and Reynolds followed behind us in a BMW, their headlights ghostly and inexplicably sinister. All of us gathering, each for different reasons, the Low-country spreading out its ancient, mossy welcome mat.

I turned to Trey. "So you're creating a security plan for Reyn-old's very own golf tournament."

Trey hesitated, then nodded. "The Harrington Lowcountry Classic."

"Is he coming to the Expo too?"

"Yes. And the reenactment at Skidaway Island. And the Black and White Ball."

"Busy man, Mr. Harrington, when he's not trying to snatch my Bible."

Trey tightened his fingers on the wheel and said nothing. He missed the sensory feedback and response of the Ferrari. I'd once thought Ferraris were about indulgence, but after spending time with Trey, I knew they were really about control.

Not that I'd ever gotten my sticky fingers on the wheel. Not yet anyway.

Despite the rain, I rolled down the window and let the smell of the Lowcountry into the car—the humid air thick as vegeta-tion, the chemical pong of the paper mill, the salt-clean top notes of the ocean. It was impossible to separate the land and the sea in Savannah. They encroached and flowed, sometimes antagonistic, always intimate, island and marsh and estuary in sustained restless cycles.

I turned back to Trey. "Are you working tonight?"

"Yes. Are you?"

"Not officially. There is someone I'd like to see, though."

"Who?"

"Winston. My former employer. He runs a tour shop on River Street. John thinks that Hope might have contacted him about finding a buyer for the Bible."

"Do you think John's right?"

"I think Winston is a good place to start. Like a reunion, only…not."

"Tai—"

"I'll stick to places I know, and I'll tell you where I'm going and what I'm doing at all times."

In profile, Trey always looked older, sterner, the first hint of wrinkles visible at the corner of his eye. He flexed his fingers on the wheel yet again, softening his grip.

"Okay," he said. "That seems sensible."

◇◇◇

We'd booked an executive suite at the Westin, on the seventh floor. The room sprawled like a drunken debutante, overflowing onto a balcony with a river view. Below us, the dock lay like a charm bracelet, bordered by a courtyard and swimming pool. Across the water, the blocky River Street skyline glowed gray and amber. The drizzle had dampened the party somewhat, but I saw pedestrians up and down the cobblestones, umbrellas bobbing.

Trey unlocked the interior door and opened up an adjoining room. This was going to be his office while we were there. Mine too apparently. My boxes of Confederate gear were stacked in the corner, rain-dappled but obviously towel-dried by efficient hands. Trey opened his briefcase on the desk and pulled out a sheaf of paperwork.

I linked my elbow with his. "Not yet. Come here first."

He let me pull him onto the canopied balcony. I pointed across the river, to a small shop next to a docked riverboat on the east end, the touristy section. "That's Lowcountry Excursions. I watched them build this hotel from right there."

"You gave tours there."

"Yep." I patted the balcony. "This place we're standing used to be scrubland. When General Sherman threatened the city, the Confederate army escaped across the river to this island, then fled for South Carolina under cover of night. The mayor, waking up the next morning to an undefended city, wisely surrendered. And Sherman decided not to burn down the place."

A massive freighter ship plowed its way past, blocking our view. It was as big as an office building, colossal, with Cyrillic characters spelling out its name.

I shook my head. "Every summer, some drunken tourist tries to swim across the river, with ships like that coming through."

Trey measured the distance with his eyes. "That's seven hundred and fifty feet from bank to bank."

"Correct. But drunk people sometimes make unsound decisions."

I didn't tell him I'd almost done it myself once, chock full of hurrah and stupidity. And bourbon. I'd chickened out, but one of my classmates had taken the plunge. The Coast Guard pulled him out half-drowned fifteen minutes later, upchucking algae and brackish brown water.

I looked over Trey's shoulder to his desk. It was a collection of golf course maps, hotel blueprints, graphs, and charts.

Trey followed my gaze. "I'm studying the basic protocols for some of the major tournaments. Of course this one will be on a smaller scale. Most of the work for Mr. Harrington will be his own personal protection plan."

"To keep him out of trouble?"

"To minimize the potential for liability."

"Same difference."

Trey didn't disagree. "I have to finish the intake report tonight."

"I know. It's okay. I'm going to try to catch Winston." I leaned against the railing, and the wet breeze flipped my hair across my face. "Hope worked for him too, you know. That's where we met. I specialized in ghosts and the Civil War, she knew architecture and famous people."

Trey didn't reply. He was half a second from telling me he didn't want me to go by myself.

"Oh no, you don't," I said. "We made a deal, fair and square."

He shot me a look. "Hardly fair."

"But a deal nonetheless." I rubbed his arm. "Winston is an old friend. I've known him for years. I'll be fine."

Trey examined me, his head tilted. Finally, he squared his shoulders and pulled the keys to the Lincoln out of his pocket.

"Remember," he said. "Sensible."

◇◇◇

He insisted on escorting me downstairs. In the fifteen seconds it took to reach the lobby, he paced off the elevator's dimensions and scanned the ceiling, finally locating the barely perceptible security camera in the corner. Its presence seemed to reassure him.

In the lobby, a uniformed bellhop approached us with a little half-bow. "Mr. Seaver?"

Trey stopped. "Yes?"

The bellhop handed him a card. "You have a delivery, sir. Ms. Randolph too."

Trey looked over the bellhop's shoulder. Two sets of golf clubs leaned against the front desk like incognito celebrities, a men's set and a women's. Callaways, top of the line. Trey opened the card.

"From Reynolds Harrington," he said. He handed the card back to the bellhop. "Take them to the room, please. I'll be right up."

Then he put his hands on his hips and looked hard at me. "Do you have your keys?"

"Room key, car key, cell phone, pepper spray. I even have the .38." I stood on tiptoe and kissed his cheek. "This is my home turf. I know these streets like I know my own bones."

He softened a bit. A peck on the cheek usually had that effect. I headed out the doors, tossing him a wave. "Back in two hours. Be careful with my new clubs."

Chapter Ten

The rain had cleared out all but the most intrepid tourists, the sweetgrass rose-makers and the buskers too, leaving behind a layer of mineral-rich ozone. The street blossomed with familiar sounds and smells—fried shrimp and warm pralines, spilled beer and pipe tobacco, the echoing churn of the paddleboats plowing the water.

I walked carefully on the cobbled walkway, old ballast stones from centuries of ships; they were slippery and treacherous, downright deadly for the high-heeled and inebriated. I was neither, but still cautious. The last thing I wanted to do was call Trey to come and rescue me because I'd sprained my ankle.

So I was moving slow. Paying attention. Which was why I noticed the shadowy figure duck into the alley.

I stopped at the candy shop and pretended to watch a man dump a vat of glazed pecans on a marble slab. I tried to scan the sidewalk with my peripheral vision, but saw only a couple walking arm in arm, a gaggle of art students laughing and elbowing each other.

I shoved my hands in my pockets and kept walking. When I passed the alley, I paused and looked inside. River Street had several of these passages, some stair-stepped, some simple inclines, some narrow, some wide. They all led from River Street to a single long passageway running parallel to the sidewalks and the river, behind the shops. This particular alley had a fire-escape at its entrance, and I waited under it, back against the wet limestone, listening and watching.

But the shadow had vanished.

I knew it wasn't my imagination, however. I also knew I'd shown my hand. Whoever was following me knew I'd burned them—they'd be extra-careful next time, and I was certain there'd be a next time.

Five more minutes of walking took me to the front door of Lowcountry Excursions. I was disappointed to see a CLOSED sign. Granted, it was a Monday afternoon in the off season, and rainy to boot, but rule one of the tour industry was "always be open." I put my hands to the glass and peered inside.

I saw a faint glow toward the back, like a small lamp burning. I followed another side alley around back, the memories crowding like fog, irresistible. I remembered River Street ablaze with summer heat, bursting with tourists, Hope and I taking our break together in this narrow lane behind the shops. It was shaded and cool there, even if it smelled of shrimp shells and standing water and slick stone. We'd sucked down cigarettes, joined by the waitresses and busboys, bound in the camaraderie of exhaustion and nicotine.

I tried the back door to Winston's shop, the one marked EMPLOYEES ONLY. I gave it a push, and soft blurry light squeezed out the sliver, accompanied by the sounds of human activity. I peered inside and saw Winston.

He hadn't changed a bit—mouse-brown hair sticking up in points all over his head, a round face like a harvest moon, one of his eye-blinding Hawaiian shirts paired with worn jeans. He crouched behind the counter on one knee, shoving a box into the storage area, muttering to himself.

I leaned against the wall. "Good help is so hard to find these days."

He jumped and cursed, banging into the counter. The box jangled, the sound of glass against glass, and he moved in front of it quickly, like it contained the crown jewels. Already he was acting suspiciously, and I hadn't even asked the first question.

He squinted. "Tai? Is that you?"

I stepped into the circle of light. "Hey, boss man."

He forced a grin. "Well, I'll be damned. It is you."

The front of the shop lay dark and deserted behind him, but I could make out hazy details. Rows of brochures, a display of Savannah-themed trinkets, a stand of guidebooks. And there, perched beside the cash register, a cage containing a familiar wad of feathers and fluff. It croaked at me, a crooning demented noise.

"You've still got Jezebel, I see."

He snorted. "Damn bird won't die."

The parrot glared at me, then trilled in exact mimicry of a cell phone. The bird was violent emerald green splattered with white and blue, one eye cocked like a lunatic peeking through a keyhole.

Winston grimaced. "Stupid bird. I swear it's possessed."

I pulled a pack of gum from my pocket, shoved two sticks in my mouth. "So how are things with you?"

Winston leaned against the counter, firmly between me and the box. "Pretty good. You looking to get your old job back?"

"Jeez, no. I'm here for the Expo. Got a new gig now."

"Doing what?"

I told him. He laughed. But he didn't move from his spot in front of the counter.

"How about you?" I said. "Still making money hand over fist?"

"Not so much. Lots of competition now—tour buses, tour carriages, tour hearses. Tourists are getting too lazy to walk."

I remembered hanging out with the other guides. We often held contests to see who'd spun the biggest sensationalistic lie and passed it off as fact. Tourists would believe any story, it seemed, if it had a bloodthirsty rogue slave or star-crossed lovers in it. And the tips would increase accordingly.

I tried to look nonchalant. "You haven't seen Hope around by any chance?"

"Hope? Is she back in town?"

He delivered the line smoothly, his eyes wide. I realized then that I didn't need Trey at all—Winston's lie glowed like the Vegas strip on his round innocent cheeks.

I shrugged. "So I've heard."

"I'm surprised you're still speaking to her."

"I'm not. But we have some business."

Winston frowned. "You're not looking to beat her up, are you?"

"No. It's a long story. I figured if she really were back in town, you'd have been her first stop."

"Why would she come looking for me?"

"Because that's what people do—they stick with what they know. Here I am, after all, back in Savannah. Back in this shop, talking to you."

"Sorry. Haven't seen her." He gave me a curious look. "I heard Boone got out of prison. Is that for real?"

Boone again. I was wondering when people would forget we were connected. As long as he was a local legend, however, I guessed that would be never.

"It's for real."

"You been to the compound since he got out?"

"It's not a compound, and no, I haven't. I have no reason to see him, and if he wants to see me, he'll let me know."

Winston's eyes gleamed. "I heard he keeps a gator pit out back, just in case he needs to make somebody disappear." He clapped his hands like two jaws snapping together. "And that on the night of the full moon—"

"Never mind Boone. I have another question." I pulled the old man's photograph from my tote bag and handed it to Winston. "You know this guy?"

Winston examined it. His perplexed expression was genuine this time. "No. Who is he?"

"Vincent DiSilva, of Jacksonville. He might be connected to my situation with Hope."

"How?"

"That's what I'm trying to find out."

Winston examined the photograph deliberately. Good. If Hope had been keeping secrets from him about the origins of that Bible, he might have some questions for her when she showed up again. Because bet my bottom dollar, she was showing up, and soon.

I jabbed my chin at the box under the counter. "That didn't break, did it?"

He paled. "What?"

"Whatever it is in that box. Sounds delicate."

He laughed nervously. "Souvenir shot glasses. You know how tourists are, always wanting something with a shamrock."

I kept the smile plastered on my face. I didn't believe a word coming out of his mouth. But there wasn't much I could do about it at the moment.

I fished out one of my cards and handed it to him. "If you do see Hope, will you let me know? She may have gotten herself in over her head."

"With what?"

"Bad stuff."

He examined the card as if it were possibly counterfeit. "Sure. If she comes around. Which I doubt. Should I tell her you're looking for her?"

I handed him a second card. "Yeah, do that. Tell her I'd like to make a deal. No tricks."

His eyes went shrewd. He tapped my card against the hard grain of the counter. "Sure. But even if she is back in town, she's got no friends in this quarter, not anymore."

"She doesn't need a friend, she needs an accomplice. And in Savannah, those are a dime a dozen."

Chapter Eleven

Back at the hotel, I found Trey engrossed in paperwork in the adjoining room. I hopped up on the edge of his desk.

He moved his papers to the other side of his work space. "You're wet."

"It's raining again." I ran a finger across his shoulders. "You're perfectly dry."

"Of course I am. I haven't left the room."

"Are you sure?"

He frowned at me. "Of course. Why do you ask?"

"Because somebody was following me."

His expression sharpened. "Where?"

"On River Street."

"Why?"

"Good question." I shook rain from my hair, which earned me a reproachful look. "Do you know why anybody would be tailing me?"

"No. Are you sure you were being tailed?"

"Yes. Are you sure you don't know?"

"Yes." He narrowed his eyes. "Was that an accusation?"

"No. Was that an evasion?"

"No."

I smiled. "You sure about that?"

He put down his pen. "Tai. I wasn't following you. We had a deal." He sat back in his chair, his expression razor-sharp, but no longer annoyed. "I had no reason to follow you. If I'd wanted to see what you were doing, I could have gone with you."

"The whole reason for following someone is that you suspect they're up to something they wouldn't otherwise be up to if you were actually right there with them."

"I don't suspect you of anything. And even if I did, that's not my job." He gestured toward the paperwork on his desk. "This is my job. Which I have been doing since you left."

I examined the desktop. It was smothered in complex dense reports, with his neat notes on the yellow pad beside. He'd obviously been hard at work.

"Could it have been Phoenix?" I said.

"Marisa was with me."

"She could have sent one of her minions."

"I'm her minion." He shooed me off the desk and pulled a clean handkerchief from his pocket. "She could have engaged another agent for the assignment. I don't know. But that's not my main concern."

"Mine either. I'm concerned about a wild card stalker. That's why I was hoping it was Marisa."

He polished the wood dry. Handkerchiefs were such useful things, good for evidence collection, first aid, turning hot doorknobs during a fire. Trey was the first guy I'd dated who always had one in pocket.

"Did you get a description?"

"No. The most likely culprit is Hope, but how would she know where to find me?" I had a sudden rush of suspicion. "You think John told her? Somebody at the hotel maybe?"

"I don't know. But I'm filling out a 302 regardless."

Trey tucked the handkerchief in his pocket and returned to the computer. He tapped out a lightning fast sequence, and the Phoenix log-in screen appeared. I grabbed a towel from the bathroom and scrubbed at my damp hair. Trey was always filling out 302s, Phoenix's version of an incident report. They were the first step to going full corporate agent bad ass on some troublemaker.

He typed in the date and time. "Do you have a recent photo of Hope?"

"Sorry. I burned them all."

Trey typed *no photograph available*. "Can you give me a description?"

"About my height, coffee-colored hair, thick and straight and hanging to her butt. Fashion model skinny. She's got puppy-dog brown eyes, a Barbie-doll nose, a rosebud mouth, and no soul."

Trey rendered my description into concrete info: five-six, dark brown hair, slim build. He stared at the screen, his index finger suddenly tapping out a syncopated rhythm. Cognition gear. Some idea trying to find purchase.

"Trey?" I moved to look over his shoulder. "What's wrong?"

He held up one finger. *Wait.* I waited. Another thirty seconds of wildfire typing, and the screen divided itself into a foursquare grid. I recognized this set-up.

"Four-plex security footage," I said.

He nodded, kept typing.

"Of this hotel?"

"Yes. The main elevator specifically, the one we took."

Indeed, there we were, getting off the elevator. The time stamp confirmed that the footage had been taken two hours ago. Trey fast-forwarded a few more seconds, then slowed the footage to real time. He pointed at the upper-left square. "Watch."

I followed his finger. The footage wasn't high resolution, but it was clear enough to make out Trey getting back on the elevator, the bellhop with the clubs too. Trey pressed the button for our floor. A woman swooped in as the doors started to close, smiling an apology.

My stomach dropped. "Omigod! That's Hope!"

Trey blew out a breath. "I suspected as much."

Onscreen, Hope stood closer to him than the space dictated. She was dressed in business attire, a fitted dark jacket and a pencil skirt chopped above the knee. She looked at Trey and her lips moved. Trey made some reply, and she nodded. And then she reached over and patted his bicep, her mouth curved in a flirtatious smile.

I got a surge of anger. "Oh no, she did *not* just put her hand on you."

"Tai."

"And you let her get close enough to do it!" I threw my towel on the floor. "You keep a five-foot barrier around you, all the time, and yet—"

"Tai—"

"You tell me to be careful and there you are, letting her paw you! I cannot believe you fell for that simpering, come-hither—"

"Tai!" He shook his head, eyes on the screen. "I didn't fall for anything. Look again."

Onscreen, the elevator stopped, and Hope got off. She cast one last lingering look, but not at Trey. At the security camera itself. And I saw smug satisfaction shining there, like a warrior counting coup.

I swore fiercely. "I swear to God, I will claw her eyes out if she—"

"Pay attention." Trey rewound to the moment she got on the elevator. "Watch it again."

"Why? So I can get madder?"

"So you can tell me what you see."

I refocused on the screen. As Hope got on, Trey took one step backwards to accommodate her. His feet remained shoulder-width apart, his eyes straight ahead in the disinterested pose of elevator riders everywhere.

Except that Trey's seemingly casual posture was also neutral stance. Except that Trey's body was a weapon, cocked and loaded.

"Tell me what you see," he said.

I sighed. "I see you move out of range when she touches you. I see your left hand preparing for a block and strike. I see your right hand loose and empty and hovering near your gun, in case you need to draw."

He waited. "And?"

I caught his drift and shook my head. He'd displayed not a single marker of sexual interest. And I knew what those looked like. I'd developed a handy playbook based on those.

"Nothing," I admitted. "Not one iota of attraction."

He blinked at me. "What?"

"Which means I owe you an apology. You're not a libido-addled idiot."

"No, I...I mean, yes, that's true, but...that's not..." He shook his head, frustrated, and returned his attention to the screen. "Watch."

The scene played out, yet again. "She gets on, touches you, you back away, she notices the security camera—"

"No." He tapped the screen. "She's not looking *for* the camera. She's looking *at* the camera."

His point finally dawned on me. "She knew it was there."

"Yes."

"Which means she didn't follow us here. She was already at the hotel, she knew we were coming."

"And she'd already surveilled the premises."

We sat there. Hope stared back, her black and white image mocking us, smarter than us, two steps ahead of us.

I whistled softly. "Damn. I need to up my game."

Trey handed me the towel I'd thrown down, now folded into a neat square. "So do I," he said.

Chapter Twelve

The next morning dawned gray, with sodden dense clouds in a low sky. The weatherwoman said to blame the tropical storm hovering offshore east of the Gulf Stream, sending sunshine and thunderstorms in alternating bands of clear and foul weather.

I'd showed up at the driving range anyway, hopeful that the deluge would hold off long enough for at least nine holes. I gave my new driver a practice swing, then retucked the cell phone between my ear and shoulder.

John's voice sounded frustrated. "Look, I didn't have anything to do with Hope showing up at your hotel!"

"So you keep saying."

"Because it's the truth."

"Then how…hang on a second."

I fished a tee out of my pocket and stuck it in the ground. Trey watched from behind the line, sticking out like an Armani-clad sore thumb. He'd agreed to go on the course, but refused to wear golf clothes, insisting that he wasn't golfing.

I jammed the phone back against my ear. "So you have no idea who might have been following me? Or how Hope found out where we were staying?"

"No idea at all."

"You'd better be telling the truth, or I swear—"

"Whole truth, Tai. Why would I lie?"

"Good question. I gotta go. But keep your mouth zipped, you hear me?"

I hung up before he could answer and shoved the phone in the pocket of my khakis. Trey checked his watch. Marisa and Reynolds were still in the pro shop with only ten minutes until tee time.

I picked up a ball from my bucket. "John says he didn't leak our whereabouts to anybody, especially not Hope. He blames somebody at your end."

"I checked with Marisa. There are no leaks at my end."

"You sure about that? Reynolds seems like the talkative type."

"He has no connection to Hope."

"That you know about."

Trey didn't reply. He had his eyes on the horizon, where a curdled mass of clouds lay piled like wet laundry. He checked his watch again, brushing a piece of grass from his immaculate cuff.

"I'm taking care of the situation," he said.

I gave my new driver a practice swing. "You know, Armani does make golf clothes."

"I'm not golfing."

"I saw some Italian leather golf shoes in the pro shop. Removable cleats, black on black."

"I'm not—"

"Yeah, yeah. Not golfing. But Marisa's right—how are you going to put together a security plan for a golf tournament if you don't understand golf?"

"That's why I agreed to come out here. To understand."

"Can't understand if you don't play."

I popped a ball on the tee, took my stance, then swung. It was a clean hit, a little hooky, but powerful. Trey watched, a glimmer of curiosity in his eyes.

I pulled the driver from his bag and handed it to him. "Forged titanium construction. Nice big sweet spot, good for newbies."

He accepted the club, his brain calculating its measurements, heft, and tensile strength. He scrutinized the head, running his thumb along the grooves in the club face.

I shook my head. "Not like that. You're holding it like a weapon." I came up behind him, reaching around to place his hands properly on the grip. "Hold it like this, firm but light. Let the club do its thing."

"What's a club's thing?"

"The swing is its thing." I put my hands on his waist. "Head down, eyes on the ball. Ease it back on the diagonal, then… swish." I moved him through a practice swing, feeling the ripple of his lats on the pivot, then stepped back. "Now try it for real."

He swung the club back and forth gently, testing its balance. And then he pulled back, swung through, and sent the ball straight into the air with a sweet thwack like a champagne cork popping. It sailed through the air in a precise arc and landed two hundred yards downrange like it had followed a plumb line.

I stared at him. "Can't you suck at something just once?"

He examined the club, then peered at the ball. "Apparently not golf."

"So you'll play?"

He handed the club back to me. "No."

"Why not?"

"Because I'm here to understand the overall structure of the game. I can do that best by observing, not interacting."

I dropped his driver back in the bag and didn't argue further. His mind required distance and objectivity, and a golf course was an organic, almost sentient thing, ripe with chaos and distraction. He'd need every ounce of his formidable focus to get a grip on it.

I heard Marisa and Reynolds approaching from the club-house, Reynolds with his deep rich baritone, Marisa…laughing? She had her bag on her shoulder, a smile on her face. She even wore a skort, her platinum hair in a tidy knot at her nape.

She hoisted her bag into the back of her cart. "Are we ready?"

"We will be," I replied. "As soon as we get Trey some shoes."

He opened his mouth to protest, but I cut him off. "You can keep the suit, but we're going back for the shoes. If you think pizza is hard on the Prada, you should try marsh mud."

◇◇◇

I rode with Reynolds, Trey with Marisa. The first eight holes went smoothly, but then on the ninth, she sliced one into the out-of-bounds and sent Trey to fetch it while she took a phone call. Reynolds and I sat in our cart and waited.

"You're looking good," he said. "Play much?"

"Not anymore."

I didn't tell him I'd grown up on the golf course, my dad usually being the club champion. I'd inherited his swing, but not his discipline, and got banned after I broke in one night and did some drag racing with the carts, sending one of them into the drink. I still remembered the sky that night, as open and limitless and miraculous as a fairy tale.

Reynolds pulled a beer from the cooler. "I hear you're headed for the Expo tomorrow. I didn't think that started until Friday."

"It's the vendor's welcome barbecue. I'm meeting my aunt Dee Lynn there."

"Does she sell guns too?"

"No, she's a relic hunter. Digs and dives. Her specialty is Civil War artifacts, but she also finds jewelry, fossils, bottles."

He stuck a cigar between his teeth. "Is she single?"

I laughed. "As single as they come, but you gotta be a brave man to tap that."

Up ahead, Trey poked at the edge of the cattails, squinting at something beyond the waist-high sedge. I stuck some tees into my ponytail and reached for a beer. This could take a while.

I popped the cap. "A fundraising tournament, huh? Whose idea was that, yours or your sister's?"

"Mine, but this is the first time she's actually gone along with it. We're reaching that age, you know. Legacy. She's afraid I'll fritter away my half of the estate. A tournament would keep me busy and fill the foundation coffers with friends and funds."

I smiled at him. "Do you fritter, Mr. Harrington?"

He grinned around his cigar. "It's Reynolds, m'dear, and yes, I fritter. Drives the old girl batty."

Marisa waved us to go on without them, so Reynolds took the cart up to the green. I had the better lie, uphill from the cup, but he had three strokes on me. Reynolds was a steady, smart golfer, strong and long on the fairway, indolently precise with his short game.

We pulled our putters and headed for the green. "Do you collect Civil War memorabilia too?"

"No, I'm more of the genteel ne'er-do-well. Audrina's the collector."

I remembered my afternoon at her mansion—the hundreds of papers and books, the black-haired, blue-eyed wait staff. Yes, once Audrina wanted something, she wanted all of it, all for her.

"Everybody has their interests," I agreed.

"Indeed. So I leave the business of collection to Audrina and that narrow-headed authenticator of hers, and I work the crowds. So to speak."

I stepped over the cart rope and headed for the pin, dodging goose droppings. "You and Mr. Fitzhugh don't get along?"

"That twit? He keeps trying to convince Audrina to cut me off. But she can't—that's not how our father set up the foundation. I control half, she controls half. Fitzhugh seems to think he should have a half too."

He pulled the flag for me and stepped out of the way. I could feel his eyes on my butt as I lined up the shot, but I popped the ball too hard, and it lipped out. I called the thing a foul name, and Reynolds barked a hearty laugh.

I held the flag for him. As he approached, a blue heron took flight from the flat gray pond behind us, beating its wings hard against a slanting brisk wind. Everything was manicured and velvety green, tidy and precise, but the weather had a temper that no groundskeeper could tame.

"So you're here to make friends in the Lowcountry?" I said.

"That's the idea." He blew out a plume of rich blue smoke. "Unless Audrina manages to kill me first. Then the whole plan's shot to hell."

I stared at him. He placed his cigar on the ground, lined up the putt, and sank it quickly and cleanly.

I wasn't sure I'd heard him right. "Did you say she's trying to kill you?"

He picked up his cigar and stuck it in his mouth. "Last year for Christmas, she got me skydiving lessons. For my birthday, a Kodiak bear hunting expedition in Alaska. In six weeks, she's sending me diving with great whites in Australia. What does that sound like to you?"

"Like she's trying to kill you."

"See?" Reynolds chuckled. "I'm kidding, of course. What she's trying to do is keep me far away from the foundation."

"Why?"

"Because deep in my sister's tight little heart, she wants to control everything—the foundation, the collection, the family name. Having me out of the way makes that easier, which makes Fitzhugh happy too. He's always telling her what a tragedy it would be to let the infidels get their filthy hands on the family treasures. Audrina falls for that 'great privilege, great responsibility' argument every time."

"But you think differently?"

"I do. Those items belong to history, not us. Creating a museum will make sure they're cared for properly for the long haul *and* accessible to all." He waggled his putter at the hole. "Now sink that gimme already. I've got a poker game with the mayor, and you've got to chase that Bible."

I took my stance, eyes on the ball. "What Bible?"

He laughed again. "Let's drop the pretense. The tournament is a bribe. In return, I'm supposed to spy on you and let Audrina know if you find the Bible so that Fitzhugh can convince you to sell it."

I tapped the ball lightly, and it rattled into the cup. "Or steal it out from under me."

"Or that. And Trey's here to keep me out of trouble while I perpetrate all this nefariousness, even though I'm not supposed to know that."

"I'm pretty sure Trey doesn't know that."

"And Marisa's here to grease the slippery wheels of her profit margin. It's a game of monkey-in-the-middle, with that Bible the grand prize. And some of the other players don't play nice."

"You mean like Hope Lyle?"

He squinted in what looked like genuine confusion. "Who?"

I hurried back to my bag and pulled out the screenshot of Hope smirking with tart satisfaction at the surveillance camera. I handed it to Reynolds.

He grinned. "Goodness gracious. Is she single?"

"No. You recognize her?"

He shook his head. "What's she got to do with the Bible?"

"Long story." I took the photo back. "But if she shows up, you need to tell me."

"Why?"

"Because it will put me one step closer to finding that Bible. Which puts you one step closer to getting it without Fitzhugh's involvement." I smiled. "But don't forget I don't always play nice either."

"Some people play especially not-nice."

"Like who?"

"You know who. The Invisible Empire. Well-moneyed and ruthless, with a taste for Confederate memorabilia. If she's one of them…"

I got a shiver, and it wasn't from the suddenly chill wind. The Ku Klux Klan. The great Southern shadow, still long, still dark, still thick in the least expected places.

"What would the KKK want with a Bible signed by Lincoln and Sherman? They're Yankees."

"You got me. But whenever big money items show up, so does the Klan. And they pay well. But my sister and I will pay you better, and we're not evil."

He said this pleasantly, but a vague feeling of apprehension washed over me anyway. We returned to the cart just as Trey and Marisa pulled up beside us. Trey got out, but Marisa remained in the cart, still talking on her phone.

I plucked a piece of pine straw from Trey's hair. "Did you find her ball?"

"No. There were alligators."

I'd seen the reptiles in question, maybe three feet long, their knobby noses poking above the waterline. Not harmless, but no cause for panic. Of course, I'd watched Trey become practically unglued around a rather petite reticulated python.

"So you gave up?"

He looked at me as if I were insane. "Alligators," he repeated. "Plural."

In the distance, the clouds thickened, and the first fat drops of rain splattered on the plastic windshield. Reynolds held out his hand, palm up.

"Blast it," he said.

Marisa put her phone away. "It doesn't matter, we have to go. The director of Secure Systems says he can squeeze in a lunch meeting. We might have a hardware vendor."

"But I have poker," Reynolds protested.

"Not if you want your tournament." She turned to Trey. "How soon can you be ready?"

"I've got to shower and change and print out the specs. I'll meet you there in forty-five minutes." He turned to me. "What will you do while I'm gone?"

I remembered Reynolds' words. The KKK had their grubby fingers in this mess, although for the life of me I couldn't figure out why. But I knew who could help me start.

"I've got to make a delivery," I said.

"But I'll have the car."

"I'll take the bus. Or a cab."

He frowned. "Can't this wait until I get back?"

I put my hand on his arm. "Trey, you can't be with me every second. I have my job to do, like you have yours. Trust me, okay?"

The rain intensified, and the first rumble of thunder rolled over the horizon. He nodded, albeit reluctantly, and sat beside me in the cart. Reynolds climbed in next to Marisa. He tipped his hat in my direction and grinned wide, and for a second, I understood why Trey got squeamish around alligators. Even when they smiled, it was all teeth.

Chapter Thirteen

Billie was my favorite relative. She was a distant cousin on my mother's side, smart as a whip, with a laugh like a war whoop. She was also the most talented mechanic I'd even known. Boats, cars, motorcycles, it didn't matter—they all loved her, and she loved them back. So I wasn't surprised that when I spotted her overall-clad backside, she was working on an old Buick, arms deep in the heart of the vehicle.

"That's where you were last time I saw you," I said.

She spun around. "Tai!"

She wiped her hands on her thighs and came around to give me a hug. She had the same build as I did, the broad shoulders and generous girl curves of my mother's people, but where I tended to freckled and frizzy blond, she had ivory skin and close-cropped dark hair.

"Special delivery," I said, pulling the jewelry box from my pocket and opening it for her.

She peered inside, eyes wide. "I swear, it's just like the one in the picture!"

A cameo brooch nestled in the velvet folds, a silhouette in creamy blue and ivory porcelain, exactly like the one belonging to our great-great-grandmother. Our common ancestor had lived to ninety-seven, and most stories described her as a real pistol ball who smoked a pipe and pulled her skirts up too high when she danced. When I'd seen the pin in an online auction,

I'd snapped it up for Billie. She looked like motor oil and overalls on the outside, but she was violets and lace on the inside.

Her grease-stained finger hovered over the delicate filigree. "It's beautiful."

"It's yours."

"How much?"

"On the house."

"I can't—"

"You can. And all I ask in return is a little information. And maybe some wheels."

She grinned at me. "That I can do."

◇◇◇

We shared Cokes in the tiny windowed office next to the garage bays, a dinky window unit AC doing its best to make the air temperate. Two of her employees changed the oil in a Ford flatbed, laughing and cutting up. The dusty grease on the walls was as ancient as cave art, but Billie kept the space neat and organized.

"What kind of wheels you need?" she said.

"The kind that can get me out to Boone's and back."

Her face went serious. She knew the complicated dynamics of that situation as well as I did.

"What you want with Boone?"

"I'm hearing rumors."

"What kind of rumors?"

"Klan rumors."

She sat back in her seat abruptly. "Tai—"

"I know. But if anybody can give me the lowdown on what those sons of bitches are up to, it's Boone."

She shook her head. "He got out of that in prison."

"I know. That's why he's the perfect source. He still keeps his finger on that pulse, but he's got no loyalty to the cause. No reason to tell them I'm snooping around."

She toyed with a random screw, tapping it against the oilcloth-covered table. "Doesn't matter, they'll know the second you show up. His boys are still in it, both of them on the selectmen council, from what I hear."

"The what?"

"Klan's not what it used to be. It's all committees now, and meetings, and agendas." Her face wrinkled in disgust. "They've got lobbyists and lawyers."

"Any reason they'd be interested in a fancy Bible?"

And then I explained. She shook her head, staring at her Coke.

"They're in the antique trade, but I can't see them wanting that particular Bible." She drained the rest of her Coke and put the bottle down hard. "Which one of the boys did you talk to about meeting Boone, Jasper or Jefferson?"

"Jasper."

Her lip curled. "I heard he has his own little militia group within the ranks. Like a racist SWAT team. Still playing second dog to Jefferson, though, still looking for a way up the ladder."

That sounded exactly like the Jasper I remembered, always wanting what his big brother had. "Jasper said he'd ask Boone and let me know. So that's the other reason I'm here. Boone's gonna want to see me alone. And I have this problematic boyfriend—"

"What?" Billie frowned. "He's not giving you trouble, is he? You need me to explain things to him?"

She was serious. If she thought Trey was mistreating me, she would wade in on him with a wrench in one hand and a blowtorch in the other. She'd get her pretty ass handed to her on a hubcap, but she'd go down bloody and beaten and glowing with righteousness.

"Nothing like that. But he's somewhat overprotective, and I occasionally need room to maneuver. Which means I need my own ride. And I was hoping you could help me with that."

She smiled. "You are gonna love me forever for this."

◇◇◇

She took me out back, and I froze in my tracks. "My Camaro!"

I approached it as a pilgrim might approach the Grail. The Z-28 glowed even in the cloud-dimmed light, a glorious stretch of cherry-red zoom-zoom with four on the floor and a performance-enhanced engine that would streak from zero to sixty in 6.7 seconds. When I'd sold it to her, it had been sun-bleached to a dull rouge, its console cracked and warped. But Billie had restored its former glory. It glistened now as lush as ripe fruit.

She stroked the hood. "You can borrow it, no problem. But I was thinking you might want to buy it back."

"Really? Why?"

"It's been fun, Lord has it. But I need something a little more grown-up." She looked down, blushing. "Something big enough for a car seat, you know?"

She put her hands on her belly. It took a minute for her meaning to sink in. "Are you telling me what I think you're telling me?"

She grinned. "Three months along now. Me and Travis love that car, but it won't do for us anymore, and I'd rather you have it than some stranger."

Oh, how I'd missed that car, putting the pedal to the floor and feeling those horses rear and snort. I'd had my fifth kiss, third make-out session, and first cigarette on those leather seats.

She ran one finger along the chrome. "So what do you say?"

I felt luckier than I ever had in my life, like I might go buy a hundred lottery tickets. "God, Billie. Yes. Absolutely yes."

◇◇◇

The leather squeaked against my khakis as I slid into the driver's seat. I adjusted the mirror, seeing Billie standing there in my rearview. When I twisted the key in the ignition, the engine snarled, then vibrated into a rumble. I put the accelerator down, and the whole chassis shimmied.

I pulled out slowly at first, getting reacquainted with the beast. Every time I sat in the passenger seat of the Ferrari, the speedometer pinned to fifty-five, my skin itched. But the Camaro was *mine*. I could let her off the chain, take her screaming over the bridge into South Carolina, find some oysters and cold beer.

Instead, I turned down White Bluff and headed south. The live oaks held their moss-draped branches in a soft canopy over the road, every tree I passed a step backward in time.

I'd spent my whole life with my rearview mirror angled so that I didn't have to look at where I'd been. I'd kept my eyes on the horizon, my foot on the gas, and there was only one U-turn on my record—the one that had taken me back to Trey, the one that had ended less than ten minutes later with me in his bed.

That was history, our history. And now I was back in Savannah, steeping in my own history. There and back again. Wasn't that the oldest story in the book?

Only my back-again was Atlanta now, that place of ashes and rising, not this place of salt and tides. Atlanta sprawled like an enormous amoeba, a city as transitory as its airport, nobody ever touching down for long. In Atlanta, you could write your own history, revise the story until even you yourself believed it.

Nobody in Atlanta knew that my dad drank himself into an oblivion so deep that when the heart attack came, it must have been a gentle push over the edge. Nobody knew that my mother watched him sink into that oblivion, this man who was supposed to take her away from Georgia but who instead had joined her here. Nobody knew that I was an unplanned and probably unwelcome surprise. Nobody knew.

Nobody except my brother. And Rico.

I parked outside the gates of Plantation Cove—still exclusive, still sequestered. I didn't know the access code anymore, so the wrought iron and boxwood barrier was as close as I could get. I called Rico, not expecting him to answer. When he did, my voice cracked.

"Hey you," I said.

"Hey, baby girl, I was about to call you."

"You always say that."

He hesitated, and his voice went gentle. "Uh oh. What's wrong?"

"Nothing." I wiped my eyes. "I'm sitting here outside Plantation Cove, that's all."

Rico was silent. My childhood home lay beyond that gate. It had a rectangular swimming pool and a patio clouded with crepe myrtle, a cookie-cutter McMansion like dozens of others.

Rico's house sat across the street from it. Strangers lived in mine now. Rico's parents still lived in his, I supposed, although I didn't know for sure since they didn't speak to me anymore. Or to Rico. Not since he'd come out of the closet.

"Damn," I said.

"Damn straight."

"It's too big, Rico."

"Then leave it be until you're bigger than it is."

We sat in silence, tethered to each other by the past and the phone line. Finally, he sighed. "We done reminiscing now?"

"Yep. Thanks."

"You're welcome. Wanna hear what I found out about your dead guy in Florida?"

I sat up straight. "You found something?"

He laughed. "I knew that would cheer you up."

"Rico—"

"DiSilva was a pretty vanilla dude—no criminal records, no wants and warrants, no divorces or paternity suits. Only one soft spot. He had a whole set of e-mails linked to the same IP address in Jacksonville. Each had a separate registration name, each would be active for a while and then deleted."

"He had an alter ego?"

"More like a new identity every six months or so. Now some people do legitimate business under a pseudonym, but that looks a whole lot different than this."

"This looks like a scam artist."

"It does."

I drummed on the dashboard. "Black market antiques maybe, to supplement the retirement?"

"Dunno. You said you talked to the cops down in Jacksonville?"

"Garrity did."

"Nobody said nothing about this?"

"No. You think I should put them on it?"

"I would. Your old guy may have died innocent, but I'm thinking he didn't live that way."

Chapter Fourteen

When I got back to the hotel room, the first thing I did was download and print the files Rico had sent. The mass of new, neatly organized paperwork on the desk told that that Trey had come and gone again. He'd also rearranged the sofa cushions and re-made the bed with surgical precision. Our golf bags now stood sentinel in the corner of the bedroom, not sprawled next to the sofa, and my shoes were lined up in a soldierly row in the closet.

I sighed. Sometimes that man...

I changed out of my khakis and golf shirt and ducked into the shower, leaving my phone on the countertop where I could hear it. I turned the water as hot as I could stand it and stuck my face in the spray. I knew why the memories rose—I was in the cauldron that created them. I'd underestimated their power, however, like I'd underestimated a lot of things.

The KKK, for example. I was not naïve—I knew the Confederate cause was dear to the racist heart. People dismissed my reenactor clients as crazy for running around in fields, eating from cast iron pots, sleeping in primitive tents. But they were living a memory the rest of us were trying to forget.

So was the Klan, in their own way. A memory we didn't deserve to forget, not yet.

I wrapped up in one of the hotel's robes and pulled my copies from the printer. Trey's desk now sported fresh sketches from our golf game—the front nine, the clubhouse, the parking lot.

In the middle of the desk sat a stack of file folders, including surveillance system installation materials from Secure Systems. New maps too, a multitude of them making a pastel patchwork.

I turned the Hutchinson Island map around to see the details better. The hotel and the convention center stood side by side, sandwiched between the acres of manicured golf courses on the northern border and the gray skein of the Savannah River to the south. Undeveloped scrub land lay to the east and west, with the twin buildings like paired jewels not yet set into a crown. But they would be, and soon. The cranes were already in place.

I sat on the bed and dumped out my tote bag, sorting the research into four piles—one for Hope, one for Winston, one for Vincent DiSilva down in Florida, and one for the Harringtons. I knew I'd need a fifth pile eventually—for the KKK—but I didn't want to think about that yet.

My phone rang. I checked the number, then took a deep steadying breath. "Hey, Jasper."

"Got your message."

His voice was familiar, another memory surfacing. I waited, but he didn't offer any pleasantries. I took the cue and got to business.

"Did you talk to Boone?"

"Yeah."

"And?"

"He said he'll meet you at Oatland Island. Three o'clock."

I snatched a pen from Trey's desk. "I thought he was on electronic monitoring?"

"He gets to leave the house twice a week. Today's one of his days."

"Can't I meet him at the house?"

"He don't take visitors anymore."

"Come on, Jasper, I—"

"That's his offer. You don't want it, I'll tell him so."

"No, no. I'll be there." I scribbled the info on my palm. "Oatland Island. Three o'clock."

"At the wolf den. And come alone."

I recapped the pen and placed it back exactly where I'd left it, precisely aligned with the pencil and highlighter. "Don't worry, Jasper. You didn't have to tell me that part."

Chapter Fifteen

I'd been to Oatland Island more times than I could count. Science teachers loved the nature preserve, and today was no exception. Three fat yellow school buses hunkered on the grassy field that served as a parking lot. I noticed a silver Hummer, incongruous and menacing. Boone's car, I was betting.

I crumpled up the sandwich bag from my lunch and parked. And then I froze, stunned. No. It couldn't be.

But it was.

The black Lincoln rested in the shade of a sprawling live oak. A familiar figure leaned against the driver's side, making notations in a palm-sized leather notebook.

I got out. "Trey? What the hell?"

He looked up. One eyebrow rose as he took in the Camaro. "Where did you get that?"

"I asked you a question."

"No, you didn't. You—"

"What are you doing here?"

"The same thing you are." He checked his notes. "Meeting Beauregard Forrest Boone. Two-time felon, assorted charges for alcohol, tobacco, and marijuana smuggling, two counts involuntary manslaughter. Ties to several white supremacist organizations, including serving as a Grand Dragon in the KKK. Out now on compassionate parole."

He snapped the notebook shut and looked at me, eyes hard. Felons belonged behind bars in Trey's worldview. Not meeting me, his all-by-herself girlfriend, on some island.

I glared at him. "You followed me."

"Of course I didn't. I got here first."

"But how…" Then it hit me. "Omigod, you bugged my phone!"

Trey looked insulted. "I did not. Georgia law forbids tele-communications interception without consent of both parties." He paused, then cocked his head. "I bugged the hotel room."

It took me a second for his words to register. "You did what?"

"It's a simple infrared signal burst device. I installed it right after lunch. It saves each session as a separate MP3 file, time coded, smart phone accessible. See?"

He held the phone out. Sure enough, the screen displayed a neat listing of several recordings, each time-stamped, including my most recent visit to the room.

I felt a hot geyser of mad bubbling in my chest. "And you didn't think to tell me this?"

"You were gone."

"So? You had no right to bug our room!"

"It's not *our* room, it's *my* room, and as the primary registrant, I had the legal authority—"

"Don't throw legal bullshit at me! I'm your girlfriend, for crying out loud!"

"That has no relevance."

I held out my hand. "Give me that phone! I'm dismantling this set-up right now."

"Not until we've talked to Boone."

"We? No way. I'm talking to Boone all by myself, and you're waiting here until I come back."

He shook his head. "That's not how this works."

"It bloody well is. We made a deal. You agreed to drop the overprotective routine."

"And you agreed to be sensible."

"This is sensible!"

He folded his arms. "You're meeting a convicted felon, alone, without telling anyone where you are. You've got no back-up and no secondary escape options, which means that what you're doing is not only not sensible, it is, in any reasonable estimation, stupid."

I stared up at him. His expression was serious, but not bland. And not passive. He was angry—I saw it in the flash of his eyes, the set of his jaw. I remembered the last time he'd gotten angry with me and swallowed hard. Anger got the juices flowing in more ways than one. I knew the hormonal cascade—cortisol then adrenalin—and I knew what happened with a dose of dopamine in the cocktail. It had happened before, red-eyed fury burning into something equally hot, and maybe even more dangerous.

I bit back the curse. This was getting us nowhere. I had Boone to deal with. The last thing I needed was a lover's spat with my pissed-off, chemically unstable powder keg of a boyfriend.

I kept my voice calm. "One question."

"What?"

"When you installed that system, were you being my boyfriend? Or were you being a corporate security agent?"

He looked startled. "What?"

"How about showing up here? Boyfriend or security agent?"

He shook his head. "I don't know. But I'm here. And I've presented a valid interpretation of the scenario. You know I have."

How had we gotten into this mess? Which had come first, the stupid chicken or the overprotective egg?

I rubbed my eyes. "It's valid based on the facts you have. But there are things you don't know."

"Then tell me."

"I will. On the way."

"To where?"

"To see Boone."

He frowned suspiciously. "You're letting me come?"

"You may as well. You probably slipped some bugging device in my underwear when I wasn't looking."

He made a soft noise of affront. "I did not."

He started to walk around me, but I planted myself in front of him. "One condition—you have to let me talk to Boone alone. You can watch. There's an observation area. But he wants to see me alone, and I agreed, so that's the situation."

"It's too risky."

"I'll be perfectly safe."

"He's a convicted felon."

"Who is also my uncle."

Trey blinked at me. The forest wove a tapestry of sound around us, including the long piercing cry of a red-tailed hawk, followed by a cacophony of shrieks and harsh calls, like the soundtrack of a Tarzan movie.

"I've known him since I was a baby," I continued. "And he'd sooner cut off his own head than hurt me, but he does not like tardiness any more than you do. So come on. The wolf den is this way."

◇◇◇

Trey and I took the path backwards. Normally the trail ran counterclockwise, winding first through the gator pond, then past the bobcats and foxes, the eagles and panthers. But we weren't sightseeing. We had one goal in mind.

The wolves.

We took the path side by side, and I explained my complicated ties to Boone. "He married my mama's sister fresh out of high school. They opened a boat servicing business and marina, a very successful one. When I was little, our families used to spend Saturdays together at Boone's place. I'd play hide and seek with Jefferson and Jasper— Boone's kids, my cousins—and the grown-ups would drink."

The memories flooded me as I talked, incandescent and idyllic and almost tangible, like mental postcards. Trey didn't interrupt. He let me set the pace, our shoes crushing gravel.

I sighed. "But Boone and Aunt Rowena got involved with the KKK. She eventually ran off with another Klansman, dumped the boys on Boone and vanished. Mama said I wasn't allowed out there anymore, so I didn't seen any of them until I became a teenager and could sneak out on my own. Jasper and Jefferson were too grown-up to hang around with me then, but Boone always had time."

Trey held a moss-tangled branch out of the way. He was back to his usual patient chivalry. As we walked, I told him the stories I'd grown up with, hissed under my mother's breath in the kitchen when I was supposed to be in bed. Told with a grin by my other cousins at the family reunions. Spread by the kids in high school who counted on him for their underage libations.

Boone was a legend. And as his niece, I was a legend by proxy. Many a school bully left me the hell alone when someone whispered his name. For several years, I couldn't pick a fight on any playground in town.

I shoved my hands in my pockets. "He ditched the KKK when he went to prison the first time. Saw the error of his ways and repented."

Trey arched one eyebrow. "Really?"

"I know, hard to believe. But these days, if you wanna be a successful smuggler, you gotta deal with the melting pot."

"You said he repented."

"Oh, the violence and race hating, yeah. But not the moonshining and tobacco smuggling, which is why he eventually went back to prison. Now he's home servicing boats again, him and Jefferson and Jasper all on their best behavior, although the rumor mill proclaims otherwise."

Trey stopped. In the distance a whooping crane made an unearthly racket. "Why did you arrange this meeting?"

"Because I'm trying to decide if the KKK is involved in the hunt for the Bible. If they are, Boone will know."

"And he'll tell you?"

"Of course." I stopped and pointed. "There it is."

What looked like a log cabin was actually the entrance to the wolf pack observation area. We went into the cool dark interior, a rustic room with a dirt floor and three exposed log walls. The fourth wall was thick clear plastic, a transparent barrier between the visiting humans and the resident wolves.

A pack of five, they moved like ghosts through the shifting green shadows and wan afternoon light, three of them loping the perimeter of their territory, two others resting in the shade. At the other end of the enclosure, waiting in the outdoor observation area, I saw Boone.

He was shorter than average, but it took looking twice to notice because he carried himself tall. He wore his thin blond hair in a perpetual crew cut and shaded his pale white skin under the brim of a slouchy Panama hat. Still as lean as a whippet, he could arm wrestle men twice his size into submission.

"That's Jefferson out there with Boone," I said, "which means Jasper's at the door. Both of them are mean as snakes and very good at hide and seek."

"So one stays with Boone, and the other stays with me?"

"Most likely."

"I don't like that."

"It's the rule."

Trey didn't argue; he understood rules. He kept his eyes on Boone even when I put my hand under his jacket and rubbed his back. He was fully strapped, the H&K nestled in the shoulder holster.

I dropped my voice. "Listen, Jasper's the meanest, the sneakiest too. But he's no match for you. And I'll be right there, on the other side of that door, two seconds away. Okay?"

Trey nodded. "Okay."

Jasper opened the door leading to the outdoor viewing area. He had Boone's raw looks, but none of his cool Nordic temperament. Like his brother standing outside, he wore combat boots and camo and probably had six different weapons on him.

He glared at Trey, then turned the glare on me. "Daddy said alone."

Through the open door, I saw Boone leaning against the wooden railing. He gave Trey a cursory glance, then nodded.

Trey didn't react. His hands were open, shoulders dropped, backbone straight. He was calm and collected, but it was the poise of an unsplit atom. He wasn't happy about this, but he was willing to trust me. The thought made my heart pound.

Or maybe that was Jasper with the .45 in his waistband.

Too late to reconsider.

I went through the door, and Jasper shut it behind me.

Chapter Sixteen

Boone watched me approach. He wore tiny round spectacles that intensified his eyes, hazel green going to ice-gray at the edges, like moss caught in a frost.

He pulled off the glasses. "Well, look at you."

I stepped into his embrace. His chest felt thin against mine, and I realized he was skin and bone under his jacket. His scent was a punch in the memory banks—Red Man chewing tobacco and Lifebuoy soap.

Jefferson watched from the edge of the wooded trail. Darker in hair, keener of eye, and swarthier than his brother, he had the calm authority of the eldest son. Despite his demeanor, I knew he was on red alert. So were Jasper and Trey back in the observation room. Boone and I were the epicenter of so much aggression-fueled focus, I thought we might combust like ants under a magnifying glass.

Boone examined Trey with sharp appraisal. "You brought muscle?"

"No. That's my boyfriend."

"He's a cop."

"Ex-cop."

"Same difference." Boone polished his glasses on his sleeve. "He's got Black Irish in him."

"On his mother's side, yes."

"And his father?"

"Your guess is as good as mine. The man abandoned his family when Trey was two."

Boone regarded Trey with new eyes. In the enclosure, the wolf closest to us stopped pacing and turned its nose into the wind. It was colored the hard pale white of quartz, its every movement honed and deliberate.

Boone put his glasses back on. "So what ant hill you gone and stirred up now?"

I told him the story. He eyed me with curiosity. "You think somebody killed that old man down in Florida?"

"The autopsy said natural causes."

Boone smiled wryly. "Every death's from natural causes."

"You know what I mean."

"I do. But you got this story secondhand from John Wilde." He spat on the ground. "Why concern yourself with his business?"

"Because that's all it is—business. You know how that goes."

He clucked his tongue. "So what do you want from me?"

"Information."

"Why should I help you now?"

"Oh, come on, Boone!"

"I haven't heard a word from you since your mama's funeral."

"And you know that's not true. I sent you a thank-you card for those flowers. The ones you didn't put your name on? The pot of marigolds? Don't even pretend that wasn't you."

He didn't deny the accusation.

"So help me or don't help me, but don't make it about what an ungrateful wretch I am."

He smiled. "Did I say I wouldn't help you? I made up my mind when I heard you were coming back home."

I didn't ask him how he'd heard. He kept his ears pricked, like the wolves.

"I'm out of my league here," I said. "Trey's equipped to deal with this kind of stuff—"

"He looks like it."

I laughed. Boone wasn't one to be fooled by a little Armani. I glanced over at the observation area. Trey was watching one of the wolves, a dark gray creature as lean as a shadow. The wolf was watching him right back.

I turned back to Boone. "But this is my battle, not Trey's. And I don't want it following me back to Atlanta."

"Makes sense. Anything in particular you want to know about?"

"This woman, for starters." I handed him the still shot from the elevator footage. "Her name is Hope Lyle, although she may be using an alias."

He examined the image, then shook his head. "Nothing on her."

"How about this guy, Winston Cargill?" I handed him another printout, pulled from the Lowcountry Excursion website, featuring Winston resplendent in one of his Hawaiian shirts. "He's hiding something, for sure, including a big box of something under his front counter."

Boone looked at me over his glasses. "You heard I'm on the straight and narrow, right? Don't reckon I'll be peeking under any man's front counter."

"I'm not here to sic a burglar on anybody. All I want is information."

"About these two?"

"Yes. And the local Klan. Rumor has it they're poking about in the same spots I am."

The words fell between us into a flat uncomfortable silence. Boone looked significantly at Jefferson, who returned the gaze evenly. Then he looked at me.

"I don't run with that crowd anymore. But they know better than to lay a hand on you."

"Are they in the trade right now?"

"What trade?"

"The Confederate relic trade."

Boone scratched the back of his neck. "I suppose so."

"Will they be at the Expo?"

"Guess you'll find out tomorrow, won't you?"

"So—"

"That's all I'm saying. You'll have to figure out the rest yourself. But watch yourself, girl. The brotherhood does not play."

I didn't ask any more questions. Information was a commodity, after all; it had its own systems of commerce. I leaned on the wooden railing next to Boone. The wolves went about their business.

Boone waved his hand at the gathered pack. "Which one you think is the alpha?"

The slate-colored wolf was now sitting right in front of Boone, staring at him with challenge in its clear gray eyes. I pointed.

Boone shook his head. "Nah. That's Cheyenne. He's the beta."

I looked over to where Trey stood. A large silver-gray wolf now paced back and forth in front of him. It reminded me of the way Trey paced sometimes, tight turns, repetitive.

"That one?"

"Nope. That's Brook. Mid-level." Boone pointed. "See the white one over there, next to the den?"

"The one that's asleep?"

"Pfft. He's not asleep. That's Odin. All the other guys are scrambling for any opportunity that comes, but Odin? He knows he's top dog." Boone put a foot against the fence and leaned forward. "Your feller over there? He's all alpha. Probably quiet, though, when he's not knocking heads. Real clear ideas about right and wrong. Reads people like a book."

I kept my expression blank. Yes, Trey could read people, but only the lies, which lit up their faces like Times Square billboards. The motives behind the lies remained opaque to him.

I smiled Boone's way. "They teach you that psychology stuff in the big house? Or you been watching Dr. Phil?"

Boone laughed until he started coughing. Jefferson took a step closer, his features knit in concern, but Boone waved him back. Eventually he got his breath again, and Jefferson settled down.

Across the enclosure, I noticed another wolf rise, this time a mottled black and gray one. It shook off the dust, dipped its nose into the stream. Every other wolf in the enclosure looked its way, suddenly on point.

Boone jabbed his chin in its direction. "See that one?"

I squinted across the enclosure. The wolf was smaller than the others, self-contained and compact. "Another beta?"

"No, that's Buckeye. A female, the only one in the pack right now." Boone looked at me out of the corner of his eye. "And that makes her the most powerful creature out there."

Chapter Seventeen

Once we were in the room, Trey went straight to his desk and unloaded his pockets—the leather notebook, primary pen, handkerchief, phone, secondary pen. I closed the door behind me.

"Are we being recorded now?"

"The system is sound-activated."

"So that's a yes?"

"Yes."

He arranged his things according to some personal geometry, then took off his jacket and draped it on the back of the chair. I wasn't used to seeing him against a backdrop of beiges and neutrals, thick curtains and pillowed upholstery. The suite looked so innocuous, and he looked so…not innocuous.

I locked the door behind me. "When you said you were taking care of the Hope situation, I didn't think you meant this."

"It seemed a prudent option. Considering."

"And you just happened to have an audio surveillance system lying around?"

"I asked the director of Secure Systems if I could field test one. He agreed."

"Why didn't you tell me?"

"I planned to tell you as soon as I saw you. But then I heard the first transmission and decided instead to meet you at Oatland Island." He moved to the safe. "Why didn't you tell me about Boone?"

"I didn't think you'd let me go alone. But I was going to tell you when I got back."

He unholstered his gun and unloaded it, then the mag. Everything went into the safe, joining his spare H&K in its travel case. I handed him my bag. It was specially designed for concealed carry, with a lockable holster and separate compartment for ammo. It held my S&W .38 and a speed loader. He double-checked each item before placing it inside the safe.

Through the window, a ripple of lightning fractured the dusk-dimmed sky. Another storm was coming, spawned by the weather system still spinning in the ocean.

I crossed my arms. "We're not doing a grand job of trusting each other."

He shook his head, eyes on the weapons. "No, we're not."

I moved behind him. "Remember when I said that I needed to up my game? And you agreed that you did too?"

"Yes."

I turned him around to face me. "This isn't how we do that."

"I know."

"So let's start doing things differently. Let's start right now."

I unsnapped his holster, an Alessi custom-made that was practically unnoticeable under the well-tailored drape of an Armani jacket. I eased it off his shoulders, then leaned forward and put it in the safe with our respective armaments. He didn't move, not even when my breasts brushed against his chest.

He put his hands on his hips. "You're doing it again."

"Doing what?"

"Trying to seduce me into a deal of some kind."

"Not a deal. A compromise. You can keep your surveillance set-up, but I want the codes. I want to be able to turn it off when I'm in here." I looked him in the eye. "When we're in here. You and me. Doing certain you and me things."

Trey cocked his head. "What if I reject this compromise?"

"Trey. Boyfriend of mine. I am asking sweetly—"

"That never works in interrogations."

I pulled back. "Interrogation?"

"Technically, yes. You want the codes to the surveillance system. I am, however, resisting the idea of giving them to you."

"Why?"

He kept his head tilted, scrutinizing me. "Because I still don't trust you. Not completely. And I need to trust you."

"So what do you suggest?"

"I suggest we return to your first suggestion."

"Which was?"

His eyes never left mine, and the challenge in them was acute and erotic and potent. "Trying something different."

Now I was the wary one, especially when he shifted his weight into a neutral stance, his shoulders dropping. I was two seconds from ending up flat on my back. Again. Which was, I realized with a hot flush, a development ripe with possibility.

I stood on tip-toe, my mouth inches from his. "I want those codes."

"They're useless without the password."

"Then I want your password too."

He inclined his head lower. "I know."

"Give it up, Trey."

And then it happened. His mouth curved against my lips, and when I put my hand against his cheek, I felt the deep-set dimples revealing themselves. A smile, a slow deliberate one, brazen and enticing. My knees went weak as a wallop of thunder rolled in from the ocean and rippled through me in a wave.

"Make me," he said.

◇◇◇

Forty-five minutes later, I sat propped up against the cushioned headboard staring at his phone. The thunderstorm had arrived in full force, dragging sheets of rain behind it. The drops drummed on the balcony, occasionally hitting the window like bullets, almost as fierce as the lightning and keening wind.

I squinted at the screen. "Okay, where do I type the code?"

"You have to input the password first."

"So what's the password?"

"It changes daily. Every morning, I feed a new starter sequence into this program, and it creates a numeric password for me." He tapped an icon. "And then I memorize it and erase it."

I saw several grids, each like a tic-tac-toe square, numbers one through nine in the boxes. "This looks like Sudoko."

"What do you know about matrices and determinants?"

"Nothing. You have to start at the beginning."

He was still naked. So was I. It was a testament to my time with Trey that lying naked in bed talking about higher math felt perfectly normal.

"Okay. The beginning. Matrix codes are very difficult to crack. Using one to create a password is almost as secure as a randomly generated password, but there's a repeatability factor in case I forget."

"You don't forget shit."

"Mostly true. But if I ever do, I'll need a way to generate the password again. Sequenced input generates a coded output. And even if the program is compromised, I can create the inverse matrix with a calculator and still access my data."

"Sequenced?"

"A changing formula based on the day and date."

He typed in tuesdayfifteen, then fed the letters into one of the seven matrixes. "Tuesday is the second day of the week, so… matrix number two."

A numeric sequence appeared. He typed it in, then dragged another icon with his finger. "Once you're in, finding the audio files is simple. They're chronological."

He clicked on the day's collection, seven files. Some were only five minutes long; others lasted almost an hour. I looked at the most recent file, which was still taping, then handed his phone back to him. He logged out and put it on the bedside table. Such a remarkably simple system, but virtually impenetrable unless you knew the key. Which in many ways was exactly like the man himself.

I poured a glass of water from the bedside carafe. "I forgot to tell you Rico called. He discovered some suspicious material on the dead guy in Florida."

"How suspicious?"

I filled him in, including the part when I went all good citizen and called Garrity with the info.

"And another thing," I said. "Boone and Reynolds both told me that the Klan may be involved in the case."

"How?"

"Reynolds implied they're big behind-the-scenes Confederate collectors. Boone was less specific what they might be up to, but he said to start with the Expo. So I guess that's what I'll be doing tomorrow morning."

Trey frowned. He had an appointment with Marisa and Reynolds to scout alternate locations for the tournament. I could see the worry in his eyes suddenly sharpen.

"It's ridiculously safe," I assured him. "Cops and private security in spades. I'm meeting Dee Lynn there for the vendor's lunch, and she's like a mother hen sometimes."

"Are you ready?"

"Sure. I don't know what I'll find out, but I have a tote bag full of research to prime the pump."

He shook his head. "I mean, are you ready for the sale?"

"Oh." I did a quick calculation. "I guess so. It doesn't start until Saturday. Between then I have the business meeting on Thursday and the reenactment on Friday. But yeah, I'm ready."

"Good."

He was almost asleep, hanging out in that fuzzy realm between wakefulness and dozing. I lay down beside him. "Trey?"

"Yes?"

"Why didn't you just give me the code? Why'd you make me pry it out of you number by number?"

He yawned. "I don't know. It seemed...I can't think of the word."

"Fun?"

"No." He slipped me a sideways look. "Not that it wasn't. But that's not the reason."

I stretched against him. Just when I thought I knew the rules, the rules shifted. Oh, there were always rules, dense as jungle undergrowth. And I could machete my way right through them. But I was also learning that I could ease around them. That for every rule, there was a loophole. For every obstacle, there was a way around it. Exactly like…

"Sparring," I said.

"What?"

I propped up on my elbow. "Making me get those codes from you. It was sparring."

"How?"

"Not dominating, not surrendering. Give and take the whole way. Which is why it's got the same kick."

He didn't argue. His heart was still thumping faster than its normal sub-sixty beats per minute, his skin still warm from the blood rush. The collision of chemicals, as irresistible as physics.

I sat up all the way. "Is that why you've been backing down in sparring? The kick?"

"Which kick?"

"Not a literal kick, the hormonal one." The realization came like the crack of dawn. "That's it, isn't it? You're not just afraid of hurting me—you're afraid of liking it."

Trey froze. I watched the gears of his brain turn and mesh as the understanding caught. Adrenalin, testosterone, neuronal circuits crossing and crisscrossing. Arousal was arousal, after all, no matter what followed it.

He stared at the ceiling. "I can't."

"Can't what?"

"Just…can't."

"Can't talk about it, think about it, what?"

He exhaled and shook his head.

"Trey—"

"Please, Tai." He rolled his head to the side and looked at me. "Not now. Please."

Please. The most intimate word in his vocabulary. Of course he'd held onto those secret numbers, sharing them with me one at a time—they were a vulnerability. And even though he'd trusted me with them eventually, it was only after we'd hit that middle ground, the surprising and unsteady territory of give and take. And I knew he'd trust me with this new weirdness we'd tapped. Eventually.

I rested my head against his chest. He flinched at my touch, but I moved his hand to my hip and stretched under the covers, all of me against all of him, skin to skin.

"Not going anywhere," I said. "Get used to it."

He let out the breath he was holding and closed his eyes. This was how we'd make it work, breach and then fortification, break down and build up. One strange and shaky step at a time.

Chapter Eighteen

I'd noticed something was wrong the second I pulled into the parking lot at the Convention Center. Instead of vendors moving their wares inside, a knot of people clustered around the front entrance. Two Savannah Metro police department cruisers parked catty-corner, practically on the sidewalk, blue lights flashing. Almost a dozen cops worked the crowd, holding back the main swell while people screamed obscenities.

Not at the cops. At the man on the sidewalk, clutching pamphlets. The man wearing the triple tau t-shirt, the three-pronged symbol of the Ku Klux Klan.

"We have the Constitutional right to be here!" he yelled. "We are a legal political entity, and we have the right to share our message!"

Two uniformed policemen protected him from the surging edges of the crowd, a kaleidoscope of rage and volatility. He was pure white-bread, this Klansman—thinning brown hair, close-set eyes, pale freckled skin. And he was enjoying the hatred. It justified every vile thought in his head.

I heard the squawk of a police radio right behind me, and then a voice from my past. "Oh no. Not you. Like I haven't had a rough enough morning."

I whirled around. A short dark cop with biceps the size of pork loins stared at me, a wry grin at the corner of his mouth. His muscles strained the black uniform, and a sergeant's badge glimmered on his chest.

I squinted at him. "Kendrick? Is that you?"

"Yeah, Tai. How you been?"

To our left, the Klansman held his arms in the air. "We support the rights of all people to peaceably assemble! Equal rights for everyone, special rights for none!"

I jerked a thumb in his direction. "Seriously, Kendrick? Y'all just gonna let him spew all over the steps?"

"He's not the one I'm worried about, it's the people he's pissing off."

Kendrick was as wide and brown as the delta of a river. He hadn't grown an inch taller since high school—his nickname on the football team had been Fireplug—but the body under the uniform was hard, like a flint-napped arrowhead. He'd sported a crew cut then too, only now it revealed a man's skull, with muscle at the neck.

"Heard you were running a gun shop up in Atlanta," he said.

"You heard right."

"Back for the Expo, huh?"

"Right again."

The officers bum-rushed the Klansman into the convention center, the sleek glass doors closing behind them, leaving the protestors to churn in their anger with no clear target anymore.

"So what's going on here?" I said.

Kendrick sighed. "The Klan applied for a booth permit. They were denied. The organizer said they didn't get the paperwork in on time. The KKK says that's a lie and that they're being discriminated against, and now the ACLU is involved. So this is my morning."

Mine too. I remembered Boone's warning about stirring things up. Damn. The Klan was one big anthill.

I looked back at my car. "So when will those of us nonracists who *do* have a valid permit get to set up?"

He poked his chin toward the back. "This way."

◇◇◇

I found Dee Lynn in her usual spot, right inside the entrance, the first and last vendor the customers would see. She'd rented two tables and had them covered with old bullets, buttons, coins, the smaller detritus of her trade illuminated in the high fluorescent overheads. Behind her, an eight-foot-tall triptych displayed poster-sized portraits of her at work—Dee Lynn underwater in SCUBA gear, Dee Lynn standing erect at the wheel of her boat. When she saw me, she put down her barbecue plate and stood.

"Lord, what a mess. Fucking Klan. Come here and hug my neck."

She'd changed little, still tall and wiry, still sporting the salt-cured tan that came from hours of exposure to ocean wind and the merciless coastal sun. The skin around her eyes was the soft white of well-milked tea, however, her ever-present sunglasses shoved on top of a baseball-capped head. Gray now liberally streaked her black hair, which she kept pony-tailed in a kinky rope as thick as my wrist.

She threw herself around me before I could move. She was the twin sister of my Aunt Dotty, who had been married to my Uncle Dexter. Dotty had been gone for five years, but this was Dee Lynn's first event without Dexter at the table next to hers.

Her eyes were bright. "Dex would be so proud to see you here. Where's your stuff?"

"Still in the car. I'm waiting for the crazy to die down."

"It's not. They'll have to give 'em a booth. Not giving them one is giving them a soapbox, and that's more dangerous." She shoved a folding chair at the back of my knees. "So sit for a minute. Catch me up."

I sat. And we talked. This was the way with Southern business folk of a certain age, as if the whole world were a wide front porch. This approach was fast disappearing, thanks to generations like mine, with our earbuds in place, eyes on our phones, thumbs constantly texting. Eventually, though—and it's a fine art to be able to tell when this moment is—talk always shifts to the commercial.

"It's a tough market." Dee Lynn picked up her sandwich again. "The finder's game is overrun with people who don't know what they're doing—digging on protected land, desecrating burials, leaving trash all over the place. On the upside, I'm getting more calls from people who want to search right. There's still a lot of good finds out there if you know where to look."

I scooched my chair closer and dropped my voice. "Speaking of."

Her ears perked up. "What? You got the trail on something?"

I told her the story. She listened, wide-eyed. All around us the other vendors continued setting up, laughing and back-smacking in a genial hubbub, their voices echoing in the gymnasium-sized room. The man across from me, bearded and overall-clad, specialized in mid-nineteenth century medical equipment. His display case of glass eyes unsettled me even more than the bone saws gracing the ivory tablecloth.

When I was finished, Dee Lynn gave me a look that could have curdled milk. "Did you say Audrina Harrington?"

I sighed. "I did."

"You working for her?"

"No."

"Good. Keep it that way." Dee Lynn made a noise of disgust. "Ignorant high-minded bitch. Doesn't even appreciate what she has. She's a thief, that's what she is, and you can't convince me otherwise."

I didn't try. Dee Lynn was hardly alone in her condemnation, which I shared. Somewhat.

"Unfortunately, Audrina's not the only one after that Bible. Rumor has it the Klan's looking for it too."

Dee Lynn's eyes hardened. "Where'd you get that rumor?"

"Lots of places."

"Including you-know-who, I bet."

I made a face. "Don't start. He's been rehabilitated, you know. Good honest businessman now."

"Right. Boone's gonna be working some angle as long as he lives. And then his boys are gonna inherit that angle and run it as long as they live."

"Which is why I need him. I tried to stay on the uncomplicated side of the line, but what with Hope stalking me, Winston being all shifty, the old man dying, and now the Klan—"

"What old man?"

"Oh. That." So I told her that story

Her eyes went even wider. "Shit."

"What?"

She pointed across the room. "See that woman?"

"The little gray-haired one surrounded by the bike gang?"

"That's Emmy Simmons. She and her husband Bob run a trinket shop. T-shirts, flags, you know."

I knew. Every backroad highway in Georgia featured at least one such shop. Heavy on cheap tourist goods emblazoned with the Confederate Battle Flag, light on actual artifacts.

"Who are the guys in bike leathers?"

"One's their son—the big one in the vest—and the rest are his crew. The important part is who isn't there—Bob."

"Why isn't he there?"

"He's missing."

I closed my eyes against the news. "What happened?"

"Went out last night and never came back. Emmy says he'd gotten real excited about an old treasure map he'd found in a box of books some customer brought in."

"Treasure like in pirates?"

"Treasure like in lost Confederate gold."

"Oh jeez."

Ever since 1865, every treasure hunter's dreams were plated with Confederate gold. That was when five wagons full of coins and bars went missing between Virginia and South Carolina, supposedly buried on the grounds of an old plantation to avoid Union confiscation. When neither the plantation nor its occupants would give up the gold's location—not even under torture—treasure hunters began searching other areas: cemeteries, lake beds, shipwrecks, family farms, submerged islands. A couple of gold coins turned up now and then, but the mother lode remained a mystery.

That cache wasn't the only missing treasure out there either. When General Sherman marched his way to the sea, many citizens buried their valuables, only to lose track of their location in the burning and pillaging, some dying with that knowledge. According to treasure hunters, a dragon's horde of loot nestled in the red clay and sand of Georgia's landscape.

"Seriously?" I said.

Dee Lynn nodded. "Emmy's freaked out, but I didn't think too much of it. You know how treasure fever is—you start digging and you don't stop. But now you're telling me your story, and there's a dead guy at the beginning of it, so…"

She shrugged and forked up a mouthful of slaw. She had a point. Gold made people do stupid things, vicious things, completely out of character things.

"Emmy saw the map?"

"She says so. She said it looked genuine."

"It's easy to make something look genuine. Does she know much about old manuscripts?"

"I doubt it. That's not their trade."

I looked over at the booth. The woman sat surrounded by a circle of burly young men. She was slight, with blue-gray hair cut in a pageboy that suited her elfin features. She was pale, though, and very thin under a denim dress a size too large.

"You think she'd talk to me?"

Dee Lynn shrugged. "You can try. But don't mention that Bible, especially not around those boys."

"Don't worry."

I went over. The woman eyed my approach with frazzled caution. When I got six feet from the table, the bikers closed ranks around her. I put on my best non-threatening expression.

"Ms. Simmons? My name is Tai Randolph. I—"

"Who?"

"Tai Randolph. I was talking to Dee Lynn over there—she's my aunt—and I heard—"

"You!" The woman bolted upright and threw a finger in my face. "You're the one brought that box of books by yesterday!

You're the one sent my Bob off on that wild goose chase, and now he's…" Her voice cracked, but her eyes blazed fury.

"But I've never been to your shop!"

The tallest biker put his arm around the old woman. He had thoughtful green eyes and bark-brown hair and a torso like a sack of concrete. "You sure it's her, Mama?"

"Of course I'm sure! I'll go back to the shop and find the receipt."

"Now, Mama—"

She shoved past him and headed for the parking lot, leaving me alone within the circle of suspicious bikers. The tall one, obviously her son, jerked his head toward the back. "Earl, go keep her out of trouble. I'll take care of this."

One of the bikers hurried after the old woman. He shot me a look—sneaky, furtive—and I shouldered my bag, heavy with my .38. Unloaded, as required by the rules of the Expo, but more reassuring than a nail file.

I tried to sound reasonable. "Look, I'm as baffled as you are. I don't know anything about any treasure map. Why would I come over here if I did? I'd sure as hell have stayed in my own booth."

"Guess we'll know when Mama gets back." Those smart eyes narrowed. "Tai, huh? You don't look like a Tai."

"I'm a Teresa Ann actually. Tai's a nickname. Long story involving my Aunt Dotty and her fanciful delusions. You knew Dotty and Dexter, right?"

He nodded. "They've been coming as long as I can remember."

"I'm their niece. I inherited the shop back in the spring. And I swear to you…what's your name?"

"Richard. But everybody calls me Rock."

"Look…Rock. I didn't try to pass off some treasure map on your dad. Somebody's trying to get me in trouble, and I have a pretty good idea who." I scribbled my cell phone number on the back of a business card and handed it to him, along with my photos of Hope and Winston.

He accepted both. "They don't look familiar."

"Show them to your mother. And if either of these people show up, please call me. Let me know what your mama finds, okay?"

He looked at the card. Then he looked me up and down. "We'll see."

◇◇◇

After that, I unloaded my car, set up the table, then I bummed a cigarette from the guy with the glass eyes and headed for the parking lot. Mrs. Simmons still hadn't returned. Rock and Company were still eyeing me suspiciously. And my nerves had been pulled as tight as guitar strings.

I'd had enough. I would have bet my entire arsenal that my mysterious impersonator was none other than Hope Lyle. Which meant that it was too late for me, I was in the web. So was a second old man, missing now under mysterious circumstances.

I found a shady spot off the beaten path, flopped on the ground, and stuck the cigarette in my mouth. Nicotine. Sometimes it was the one sure thing in my life.

Chapter Nineteen

The cigarette hit me hard on top of the nicotine patches, but it soothed the wrenching buzz. It did nothing to tamp down my anger, however.

I called Trey. Voicemail. Then I called John. When he answered, I blasted him. "There's another old guy involved."

"What? Who?"

"A vendor. He's missing. Mysterious circumstances. Plus your wife's been blackening my name all over town. And now the Klan—"

"What?"

I sucked in another lungful of smoke. "I should've never let you in my shop, you and your post-dated check and big boots. I should've known this would be the result—being stalked, being manipulated, being set up—"

"Slow down, Tai. Start at the beginning."

My cell phone beeped with an incoming call. Trey.

"I gotta go. But you and I will be discussing this further, John Wilde, you hear me?"

"But—"

I hung up on him and answered Trey. "You are not going to believe—"

"Tai?"

His voice was lost in a swooping chop and woosh, like a stainless steel tornado. "Trey?"

"I'm sorry, I….since this morning…. later?"

"I can't hear you, where are you?"

"…at the latest…the helicopter…"

"Trey, do *not* get in a helicopter with Reynolds, there is a slight chance Audrina is trying to kill him."

And then the line went dead. I tried calling back. More voicemail. So I sent a text instead, telling him to meet me back at the Expo as soon as possible. Then I stared at the phone. Now I had identity theft and a missing person to deal with. I sucked down another lungful of smoke.

The voice came from behind me. "Put down the phone and turn around."

I looked over my shoulder. It was Mrs. Simmons. She looked sick, trembling and pale.

I stood. "Are you okay?"

The gun came out of nowhere, a semi-automatic, enormous and jet black and scary as hell. It shook violently in her hands.

My cigarette dropped to the ground. "Mrs. Simmons—"

"It *was* you! Your name's in the receipt book! He even took your business card!"

I raised my hands slowly, palms forward. "Not mine, he didn't."

"You said you were Tai Randolph!"

"I am, but the person who left the card—the person who sold your husband that box of books containing that map—wanted you to think it was me. But it wasn't."

Her hands shook harder, and the big damn gun shook with them. So much for Earl the Biker Dude keeping her out of trouble.

I kept my voice slow and easy. "I'm the real Tai Randolph, and I have the credentials to prove it. But I don't know how to prove that I've never been in your shop."

"I'm calling the police!"

"Please do. And once you've figured out that I'm telling the truth, we can figure out how to find your husband."

Mrs. Simmons considered me over the barrel of the gun, her voice as shaky as her hands. "He wouldn't run off like this.

The police keep saying I have to wait to file the missing persons report, that he's only been gone twelve hours."

I lowered my hands a little. The gun stayed up, but her anger wasn't behind it anymore.

My heart panged. "I'll do what I can, Mrs. Simmons. But first...could you put the gun down?"

She seemed suddenly ashamed of herself. When she handed over the weapon, I ejected the magazine. Empty. The gun hadn't been cleaned in a while either.

"Where'd you find this?"

"Bob kept it under the register."

"He didn't take it with him on his expedition?"

She shook her head. "No. He said he didn't need it."

Most likely he'd been wrong about that, but I didn't say so. "Do you remember anything about that map?"

"It had lots of gibberish on it. Weird drawings. A moon, some stars."

Putting down the gun, I pulled a schedule from my bag and flipped it over. Then I grabbed a pen and squiggled a crescent shape. "Like this?"

"And there was other stuff too. Wavy lines."

I doodled in some spirals and circles. "Like this?"

"No." She shook her head, frustrated. "None of it made any sense. But there was a list in the middle. Bob said it was a treasure tally. He said he recognized the symbol for gold. AU."

I scribbled a list in the middle. "Like that?"

She nodded. "And there were other numbers too, strings of them. He said it was a code. But it was the paper that made him decide it was real. He said it was old, real old."

"Did he say where he was headed with it?"

"No. But I think it was a cemetery."

"Bonaventure? Laurel Grove?"

"He didn't say. But I think he managed to figure out the code. I found the piece of paper next to the register with letters and numbers and the word 'boneyard' on it."

Boneyard. Savannah had plenty of those. The whole city was a boneyard. Even the medians of Victory Drive were burial grounds.

"Was there anything more specific?"

She shook her head. "That's all I can remember."

I was staring at my makeshift map when I saw them at the edge of the parking lot. Two uniformed Savannah metro officers. They spotted us, double-checked a piece of paper, and then headed our way.

I tried to keep my voice calm. "Mrs. Simmons? Did you call the cops?"

She shook her head. And then my stomach plummeted. Because that meant there was only one reason those cops were there, looking full of duty. Mrs. Simmons followed my eyes, turning to look behind her. And then she knew too.

"No!" she said, hands to her mouth.

But the cops were headed straight for us, with stoic compassion on their faces. And they kept coming, relentlessly bearing their official burden forward.

Chapter Twenty

When I got back to the hotel, I found Trey at his desk. He'd sent me a text asking if I were okay. I'd told him I was, that I'd explain later. Now he was looking at me, the question in his eyes.

I sat on the edge of the desk. "I guess you heard."

"About the body? Yes. Dee Lynn explained."

"You went to the Expo?"

"I did, but you'd already gone to give an official statement." He put his work aside and looked at me seriously. "Do they have cause of death?"

"Not yet."

They'd found the old man's body in the shipping channel. Shrimpers going out for the day had spotted it. No boat, however. Mrs. Simmons, now a widow, had insisted she and her husband didn't own a boat, then collapsed on the officer and been taken away. Another officer had escorted me downtown and grilled me for an hour, although without much enthusiasm for my guilt, unlike every other police interview I'd ever endured.

I put my bag down inside the door. "And on top of everything, Mrs. Simmons filed a restraining order against me."

Trey rarely looked surprised, but that comment did the trick. "On what grounds?" he said.

"That I threatened to hurt her if she turned over the evidence implicating me to the cops. She's the one pulled a freaking gun on me! That sweet old lady. I could kick her ass."

"You'll need to explain."

So I did. As I told the tale, he pulled out a fresh yellow pad and made notes, lots of them. I went to the mini-fridge to get a soda.

"Dee Lynn says I need to make myself scarce at the vendors' meeting tomorrow, and she's probably right. No sense causing a confrontation."

"Restraining orders don't take effect that quickly."

"No, but rumors do. And my reputation as a purveyor of shady goods is spreading fast. Dee Lynn says I need to appear docile and cooperative and respectful to Mrs. Simmons in her time of loss. She says I'll do this better from a distance."

I kicked the fridge door closed and flopped myself on the sofa. "Besides, that frees up some time for me to figure out what the hell is going on here. Which reminds me—the Savannah police want the security footage from the night Hope came here. Can you send that?"

"Of course."

"Good. Kendrick says that's an important part of my defense, that I'm a victim of identify theft. He said I need to start collecting evidence to prove it. Apparently, this is the one time the police actually encourage a civilian to investigate."

Trey tapped at the keyboard, and the image of him and Hope in the elevator formed on the screen. She looked at the camera—smug, satisfied, deliberate. He tapped out more instructions, and the footage began downloading.

I glanced at his notebook, noticing that except for a precise diagram of the conference center, his afternoon at the Expo had netted him little information. I knew the Armani had worked against him. When death and treasure were on the agenda, people shut down the information corridors fast, especially around official-looking people in suits.

He gave me a sharply inquisitive look. "Do you really have the map?"

"I have this thing I scribbled based on what Emmy Simmons told me. But it's not *the* map." Then I frowned. "Wow. Hard to believe that information got around that fast."

"Did you do that on purpose?"

"No. But it means treasure fever has gone viral." I stretched my foot out and massaged my instep. "What are you doing here? Don't tell me Marisa let you have the night off?"

He tapped his phone. Marisa's voice leaped from the speaker. "You'd better be on your way to the mayor's reception, do you hear me? And why the hell aren't you answering your phone? I told you—"

He switched it off. "There are two other messages in a similar vein."

He sat in his chair, legs stretched out in front of him, fingers steepled across his stomach. He and Marisa had made a deal—he continued to work for her, and she got him for charts and data, not glad-handing and show pony work.

But Marisa could manipulate Trey very easily—putting things in writing, giving direct orders, evoking the hierarchy. He gave in to these machinations and did what he was told. Most of the time.

"Are you okay?"

He exhaled. "I'm confused."

I shoved myself off the sofa and went to him. "You can go off grid for one night, you know. Tell Marisa you're tired of being pimped out to the highest bidder."

He stared at his desk. It was a collage of maps, mostly aerial shots of golf courses. But he also had a map of the Savannah waterways. I ran a finger along the edge, following the flow of the Atlantic, its blue fingers spreading inland among the green. Land and sea, sea and land.

I tilted the map and examined it again. "You wanna know what's bugging me most? Why would a man going digging in graveyards be out on the water?"

I pointed to where the body was found, then drew a line from that point backwards, following last night's current. "He got caught in the storm, no doubt. The boat was swamped, sank somewhere. They assumed the map was lost with it. But they couldn't explain why he was in the middle of the channel in the first place."

"You have an idea?"

"Maybe."

He arched an eyebrow. "And it is?"

"Remember, this is a total shot in the dark." I pulled out my little faux map. "Okay, so his wife finds a piece of deciphered code. One word—boneyard. She assumes he meant a cemetery. But look."

I pointed to the map. "Here's where his body was found. But consider the flow, factor in the tides, and I'm guessing he was somewhere in this vicinity when he went in the water."

I pointed further up the map. Trey peered closer.

"Wassaw Island. Is there a graveyard there?"

"No. But there is a beach littered with driftwood logs and dead pine trees. Locals call it the Boneyard. And the only way to get there is by boat."

"But he didn't have a boat."

"I'm still working on that part of the theory."

Trey cocked his head. "Have you shared this theory with the authorities?"

"I'm coming into this theory as we speak. But I'm willing to call it in, see what happens."

We both knew what would happen. It would go onto someone's desk and they'd see it in the morning. But that was what law-abiding citizens did—they followed official channels, washed their hands of the responsibility. Trey was one of these citizens.

Except that Trey wasn't picking up his phone. And his finger was tapping the desktop.

His eyes met mine. "All right. We alert the authorities, share our information. And then what?"

I sat on the edge of the desk. "Normally I would say, let's go check out the island and see for ourselves. Unfortunately, it's almost dark. There's no getting on Wassaw Island legally after dark. And normally I would say screw that, let's chance it. But it's a National Wildlife Refuge, which makes trespassing a federal crime, and the ATF does not look upon those favorably. Inspector Cranky-Pants would snatch my federal firearms license in a heartbeat."

Trey listened, very intently. "Go on."

"So while I'm usually the run-around-sneak-over kind of girl, not this time. But believe me, if this rumor's spreading, and if anybody else makes the connection I just did, that island will be crawling with treasure hunters in the morning."

"And the scene will be destroyed."

"Definitely, especially if that next storm flares up tonight like they're predicting. Because nobody's getting on without a special permit, and those are scarce as hen's teeth."

Trey eyed me, arms folded. "Why would he have gone at night?"

"Because his wife described the map as having strange symbols on it, including a moon. And last night was the full moon."

"Wouldn't he have been afraid of getting caught?"

"Not if he had treasure on the brain."

Trey looked at me, his eyes catching the light like a scalpel. "And there's only one way to Wassaw Island?"

"Only one way—by boat. And during the day, Dee Lynn would be pulling in the dock lines and heading over. But at night? Like I said, that's a no-go."

He pulled out his phone. "Dee Lynn owns her own boat, correct?"

"Yes. But like I keep saying, there's no way...who are you calling?"

He held up a finger. A crisp formal voice at the other end of the phone answered. Trey reached for a pen and yellow pad.

"Hello, Grace, this is Trey Seaver. Is the senator available? Yes, I'll hold." He covered the phone's mouthpiece with three fingers. "There are certain benefits to...how did you put it? Being pimped out?"

◇◇◇

Within five minutes, he had a Department of Natural Resources special permit waiting for us at the ranger station. Trey didn't excel at small talk, but no matter—he'd apparently done duty for the senator during his dignitary protection days with Atlanta's SWAT team. And the senator remembered. And was grateful.

Trey made one final notation on the paper. "Thank you. I appreciate this." He looked up then, his eyes on mine. There was a sexy little crinkle at the corners. "No, Senator, it's nothing official. Simply a favor for my girlfriend."

Chapter Twenty-one

Trey had the right skill set for eating crabs—patient, with nimble fingers and singular focus. He'd dressed in clean workout clothes, storing his second set in a dry bag along with a change of clothes for me. Everything of his was fresh from the laundry despite my warning that clean clothes and blue crabs did not mix.

The evening lingered warm after the chilly morning, the sky purpled and rippled with fishtail clouds. The planked floors of the tiny waterside restaurant felt like a boat deck beneath my feet, and the breeze smelled of brine and pluff mud. We sat at a table near the marsh, pedestal fans keeping the sand gnats at bay, and watched the dock.

"Is she here?" Trey said.

I shook my head. "Not yet."

I watched him work at the crustaceans, white shirt sleeves rolled up, juice running down his wrists. He'd taken his watch off.

I grinned at him. "You look positively bohemian. Almost—"

I bit back the word. Almost normal. It was disconcerting to remember that he wasn't. I reached too quickly for my beer and knocked it over. Trey caught it in one deft move, then placed it upright on the table without spilling a single drop.

"What's the name of Dee Lynn's boat?" he said.

"*Storm Season.*"

He nodded toward the dock. The boat was pulling up, Dee Lynn at the wheel high above the deck. It was a thirty-foot sport fisher, an older craft tricked out with the latest in artifact hunting technology.

I stood. "Time to go, sailor. Our ride's here."

◇◇◇

Dee Lynn steered us down the Wilmington River, the islands and hammocks passing on both sides. She kept her eyes straight ahead, her ponytail swinging almost to the waistband of her khakis.

"Right fine boyfriend you got there."

I turned my face into the wind. "I know."

"How'd you manage that?"

"I manage that just fine."

She laughed. "He's in there messing with the side-scan sonar, like a kid with a new toy."

"I'm not surprised. Trey's a city dude all the way, but he's got a knack for graphics. Maps and charts, drawings and diagrams and blueprints."

"Treasure maps?"

"Those too, I'll bet."

Dee Lynn's eyes were bright. "I swear, Tai, if we pull Confederate gold out of the dirt—"

"We call the proper authorities."

"Don't spit the law at me, I know it backwards and forwards. I also know it's pretty gray on this particular topic."

"Don't you go catching gold fever. We're here because Trey called in a favor. I'm on my best behavior, and you'd better be too."

She grinned and took the boat into a tight turn, sloshing up a wake. "Good behavior doesn't run in our family, leastways not amongst the women. But I'll do my best."

◇◇◇

Wassaw is a barrier island just southeast of Savannah, between Little Tybee and Ossabaw. We were headed for the spit of sand on the northeastern tip, where the trails started. When the wind blew or the current was high, it was a choppy passage, even in a boat the size of Dee Lynn's.

But this night was easy. The next band of thunderstorms had yet to blow in, so the moon rose fat and almost full against a deepening indigo sky. The Blood Moon, it was called, the moon closest to Halloween, when the veil between the worlds is thinnest, they say. My ghost tour bookings had always gone up during the Blood Moon. But tonight it was as innocent as a pat of warm butter, and it would have been easy to dismiss the legends…except that we were following a dead man's tracks.

Dee Lynn went down to double-check her equipment. She'd packed a kayak full of treasure-hunting gear for us to pull ashore, including a couple of pulse induction metal detectors, plus the more mundane tools of her trade—shovels, plastic bags, hand trowels. She'd let me take the wheel, and Trey stood beside me, scrutinizing every dial and console.

"You know the way?" he said.

"I grew up with a tiller in one hand. Dad loved the water." I pointed to the left. "That's Cabbage Island. Once we're past this curve, you'll see Tybee in the distance. Skidaway to the right. Soon we'll be coming up on Dead Man Hammock."

Trey gave me a look. I shook my head.

"Not making that up. There's good fishing here, seatrout and redfish especially. Dad and I used to come here all the time."

I suddenly missed it, all of it, with a deep tidal longing. I was an orphan in this land now. No anchor, no ties. What was I really doing out here on this beautiful night chasing a dead man's fevered fantasy?

I turned my face into the wet rush of air. Beside me, Trey dropped his duffel bag and did the same.

"It's very dark," he said.

"You've gotten used to Atlanta. The dark comes solid and fast here. It can catch you off guard, especially when a storm's on the way."

"The weather looks clear."

"Don't be fooled. We only have a few hours before we have to turn back."

He didn't ask any more questions. I kept the silence too, until Dee Lynn returned from the deck and took the wheel.

She handed me a rope. "You still know how to tie a bowline?"

I made a noise. "Please."

There are no docks on Wassaw. To get to the beach, we'd have to drop anchor and swim to shore, pulling our kayak full of tools behind us. For an unseasoned sailor, it was a perilous endeavor—too small a boat, too inexpert an anchoring, too weak a swimmer. It all added up to drowning far too often.

Dee Lynn surveyed the shoreline. "I don't know, Tai. Drowning may have been the official cause of death, but it don't make a lick of sense."

"His boat got away from him, they say, and he tried to swim out to it. But he overestimated his ability, they say, and didn't make it."

"They say? You have doubts too?"

"They never found the boat. And his wife says he didn't own one, didn't know anything about them."

"Mighty suspicious, that." Dee Lynn shook her head. "Oh well. Back to business. Go get the main anchor. I'll bring her 'round and set the second."

◇◇◇

With *Storm Season* firmly tethered, Dee Lynn dropped the kayak. Fifty yards away, the beach was flooded with light from the moon, which glowed phosphorescent through the trees. Trey was barefoot already, only a sweatshirt covering the t-shirt and shorts he'd worn for the swim. The rest was in dry bags, to change into when we hit the sand.

He pulled his sweatshirt over his head. I watched him, his skin white in the moonlight.

"You undress like a Chippendale dancer," I said.

He stuffed the sweatshirt into the dry bag. "I do not." He peered over the edge of the boat. "Are there alligators?"

"No gators."

"Sharks?"

"I would never send you into dangerous shark-infested waters."

He tried to read my face, but the dappled moonlight played across my features like a shifting mask. He stared at me for five seconds, hard. And then he climbed over the edge and slid into the water.

Dee Lynn watched him swim to the equipment-stuffed kayak, then leaned closer and lowered her voice. "You lied to that man."

"Not a lie. It was what we call 'technically true but deliberately evasive.'" I pulled my own shirt over my head and stuffed it in the bag. "The sharks won't bother us unless we bother them. You know that."

She chuckled and swung herself over the edge.

Chapter Twenty-two

The Boneyard lay on the eastern shore, inaccessible during high tide, so we waded onto the rippled beach instead, dunes and sea oats tumbling to white sand, dragging the kayak behind us. Over two thousand acres of pine and oak and palm trees all to ourselves.

Dee Lynn consulted her compass. "Come on, you two. Grab your stuff."

She handed Trey and me our flashlights, showing us how to switch from regular light to black light to signal flare. Compasses next, then radios in case we got separated. Trey noted each piece of equipment with satisfaction. Dee Lynn was as prepared as a Girl Scout, and he approved.

I played the light around the deserted beach. "What do we do?"

"Keep your eyes down. Look for anything out of place—freshly turned dirt, manmade objects, broken tree limbs. There's been a storm and three tides since he disappeared. You'll have to look close and thorough."

Trey's specialty. He and Dee Lynn moved in the natural searcher's pattern, within five feet of each other. I followed behind.

The beach was clean of human evidence, the previous night's rain having beaten the sand into a flat clean plane. It crunched beneath our feet, marbled and pocked in the moonlight, strewn with seaweed clumps. The skitter of crabs sounded like stage whispers from an unseen audience.

Soon the Boneyard lay in front of us, its jagged coastline broken by the stark lines of the downed trees, some lean and gray and eroded smooth, others fresh-fallen. One weather-beaten specimen jutted upright in the water like a ghostly hand, skeletal fingers reaching for the fat moon. The wooded interior of the island lay to the right, crisscrossed by narrow trails.

I moved to Dee Lynn's side. "So where would you hide treasure?"

"Me? I'd think like a pirate, move inland."

"So let's do that."

"Fine by me. But you gotta know where he started to know where he ended up."

I looked around the beach. Vast and dark. No way to track Simmons' movements, no way to predict what he'd been up to or if he'd even made it this far. But my fingertips itched, and not from my usual nicotine withdrawal. If only I had the real map…

Trey touched my elbow. "Tai?"

"Hmmm?"

"Tell me again…what do alligator eyes look like?"

"Shiny red dots."

He sent the beam of his flashlight into the woods. A single ruby light glittered back. Then he looked at me, one eyebrow raised in accusation.

I laughed. "That's not a gator."

"Are you sure?"

"Unless it's a one-eyed gator that can climb trees, I am totally sure."

"Then what is it?"

Which was an eminently sensible question.

When we got close to the palm tree, I ran my finger along the bark. A single red triangle winked at me when I played my flashlight over it.

Trey peered closer. "What is it?"

"Reflective marker. The real question is, what's it marking?"

Dee Lynn ran the metal detector around the base. It whined in an undulating crackle, and she knelt and sifted her fingers through the leaves and crumbled sand. A few scrapes revealed a beer cap. Trey stood and sent a clear beam of light along the perimeter. Soon, another flash of red winked at him.

"It's marking a trail," he said.

We followed the light to another tiny plastic marker. Trey slowly panned the trees and sure enough, another flash of red appeared. We could barely see the boat bobbing at the horizon. The next marker would take us where we couldn't see it at all.

Dee Lynn pulled out a compass. "It's following a southwesterly heading."

I followed right behind her, Trey bringing up the rear. The last marker took us another hundred feet inland. Trey's light scanned all around, but no further red dots flared at us, only the one that would lead us back to the beach.

"The trail stops here."

Trey stood very still. Even in the dark, I knew he could take the measure of a place. Like a computer, he could feed the data into his head and reproduce a map. He'd been pacing off distance since we'd arrived.

But this wasn't the urban landscape of Atlanta, with its traffic and ever-present haze. The enormous moon and scudding clouds created shadows as thick and liquid as ink. They spilled onto patches of clear illumination, creating a black and white mosaic, growing darker as the cloud cover increased.

Trey crouched. "Dee Lynn?"

She knelt beside him. He ran his hand along the ground, a mix of sand and Spanish moss. "This is freshly turned."

Dee Lynn reached for the top layer and brushed it aside. Two sweeps and her fingers hit something hard and smooth. She looked up at me, her eyes brilliant in the flashlight.

"There's something metal under here, bigger than a bottle cap."

She pulled out her digging tools. Gently, with her fingers and trowel, she unearthed a square metal box about the size of a toaster. It was a little rusty, but otherwise in fine shape.

I sucked in a breath. "Trey?"

"I see it."

"It's a box."

"I know."

We stared at it. I knew he was running the flow chart through his head. Evidence or not evidence? If it was evidence, then there was a definite procedure, and it didn't involve prying things open and rummaging around inside. But how to determine if something was evidence without examining it?

Dee Lynn reached for the lid. I held my breath as she tugged it open.

The flashlight caught the dazzle of gold, fiery and molten. Coins, dozens of them, winked seductively in the flashlight's beam.

"Shit. Oh shit. Trey—"

"I know."

"That's—"

"I see."

He reached forward, a little gold-dazzled himself, then froze. He pulled his hand back, but peered closer. "Is that a notebook?"

"A what?"

"A small ledger." He directed his flashlight. "Right there."

I squinted at the tiny notebook. It had a dark black cover, and was in impossibly good shape for buried treasure. And then I saw the trademark. "Wait a second, that's not Confederate. That's from Office Max." I picked it up and opened it. "Oh good Lord."

I turned it around and showed it to Trey and Dee Lynn. It was a running list of signatures and dates. They both looked puzzled. I'd been too, for a second, but the ledger cinched it.

"This isn't treasure, it's a geocache site," I said. "People bury things and then post the coordinates online, and other people try to find them. They're all over Savannah. It's an obsession, especially with tourists."

I picked up a coin. It was feather-light, with a leering skull on one side and a Jolly Roger on the other. "Plastic."

Dee Lynn cursed. "So this is a hoax?"

"Not a hoax. A game. Only I'm thinking the old guy took it very seriously."

"I would too if I had an antique map."

"This part may be a game, but the map wasn't. Someone created it to tempt him and blame me, and they used geocaching coordinates to do it."

Dee Lynn stared at the plastic hoard, the light gone out of her eyes. I felt deflated too. Trey, however, was still on point. He'd switched his flashlight from incandescent to UV and was casting the bluish beam around the trees.

"Tai? Dee Lynn? I think I've found something else."

He pointed the flashlight to a fallen tree a few yards away. A piece of paper was jammed into a hollow, barely visible. It wouldn't have been seen in ordinary light—only the glow of the UV flared it into brightness.

Dee Lynn hurried over and pulled it out. It was an ordinary envelope. She reached inside and extracted a piece of old paper, crumbly with age. Trey illuminated it with his flashlight. It was a map of the island, complete with geographical codes and strange images, including a crescent moon. My excitement soared yet again.

"It's the map, the real one! He made it out here after all."

"Then where's his boat?"

A good question. Trey turned the paper in his light. I smacked my forehead.

"Look! These numbers are latitude and longitude markings. That's what brought Simmons here." I pointed to an eight-number sequence in the middle. "But I have no idea what these are."

Trey examined them. "It's an alphabet code. See? There isn't a number larger than twenty-six. A simple replacement system." He did a quick calculation, then looked at me. "It says 'boneyard.'"

"So this *is* the original map."

"The evidence suggests so."

I peered closer. In the corner next to the crescent moon was a circle with a dot in the center followed by a capital M with a tiny little tail, a fanciful flourish that looked vaguely devilish, and oddly familiar.

"I've seen this before," I said.

He nodded. "It's an astrological glyph for the sign of Scorpio. Gabriella has it tattooed on her instep."

Gabriella. His ex. Suddenly I remembered the dark curving lines against her milk-white foot, gleaming wet-black through her strappy sandals. Of course this would be how he knew this odd scrap of occult signage.

I saw the flare of lightning at the horizon. "Uh oh."

Dee Lynn gathered our things. "Yep. Time to go."

I looked at Trey. "I know the rules say this is evidence, and that we should let the authorities handle the chain on it, but if we don't take this in, the storm's gonna ruin it."

He thought for two seconds, then decided. "Okay. Take it in."

"We'll turn it in at the ranger station. They can keep it until the Savannah police can come pick it up." I tucked it under my jacket. It would fit nicely in the dry bag. "In the meantime, do you think Gabriella would help us do a little deciphering?"

Chapter Twenty-three

"Of course I will!" Gabriella said. "I'm a double Scorpio with Aquarius rising—I love arcane mysteries!"

The enthusiastic trill in her voice was contagious. We'd obviously caught her headed out the door to some high society fete, with her fire-red ringlets piled atop her head and dazzling teardrops of diamonds flickering at her earlobes. Even in Skype she looked luscious. I ran a hand through my salt-encrusted tangles. We were still on the boat, headed back to the ranger station, hours away from hot showers.

"I don't know what that means," I said, "but as long as you do, we're good. Did you get the photo?"

"It's printing now."

I heard the buzz of the machine off-screen. "Thanks for helping us out with this."

"My pleasure. Where's Trey?"

I pulled him into view of the computer's camera. Gabriella laughed.

"*Mon dieu!* Your hair is a mess!"

He didn't argue. He refused to used the word "ex-girlfriend" to describe her, but she'd been something, that was for sure. She still was—sophisticated, elegant, able to tell a Prada from a Hushpuppy.

Someone off-screen slipped the printout to her, and I caught a glimpse of a masculine hand, a tuxedo cuff. I slid a glance Trey's way. His expression was curious but not emotional.

Of course that described Trey ninety-nine percent of the time.

Gabriella bent her head over the map and bit her lip. "The circle with the dot represents the sun, and this little glyph is the sign for Scorpio, which is the sun's current astrological position." She pointed. "And this is the moon in Aries. See the little squiggle right there, like ram's horns?"

I looked down at my own copy. "Yes. What's that mean?"

"It means you're dealing with someone who doesn't know astrology. According to these notations, the Aries moon is supposedly new, but that's impossible with the sun in Scorpio. The new moon in Aries won't happen until the spring."

"Could it refer to something else, maybe the constellation of Aries? Or Scorpio?"

"I'm not an astronomer, but I don't think so. Western astrology is tropical, not sidereal."

Her explanation was going over my head in every way except one. "So you're saying this map is a fake?"

"I'm saying the information on it doesn't make sense. It's beautifully done, though, by someone with artistic, if not astrological, talent."

Behind her I saw a black-and-white blur at the door, followed by a masculine smattering of French. She looked over her shoulder and tossed out a bit of Gallic in response. "I have to go. Jean Luc is becoming sulky. Call me tomorrow, yes?"

"Sure thing."

She blew a kiss at the camera and switched it off. Trey sat on the edge of the desk, index finger tapping.

"Interesting," he said.

"Very." I propped my chin in hand. "I wonder who he is."

"Who?"

"Her date."

"Jean Luc. But that's not what I meant." He tapped the map. "This is interesting."

So much for jealousy. That didn't seem to be on the agenda. "Why?"

"The astrological information is intricately rendered, but has no function in decoding the map. The longitude and latitude coordinates were enough to pinpoint this location, even without the coded clue to start at the Boneyard."

I was beginning to get his point. "It's simultaneously too mysterious and too direct. It's a muddle of a map."

"Yes. Exactly."

"So it's fake. Just like the coins."

"Not totally fake," Dee Lynn said.

"What do you mean?"

She came up and looked over our shoulders. "You understand this isn't my specialty, right? I'm a bullets and bottles woman. But I can tell you a couple of things."

She held the paper up to the light. "This is old paper, could be circa 1860s. See the fiber patterns? Not cotton, not blued either, which is why it didn't fluoresce under your black light like the envelope did."

This wasn't what I'd been expecting to hear. "So it's real?"

"The paper is." Dee Lynn dragged a finger along the edge. "But look at the writing. See how dark it is? It should be iron-gall ink, which means it should have turned a faint red-brown by now, like old blood."

"So it's fake?"

"Some fake, some real. It's a mishmash."

"My other source says the information is a mishmash too."

She put the paper down and shrugged. "Could be old *and* fake, you know. Wherever there's lost gold, there are con men. The South was lousy with them during Reconstruction."

Trey stepped forward. "It could also be evidence."

I put a hand on his arm. "Which is why we're being extra careful with it."

And we were. We even wore gloves from the first-aid kit to protect the delicate paper. Trey remained anxious, however, and I knew he would be until the treasure map was safely in a police locker. I gave it back to Dee Lynn, who returned it to its envelope.

"So what do you think happened?" I said.

"If I had to hazard a guess, I'd say he got scammed. The usual method is to tuck one of these pretty fakes in a book, pretend you don't know it's there. Stick it in a box with some other books, take that to some shady not-so-smart dealer, ask a ridiculous price for it. The dealer takes you for a rank amateur but pays up anyway, because he thinks he's pulling one over on you and the last thing he wants is a quibble."

"You know what they say—you can't scam an honest man."

"I've seen it done."

"Me too. But it sure is harder." I chewed at my thumbnail. "So Simmons tried to cheat whoever brought this to him—and I'm convinced it was Hope using my identity—but that was the plan all along?"

She shrugged. "I sure don't think he was geocaching."

"I don't either." I stared at the map. "So he thinks he's on the trail of some treasure. He comes out to the island…and then what?"

"Maybe he notices his boat drifting off, leaves the paper in a safe place while he fetches it back?"

"Only he couldn't see the beach from where he was, hence all the little markers. So how'd he know the boat was making for open ocean? And where's the boat now?"

Dee Lynn looked at Trey. Trey looked back, one eyebrow raised.

She shoved her cap back. "Okay, you got me there. But it's a stretch from that to foul play."

She was right. It was a stretch. But my intuition made the leap no problem. Simmons' death was no accident. And that meant my case was officially complicated with an officially hinky corpse.

I blew out a breath. "Damn it."

◇◇◇

Trey sat next to me, eyes on the horizon, the muffled growl of the inboard behind us. The cloud cover had grown dense and fast-moving, banded and scudding low across the sky. No more moon.

"This stretch of water is supposedly haunted, you know. The ghosts of drowned slaves."

Trey didn't react. It took more than words to frighten him. Scales and teeth, for example.

"Not that I believe in ghosts, mind you, but they're still fascinating. The ultimate rebels. I mean, how much more spit-in-your-face can you get than refusing to die properly?"

The landscape ran along beside us, trees and docks and halos of light. We were crossing the mouth of Turner Creek, and the iron-colored water lapped in rills and ruffles, unquiet.

I slid closer to Trey. "Are you okay?"

"Yes. Why?"

"You seem...different."

"How?"

"It's hard to explain. Like things are much closer to the surface now."

"Is that bad?"

"No, no. It's good. Different but good."

The wet wind whipped our hair, the water choppy. He let me pull his arm around my shoulders, but kept his eyes on the dark line where land met water.

I sighed. "Of course, there are two dead men to be accounted for now."

"I know."

"Which means this isn't such a lark anymore. I mean, it never was, not with Hope's scheming and conniving."

"No, that's entirely too complicated to be enjoyable."

"The other part, though, that was something else."

"What other part?"

"The sparring part." I looked up at him. "We make a good team, but we make good adversaries too. Especially when it comes to interrogation."

Then I definitely saw his mouth quirk. "So we're working together now?"

"Looks like it." I put a hand on his thigh, solid and lean through the windbreaker pants. "But I'm optimistic we'll be disagreeing about something real soon."

He thought about that. "I suppose so."

"I mean, you've still got Marisa's manipulations to deal with."

"True."

"And I've still got an agenda that's decidedly at odds with Phoenix's."

"Indeed."

I reached up and turned his face to mine. "I'm sure we'll be at each other's throats any second now."

He let me pull him in for a kiss. His lips were cold and tasted of the sea, but his mouth was warm and familiar.

"At each other's throats," he repeated, and then kissed me again.

Chapter Twenty-four

The morning sun pierced the hotel room as Trey slipped his arms through the holster and adjusted the straps. "It's immaterial. Neither you nor Reynolds could have come last night. The permit was for three, no more."

Marisa stood in front of him—foot-tapping, eyes-flashing, bodice-popping incensed. She'd shown up at seven-thirty waving a piece of paper, ready to keel-haul her premises liability agent. Trey had been up for hours—running, showering, paperworking—but I was still in my bathrobe, reading the news, the remains of our room service breakfast still on the table.

"You should have told me," she said.

"I did. I typed up the 302 this morning. That's the protocol."

"Don't protocol me."

I snagged another pastry. This was the problem with trying to work the rules against Trey. He would snatch them from your hands and beat you with them, expertly and ruthlessly.

Marisa put her hands on her hips. "So what happens to it now?"

"You mean the map?"

"Of course the map."

Trey slipped his H&K into the holster, then loaded spare ammo into the holding pouch. "That's up to the authorities. I assume it will be returned to Emmy Simmons when they're finished with it. The Harringtons can approach her about purchasing it then, but I don't think they'll be interested since it's most likely a fake."

"Regardless, you can't go gallivanting all over the city without telling me."

"I was not gallivanting then, and I'm not gallivanting now. Tai is conducting a follow-up later this morning. I want to be there."

"And the objective of this little Q&A?"

I picked up my coffee. "Hope's behind the map, I know she is, but she had to have a partner, and I think I know who that is. And we're going to talk to that person this morning."

Marisa pointed to the newspaper. The headline read FOUL PLAY SUSPECTED IN LOCAL MAN'S DEATH.

"Someone who could be a suspected murderer?" she said.

I shook my head. "I don't think Winston had a thing to do with that old man's death—he runs tours, not assassinations. But I want Trey along to make sure he's telling the truth when I ask him about it."

I'd considered hard if Winston could kill. I thought not, but I wasn't about to risk my neck on a guess. I had a logical reason to believe that neither Hope nor Winston had killed Simmons— they were the ones who had put the whole map scam in motion, and he'd stumbled right along their rosy path. Killing him made no sense. But they were behind the scam, I was sure of it. And I was using my suddenly free morning—and my surprisingly free boyfriend—to find out how.

Marisa slapped the 302 on Trey's desk. "And how does this relate to your assigned duties?"

"I have no assigned duties until this afternoon. I'll be back then."

"I need you this morning."

"No, you don't."

Marisa glared. I raised the newspaper. As gratifying as it was to watch Trey stand up for himself, I had the feeling there would be shrapnel flying any second.

I was right.

Marisa's expression hardened. "I have about had it with you."

"I know."

"I'd replace you if I could. Right now."

The corner of his mouth twitched. It was the first hint of reaction I'd seen in him since she'd stormed into the room.

"I know that too," he said evenly.

Marisa closed her eyes, then rubbed the bridge of her nose. "I didn't mean that."

"Yes, you did."

"No, I didn't. Look at me."

Trey scanned her forehead and cheekbones in that chemical-peel examination of his, pausing at her mouth. For some reason, lies lay especially heavy on the mouth.

"I don't want to replace you," she said. "You're the best, and I charge accordingly, which makes you very valuable to me. But I don't sell paperwork, Trey, I sell you."

She placed one white hand on the inside of his elbow. He flinched, but didn't move. He looked at her hand. And then he looked at her.

"Go on," he said.

"I'm going to quote the Vulnerability Assessment Methodologies Report at you now, which says, in these exact words, that the quality and diligence of the assessor is the most important criteria in the success of any security plan." She tilted her head and regarded him cannily. "And you, Mr. Seaver, are my assessor."

He folded his arms. "My job description—"

"We've had this conversation before. You're a field agent, you have fieldwork, and sometimes it will involve nothing more than showing up and looking pretty. And you will do this. Because it's your job."

He didn't argue. But she'd gotten to him, I could tell, and I knew why. She'd used the phrase "showing up," and in Trey's world, showing up was everything. It was where he drew the big unbreachable line—people who showed up, and people who didn't.

He exhaled slowly. "What do you need from me?"

She smoothed the front of her blouse, calm now in victory. "I need you to finish the tiered assessment, including cost analysis. I need you to coordinate with our current secondary vendors and make sure they have lines on the proposed budget."

"I can do that."

"And I need you to spend the afternoon with Reynolds."

He opened his mouth, and she held up a hand.

"Not personal protection. He's the linchpin to bringing off this tournament because he's the only one who can convince Audrina it's doable. Listen to what he wants, then figure out how to make it happen in a way that sticks with the numbers Audrina gave us."

Trey raised an eyebrow. "And what about this morning?"

"You have four hours. I need you back here at noon."

He nodded once. "I'll be here."

He went into the bedroom to get his notebooks and pens, the materials of his craft. He may have been strapped with a nine-millimeter and honed with Krav Maga, but in his bones, Trey was a math geek.

Marisa watched him go. Then she turned her gaze on me like a firehose. "I blame you for this."

"For what?"

She pointed at the other room. "For that. He used to be my most reliable employee. Now I cringe when I see a 302 from him. What is it now? I wonder. Car chase? Dead body? Shooting? Did he really call Senator Lovejoy last night? Please tell me he didn't."

I put the newspaper back up. "That wasn't Phoenix business. It was a personal favor, for me."

"It involved Phoenix when it involved my premises liability agent in an ongoing criminal investigation."

"Hence the 302 under your door."

"He didn't follow procedure!"

"Yes, he did. To the letter."

She folded her arms. "Aren't you supposed to be working?"

"Looks like my work has merged with Trey's." I nibbled my croissant. "And don't act surprised. This is why you invited me along, after all—to poach my leads. Unfortunately, I found the map first, and I'm hot on the Bible. Try not to be a sore loser."

Her eyes held a daggered loathing. "You think this is one big adventure. I suppose I might too, if my life revolved around a backwards little gun shop. Trey must take your mind off things."

I lay the pastry on the plate and put down my newspaper. "I don't think you want to start this fight."

"I am itching to start this fight." There was heat in her voice. "Unfortunately, I have real work to do. It's not fun and games keeping Phoenix afloat, not since you darkened Fulton County with your presence." She headed for the door. "I would say keep him out of trouble, but that doesn't seem to be your M.O."

"Trey has a mind of his own."

"Indeed he does, as unique a mind as I've ever come across. I have the entire psychological profile on him, after all, compiled by your brother." She narrowed her eyes. "I know things."

"You know how to manipulate him."

"So do you. But I know the dangers too, especially of dragging him into an investigation." She made a little tsk-tsk noise. "Wish I could share that info, but it's confidential, as I'm sure your brother has explained."

She opened the door and tossed a look over her shoulder. "Be careful, sweetie. That's all I can say."

She turned on her heel and stalked out of the room, slamming the door behind her. Trey came out of the bedroom, fastening his cufflinks. He'd heard every word, of course. But his expression was clear and bland and utterly undisturbed.

He adjusted his already perfect Windsor knot. "Are you ready?"

◇◇◇

We took the bridge to Bay Street under a blue sky as brilliant and wet as fresh paint. The clouds were still present, though, tumbled and billowy and moving fast, a portent of things to come. The tropical storm continued its offshore spin, sharpening its teeth on the warm Gulf Stream waters. Landfall was imminent, said the forecaster, although its target remained unpredictable. Until then, the Lowcountry was being blessed with a temporary stretch of benevolent weather.

But I wasn't fooled one bit.

River Street lay four hundred feet below us down the sloping pavement-and-cobblestone incline, and since the day was adazzle with fresh clean light, tourists already clogged the area. Trey drove carefully, avoiding the oblivious pedestrians lurching from every sidewalk.

"Please tell me you didn't fall for that drivel," I said.

He frowned. "What drivel?"

"Marisa's drivel. I know you heard her."

He turned the car into Emmett Park, within sight of the Waving Girl. The woman depicted in the giant bronze statue— waving a flag at the incoming ships, hoping against hope for the return of her one true love—was a monument to lost causes if there ever was one.

"It wasn't drivel," he said. "She had valid points."

"That she uses to manipulate you."

"Regardless."

He eased the car into the parallel space on the curb, uneven and pocked with puddles. It was a short walk to Winston's shop. But Trey remained seated, his eyes on the steering wheel, keys in hand. Something percolating in his head.

"You can have access to the psychological profile she mentioned," he said. "I'll call Eric and sign the authorization paperwork as soon as we get back to Atlanta."

I tried not to look startled. "You don't have to do that."

"I want to. It's mostly Eric's occupational assessments. APD records and recommendations, the OPS transcripts."

The Office of Professional Standards investigation, my brain filled in. *On Trey, on the fatal shooting. The reason he resigned from the force.*

"Your brother can explain more," he said.

Are you sure you want to know? my brain countered.

I ignored my brain. "Marisa implied she knows something about you that I don't, about why I shouldn't involve you in investigations."

"I heard."

"Does she?"

"No." He kept his eyes on the dashboard. "Investigation is not my strong point. But Eric has referenced no contra-indications to such work." He turned to face me. "I'm not hiding anything from you. But there are things I don't know how to talk about, not yet. Do you understand?"

I knew what he was telling me. It was the same thing Eric and Garrity were always telling me in oblique and nonspecific ways. Be careful, they said. Depths within depths. But I also knew my brother was as professional as they came. If Trey were a hazard, Eric wouldn't have okayed him to work at Phoenix.

"I understand," I said. "Just promise me two things."

"What?"

"One, if I ever do need to know something, so matter how hard it might be to talk about, you'll tell me."

He nodded. "Okay."

I pointed toward the statue. "And two, if you ever leave me, and I start standing on the street corner waving at every Ferrari that goes by, you'll come back long enough to shoot me in the head. I'll do the same for you. Deal?"

The corner of his mouth kinked in a suppressed smile. "Deal." He opened his car door. "Shall we find Winston now?"

Chapter Twenty-five

As I suspected, River Street was a sprawling carnival, its narrow sidewalks packed and boisterous. Trey, however, threaded his way through the crowd with fluid efficiency.

I followed close behind. We passed the Olympia Café, and he caught the rhythm of the streaming people and the bouziki music, his body entraining itself to his environment, slipping in and out of it like camouflage. He brushed no one's shoulder, blocked no one's path, got trapped in no bottlenecks.

We arrived at the tour shop and stepped inside. The front room glowed with morning sunshine, bouncing off the shiny tourist faces browsing the brochures, fondling the souvenirs. Winston stepped up to the counter, his shirt a blinding explosion of red splashed with yellow and green, his professional smile in place. It wavered only the slightest when he saw me standing there.

"Hey, Tai. You change your mind about that job?"

"Not yet." I took Trey's elbow. "This is my boyfriend, Trey. Trey, Winston Cargill, my former boss."

Winston gave him the salesman grin and extended a hand. Trey didn't take it. He didn't do anything. He just stood there, a look of dazed bafflement on his face.

"Trey? What's wrong?"

He held up one finger.

"Trey?"

He sneezed, then sneezed again, violently. "I can't—" Another sneeze, this one sending him up against the wall. A blowsy woman in a sundress moved out of the way, clucking to herself. Trey buried his face in his elbow and sneezed three more times.

"Parrot," he said into his elbow, and pointed.

Jezebel cocked her head at him. Trey sneezed again. "I'm allergic. I can't…" And then he shoved open the door and threw himself back onto the sidewalk. I watched the door shut behind him, jingling cheerfully.

The parrot trilled like a ringing telephone, then screamed. Out on the cobblestones, Trey sneezed again. The bird reached up a clawed toe and preened.

Winston shook his head. "Damn. Is he okay?"

I sighed. So much for tapping Trey's cranial lie detector. Out on the sidewalk, I heard two concerned voices offering aid. Female, of course.

"He's fine." I propped my elbows on the counter and regarded Winston pleasantly. "We can talk without him."

"Talk about what?"

"Did you hear about Bob Simmons?"

"The guy who drowned? Yeah. Did you know him?"

"No. Uncle Dexter did apparently. The newspaper had a good article, but it didn't say anything about the map."

Winston tried to look innocent. "What map?"

"The one I found last night. On Wassaw Island. Somebody set that man up with a fake treasure map, and he died trying to find the gold it supposedly pointed to. But it was a hoax. Another lost cause."

Winston looked sick. "You found the real map?"

"Trey and I did. Long story. Here's the kicker. The authorities are anxious to figure out where it came from."

"What can they tell from a map?"

"Oh, lots of things. It's a CSI Wonderland out there now." I leaned forward until we were face to face. "Fingerprints, specks of dust, even DNA from skin cells. It's amazing."

Winston looked like a catfish out of water, his mouth opening and closing, his eyes wide. That was all a bunch of lies, but
the less he knew, the better.

I lowered my voice. "I'm guessing it was a game to start with,
a joke. But somebody's dead now. And the cops aren't laughing. Neither is the GBI. The Feds either. Multijurisdictional
nonamusement."

Winston collected himself. He shook his head slowly, with
manufactured regret. "That's a damn shame, that is."

"I know. But here's the thing. I'm sure Hope's behind it, and
I'm sure she's not working alone. You have any ideas about that?"

"No, n-nothing."

His eyes were clear and guileless, but the stammer gave him
away.

"Listen to me, Winston. I—"

Three loud knocks at the back door interrupted me. Winston's face went slack with relief, like he'd been tossed a life
preserver.

"Hang on a second," he said. "That's UPS."

And then he slipped out the door in back, like a rabbit making
for the underbrush. I shook my head. Six months since I'd left
town, and already he'd forgotten who he was dealing with.

I started with the shelf under the counter, whipping the cloth
cover aside. The box was gone. I hadn't really expected it to be
there, of course, but sometimes amateurs get lucky. I gave the rest
of the shelves a cursory examination to no avail. Whatever he'd
been hiding under there, he'd hidden it better somewhere else.

I moved on to his desk calendar, getting a pencil and poking
through it, flipping pages. The bird looked at me without
judgment.

"I'll bet you've heard all kinds of stuff, haven't you?" I said.
Another trill.

"Polly know a secret?"

Another croak.

I returned my attention to the desk calendar. I recognized
most of the entries as the typical tour shop agenda. But there

was an interesting bit on Friday night, a seven o'clock meeting marked with an asterisk. Unlike every other entry in the meticulous calendar, this one had no meeting place, no person to be meeting. It reeked of mysterious assignation.

I heard the back door and slammed the book shut, hurrying to the other side of the counter. Winston came thumping in with frustration written bold on his face, which was as shiny and red as the splotches on his shirt.

"Look," he said. "Hope Lyle is bad news. But are you really suggesting she killed that old guy?"

I shrugged. "Who knows? But seriously, Winston, don't get in over your head. You've got my card—call me if she shows up. I don't want to be reading about your untimely demise in tomorrow's headlines."

◇◇◇

I found Trey waiting in the Lincoln, sitting in the driver's seat, head tilted back. I climbed in and slammed the door behind me.

"Parrots? Really?"

He nodded, not raising his head. His eyes still watered, but otherwise the allergic reaction had died down.

I fastened my seat belt, annoyed despite myself. "First reptiles, now birds. Any other conflicts with the animal kingdom I should know about?"

He pulled a slip of paper from his pocket and held it in my direction. I caught a glimpse of numbers and letters.

"What's that?"

"License plate number. From the car that pulled up to the back entrance of Winston's shop."

"UPS?"

"Not UPS. Silver Mercedes convertible." Despite the watering eyes, Trey was back to his usual sharpness. "It was driven by this man. Five-six, light brown hair, slender build."

He pulled out his phone and held it my way. He'd captured an image of Winston's unexpected visitor, and Trey was right—not a delivery person. The two men looked to be arguing. Winston's expression was tight with anger, the young man's pale with anxiety. I looked closer, enlarged the image with a swipe. It was fuzzy, but I recognized the figure anyway.

"Aw, hell. That's Skip!"

"Who?"

"He used to work at the tattoo shop where I met John. Talented artist, Skip. He quit, though, before I moved. I have no idea where he is now, but I bet Train might."

"Train?"

"Yeah, he owns the tattoo shop. And I bet he can put me on Skip's trail. After all, Winston's got the knowhow and Hope's got the goods—the missing link in this equation is someone with the artistic talent to create a forgery, and Skip's got that in spades." I handed Trey's phone back to him. "Wanna come see where I got my first tattoo?"

Trey checked his watch. "I can't. It's almost noon."

"Oh yeah. The Dragon Lady Summoneth."

"Indeed."

"No problem. You take the car. I'll catch the water taxi back to the hotel."

"Are you sure?"

"Train's shop is at the other end of River Street, a five minute walk. In public, broad daylight."

Trey did the rapid calculation, factoring in all the various ways I could screw things up, multiplying that by the probability that I would, divided by the potential information coming my way. The verdict? Probably sensible.

"Okay. But call me when you leave."

"Where will you be? On some helicopter again?"

"At this point, I wouldn't be surprised."

He took my hand. The abrupt intimacy started me, but then he pulled out his pen and wrote a number in my palm.

"This goes directly to the security desk at the hotel. I'll have my phone, of course, but in case you need to access my schedule, they'll have it. Be careful."

I closed my fist tight around the number. "Careful and sensible. I promise."

◇◇◇

Soul Ink resided on the west end of River Street in the shadow of the electric plant, the funkier section of the strip. It was where I'd met John, Skip too. During work hours, Hope and I would often rendezvous with the two of them in the long connecting passageway behind the shops —sometimes at Winston's, sometimes at Train's—smoking and sneaking beers before going back to our respective workplaces.

The old tattoo parlor had been redecorated. It now felt like a slightly gothic day spa—big stained glass windows, a gold-washed concrete floor stamped with swirls, red leather seats. When I opened the door, I heard wind chimes and smelled incense.

Train looked up from one of the art books. He grinned. "Tai!"

He was a well-muscled guy, with chestnut hair and a penchant for tight white t-shirts, the better to see his intricately inked forearms and biceps, a garden of lush roses and finely-wrought crosses woven with Bible references. His face was boyish under a tough-looking goatee.

"Hey, Train. How's it going?"

"Excellently, thank the Lord."

Train took the name of his shop seriously. Soul Ink was born as spiritual outreach. The plaque above his work station read Isaiah 44:5: "And a generation will write on their hands, 'I belong to the Lord.'" But he welcomed anyone into the shop, Christian and heathen alike. I liked to imagine that if Jesus himself wanted a tattoo, he'd come to Train.

He clapped his hands to his thighs. "So what's up? You looking for new ink?"

"Yes, but not today."

I pulled out my phone and showed him the photo Trey had snapped. Train's eyes flashed with disappointment.

"What's he done now? Making fake IDs again?"

"Maybe. But I'm not out to get him for that."

"What are you out to get?"

"Information about the person who hired him."

Train looked at me skeptically. He volunteered in the prison. He knew that the vilest of all the sinners in the criminal world was a snitch.

"I know," I said, cutting him off. "Criminals don't cough up information. But Skip isn't a criminal, is he?"

Train sighed. "No. That's why he gets in trouble so much. No street smarts."

"He still work here?"

"No, not for months."

"So how's he paying the bills?"

"He's Big Nate's newest sugar baby. He never finished his degree, but he's cute, so now Nate pays for his errant ways."

"And lets him drive his convertible. A silver Mercedes, I'm guessing?"

Train nodded. I looked at the photo again. Skip was attractive enough to be a kept man, yes. But if he was living the high life now, why was he at the shop arguing with Winston? And what were they arguing about?

I put the phone away. "Trust me when I tell you that Skip has no idea the trouble he may have tapped. He's working with some low level people, but they've provoked a killer, it seems."

Train got serious. "Murder?"

"Maybe. Which is why I'm staying as far away from that end of it as I possibly can. I need to get to Skip before the people who killed Simmons get to him first. Do you know where to find him?"

"It's Thursday night—he'll be catching the show at the Speakeasy. He's got a crush on the bartender, the redhead."

"Does Nate know?"

Train fixed me with a look. "You think he'd still be letting him drive that Mercedes if he did?"

The Speakeasy. I hadn't been there since Rico left town. It was a secret bar located within Club One, the infamous glitter den and dance club. You had to ask the bouncer to let you in. He'd tell you to go up the stairs, find the door marked Employees

Only, then knock three times. A little panel would slide, and if you knew the password, they'd open up.

It was all for show. The Speakeasy trafficked in secrecy and gimmick, but it wasn't illegal. They liked to pretend, though, playing ragtime and serving absinthe and other supposedly illicit cocktails in a dark 1920s styled bar.

Train shook his head. "If he sees you coming, he's gonna run. They don't call him Skippy for nothing."

"I can run too, you know."

"Not like Skippy. Especially since he does not want to get caught there, you know what I mean?"

I did. And while Skippy's illicit crush was certainly leverage I could use, it did mean I'd have to act fast. Or have a Plan B.

◇◇◇

Plan B was sitting at his desk when I got back to the hotel. I was happy to see him there—a few hours crunching numbers always recalibrated his composure back to the cool and steady range.

I perched on the edge of his desk. "Hey you."

He didn't look up. "Hey."

"What are you doing?"

"Profit and loss calculation. Did you know that hole-in-one insurance costs three times as much as a rain cancellation policy?" He sat back and looked my way. "A fax came for you."

"A fax? Who faxes anymore?"

Trey handed me an official-looking piece of paper. "Police departments."

I scanned the information quickly and got a buzz of excitement. "Who sent this?"

"Garrity."

It was a letter from the detective in Jacksonville. Thanks to Rico's tip, they'd done some extra puttering into Vincent DiSilva's life. E-mails led to PO boxes, which led to certain dealings with a whiff of scam about them.

I looked at Trey. "He was making private antique trades using assumed names."

"He was, ever since his retirement. Documents and letters mostly, some books. The Jacksonville PD will be tracking down his customers next."

"Wanna bet his wares were as fake as that treasure map? He was a drafter, after all. He had the copywork skills to make an excellent forger."

"Whatever he was doing, it seems to be small scale; they've found only one or two trades a year. The money trail is insubstantial."

A mild-mannered retiree trafficking in forgery for beer and bingo money. It would not be the weirdest crime spree I'd heard of. I ran a finger along the edge of Trey's desk.

"So, on that note, I have this idea."

"What idea?"

"It involves going to the club."

"What club?"

"The Speakeasy."

He frowned, waiting to see where I was headed.

"Skip will be there tonight, and I would like to hear his side of things. And no, it's not illegal, or dangerous. It's a two-person job, that's all."

He tapped his pen on the yellow tablet. I told him what I'd learned at the tattoo shop. Trey listened, then shook his head.

"Criminals sometimes react violently to being confronted."

"Not this guy. I know Skip, and he knows me. Which is why when he sees me, he'll know the gig's up. Which is where you come in."

"Doing what?"

"I need somebody to block his escape route."

"Tai—"

"All you do is stand there. He won't try to go past you. Otherwise, I might have to chase him down in the parking lot and tackle the fool."

He considered that scenario. "When are you going?"

"Tonight."

He nodded reluctantly. "Okay. But there are rules."

"Of course there are. I have some too, starting with that suit."

"What's wrong with my suit?"

"People will think you're a drug dealer who can't find his way back to I-95. You have to blend."

Now he looked like he was seriously regretting his commitment. "Blend?"

I held out my hand. "Give me your phone. I know who to call."

◇◇◇

Gabriella was equally incredulous. "Blend? Tai, darling, Trey doesn't blend."

I could hear the sounds of her boutique around her—the electronic pings of the cash registers, the soft laughter of pampered customers.

"He only needs to fit in for a little while," I said. "Something between the extremes of workout wear and business formal. Normal person clothes."

"I've been trying to get him into Boglioli, but you know how he is, a Virgo all the way. Luckily, Prada's doing nice things in casual wear."

"Can he get it in Savannah?"

"I know a place. But I'm afraid he'll reject it."

"He might surprise you."

"Really? How intriguing." I heard keyboard tapping at her end. "In that case, I'll make the arrangements and let him know. And I'll have them throw in a nice shiny t-shirt for you, *ma chère*."

Chapter Twenty-six

For decades, Club One has ruled Savannah's nightlife as the most well-known party-glam establishment for gay and straight and all the shades between. It has multiple levels, expensive drinks, and well-maintained billiard tables. Back in the day, I'd been good enough with the stick to shake down the arrogant and inebriated, but my skills were too rusty to try that trick now.

Billie had accompanied me for the preliminary portion of my plan—spotting the mark. Together we kept a close eye on the street-level entrance as we racked up for eight-ball. She'd curled her hair for the occasion and sported a short pink dress that showed off her blossoming décolletage. I kept glancing at her belly, then yanking my eyes back to her face.

She sat on the edge of the table, cue in hand. "Skip's in trouble again, huh?"

I banked a clean one off the side, taking down the two. "Maybe a little. But I'm hoping I can prevent that from turning into a lot."

"I thought he'd settled down with Nate."

"You know Skip. Can't resist a redhead."

I got a flash of Gabriella suddenly and hit the shot too hard, scratching. Billie took advantage of the table and sank the eleven and the nine without even blinking.

"So when's this boyfriend of yours showing up?" she said.

"Ten sharp. He had to pick up a change of clothes."

She put a little too much spin on the cue ball, and it wobbled short of its mark. I bounced an easy rebound off the side and sank the five with a satisfying click.

Billy leaned in close. "Our mutual friend has arrived early."

I looked over her shoulder and spotted Skip, headed straight upstairs to the Speakeasy. Part one of the plan was working—Skip was effectively a rabbit in a trap now. Our plan was for me to follow him up, let him get a look at me, and then when he bolted—as he would—he'd smack right into Trey, who had a way of convincing people to do whatever he told them to do.

I checked the neon clock over the bar. Three till ten. I adjusted my Sand Gnats cap and cued up for my next shot.

Billie frowned. "Tai?"

"Yeah?"

"About your boyfriend…did you say black hair, six feet tall, dressed in black and white?"

"Yeah?"

She grinned. "Girl, your vocabulary sucks if that was the best you could do."

She nodded toward the door. I turned. And I almost choked on my beer.

It was Trey, all right, but not any Trey I knew. This Trey wore black low-slung jeans, a white t-shirt, and a black leather jacket complemented by—I clutched the edge of pool table—black leather boots.

I exhaled slowly. "Oh god. That's him. I think."

Billie gave a low whistle. "Wow. You must have been good in some former life."

Trey spotted me, and I beckoned him toward the bar with a tiny tilt of the head. He took a seat. I banged the six into the corner pocket and laid my cue on the green, then headed his way, taking my beer with me.

"A Pellegrino," Trey said. "In the bottle, the glass separate. No ice, one lime."

His presence caused a ripple of excitement to run down the bar like an electric current. He kept his eyes straight ahead, however, his finger tapping the counter.

I slid onto the seat beside him. "Skip's already here. He went into the Speakeasy two minutes ago."

"So I'm…what was your word?"

"Blending."

"Yes. Blending. I'm blending for no reason."

The bartender brought his Pellegrino, and Trey arranged the bottle in the exact center of the napkin, glass to the left.

I put my hand on his leg. "I'll give you a reason later. But for right now, do you remember the plan?"

"Of course."

"Then finish your water and let's go."

He poured the Pellegrino into the glass. I stood and took off my hat, shaking out the tousled curls hidden underneath. Then I pulled off my jacket, revealing my spanking new t-shirt, a red silk Gucci number with rhinestone accents.

I grinned at him. "Hurry up. I'm dying to see Skippy talk his way out of this one."

◇◇◇

I entered the Speakeasy to George Gershwin's "Rhapsody in Blue," Gabriella's t-shirt vamping and sparkling like a disco ball. As I'd expected, Skip had a seat at the bar. The bartender laughed at some story he was spinning, a big laugh that had strut and volume to it. She was impossible to ignore, an island of flaming red hair and bosom and luminous eyes with lashes like bottle brushes. Her manicure was impeccable, even if her hands were as big as Texas.

I took a seat, and her eyes twinkled. "Hello, sweetie!"

I smiled. "Hello!"

Skip looked down the row at me. He was a good-looking guy in a boy-toy way, with a sulky mouth and pecan-brown curls tumbling over his forehead. He recognized me instantly, and even in the dark, I saw him pale. I waved two fingers at him.

He nodded my way. And then he bolted.

I hopped up, jumped over a middle-aged couple in matching sweaters, banged into a waitress coming up the steps, then took off after him. All I saw was a flash of movement at the bottom of the stairs, and then a quick whip to the left, headed for the back exit.

I stopped running. *Rabbits and snares*, I thought, as I pushed open the exit door into the alley. Sure enough, there was Skip, face to face with Trey, who was examining him curiously.

Skip caught his breath, then jerked a thumb in Trey's direction. "The muscle's with you, huh?"

I nodded.

He sighed, resigned now to his fate. "What do you want?"

Trey glanced at me, puzzled. I was guessing that in his experience, criminals didn't roll over at the tiniest bit of intimidation from some guy in stiff new jeans and unscuffed boots. He was accustomed to SWAT raids, where the thugs got their heads banged together first, then started talking.

I sidled up to Skip, wishing I had a cigarette to tap out of the pack and offer to him. All I had was gum, however. So I pulled out a stick and held it in his direction. "Have you seen Hope Lyle lately?"

He took the gum. "Nope."

"What about Winston?"

"Nope."

I held up my phone and showed him the photograph Trey had taken. "This isn't you and Winston, arguing behind his shop?"

Skip glanced at it, his jaw working the gum. "Nope. Not me. I haven't been there in months."

"Really?" I plucked a bit of bright green down from his sleeve and showed it to him. "A little birdie says you're lying."

"So?"

"So this little birdie also says she'll tell Big Nate you were hanging around making eyes at the bartender if you don't cooperate."

Skip swallowed the gum. "She said it was a prank."

"Who did?"

"Hope. She promised me good money for the work, and it seemed harmless enough. A treasure map, for crying out loud. Like a party favor."

"Did you know what she had planned for it?"

"Didn't ask."

"You made yourself an accessory to a crime and didn't ask what it was?"

He snorted. "Now you sound like a cop."

Trey took a step forward, and Skip's attitude crumbled. He pressed himself against the concrete wall like he wanted to become a splotch of graffiti.

Trey put his hands on his hips. "This meeting is Tai's idea. She believes that if she explains herself clearly, you'll understand the seriousness of the situation and give her the information she needs."

He reached into his pocket, and both Skip and I froze. Trey pulled out his cell phone.

"I don't think that way," he said. "I think that since you admitted to a criminal act, I need to call the authorities and have them arrest you. And unless she gives me a good reason—"

"What the hell, Tai?" Skip stared at me incredulously. "Your muscle is threatening to call the five-oh!"

I folded my arms. "It's what he does. Which is why I'd start cooperating if I were you. My muscle used to be a cop, but he resigned after he shot some uncooperative punk right through the heart. And he hasn't shot anybody since. Don't tempt him."

Skip looked at Trey. Trey examined him calmly, looking for all the world like a particularly stylish serial killer.

Skip sighed. "Fine. What else do you want to know?"

"I want to know what you were doing at Winston's shop."

"We argued."

"About what?"

"I wanted out. I read about that old guy's death in the news, and I wanted Winston to take his shit back and pay me what Hope promised."

"What shit?"

"A forger's kit, a nice one too. Old ink, old paper, old pens, like somebody robbed an antiques store. I dumped it off there and left, but he still didn't pay me."

My instincts went zing, but I kept my voice calm. "Start explaining, Skip, from the beginning."

And he did, with only a few sputters and false starts. Hope had looked him up when she got back to Savannah, he said, offering him a pretty price for what she said was a prank. She supplied the materials—paper, ink, a rough sketch—and he created the treasure map.

"Were the materials in a paper box?"

"Yeah. But she didn't tell me what she was going to do with it. You gotta believe me, I didn't want to hurt anybody. Why do you think I want out now?"

Trey took his hand out of his pocket. Skip was thoughtless, not criminal. And he technically hadn't broken the law. He hadn't counterfeited bills or deeds or a driver's license. He'd made "art." What Hope has done with it, however, was a different story.

"Look, Skip, I don't know what happened to Simmons, but I'm betting somebody killed him over that map and chucked his body in the channel. And I'm betting they'll kill you too, if they think you need killing."

"But I never…"

"You need to leave town. Tonight."

Skip went pale. He looked at Trey, who nodded, and then back to me, every bit of cocky burned right out of him.

I put my hand on his shoulder. "Tell Nate you two need a long weekend. Then go someplace far away that you've never been before and stay there a while. And lay off the bartender. The last thing you want to be now is predictable."

Skip nodded. He was quiet and serious, which was good, because that meant he was listening. I squeezed his shoulder. He was shaking underneath my hand.

That was also good.

◇◇◇

Back in the hotel room, I explained things to Trey around a mouthful of toothpaste. "Guys like Skip clam up around cops. But talk to them like a thug? Works every time."

"You seem to understand criminals."

I spat in the sink. "Some of my best friends."

Trey had taken a shower and changed into his pajama pants. He was two degrees from exhausted. I was tired too, but I still had work to do. I'd already perked a pot of coffee for what was looking like a long night.

I wiped my face with the towel. "I wish I could get my hands on that box. If it really is a forger's kit, and Vincent DiSilva down in Florida really was a forger, then everybody's having a hissy fit over a Bible that's probably a piece of well-crafted fakery."

"It does seem that way."

"Which means I'm even more confused." I pulled a plain white t-shirt over my head. "Thanks for helping me out today. I really appreciate it."

"You're welcome." He leaned back against the wall, arms crossed, expression curious even if his eyes were flat and tired. "What are you doing tomorrow?"

"Tomorrow is the reenactment at Skidaway Island. I'm meeting Dee Lynn there." I put a steadying hand on his shoulder. "And don't panic when you hear this next part, but...I have a plan."

Chapter Twenty-seven

I woke the next morning to the bubble and hiss of the coffee machine. I opened my eyes and blinked into the gray blur of dawn. Trey stood at the window. He wore workout clothes, his gym bag over one shoulder, his hair damp with sweat.

I pulled my head up from the desk, eyes sticky, mouth dry and thick. "What time is it?"

"Six-fifteen." He turned to face me, a dark silhouette against the sheer curtains. "You didn't come to bed last night."

I forced myself to sit up slowly, stiffly. "I meant to. But then I had a little bit of a nervous breakdown."

"I see."

His desk was a mess. Pamphlets, printouts, garbled notes, everything I could find on the rise and fall and re-rise of the Ku Klux Klan. My cell phone lay on the floor next to the chair, along with two empty bottles of Jack from the mini bar.

I scrubbed at my eyes. "I remember calling Rico at some point and yammering at him for a while. Then I kinda fell apart. Then I fell asleep. Sorry. I'll clean it up."

"It's okay." He didn't move from the window.

"I spent all night choking down this Klan shit. It's evil, Trey, stupid and repulsive. I feel like I'm gonna throw up."

He peered at the jumble of papers. "You already knew these things. You told me about them."

"I knew the old stuff, yeah. But this is my first time getting acquainted with the new Klan, the one that's operating here."

"There's more than one Klan?"

"There's hundreds of Klans. But this is the big one—Ku Klux Klan Incorporated—and it's trying to act like a squeaky clean social club."

I got up and went to the coffee maker, stepping over a set of pamphlets I'd downloaded and printed, the ones the Klansman had been passing out at the Expo. They were professionally edited and slickly produced, featuring Gerard Dupree, self-styled Grand Wizard of the Southeastern Regional Knights of the Ku Klux Klan LLC. Sandy-haired and hatchet-nosed, smiling from the page, he looked more like a corporate CEO than the head of the Invisible Empire, or at least one head of that despicable hydra. In the old days, his identity would have been a secret to even most Klansman. Now he had a website, probably a Twitter account.

I poured a cup of coffee. "They say they're not about hate. They say they're advocates for the White Protestant Christians of America, that the violence of the past is tragic, of course, but past. It begins to seem almost reasonable, like maybe they're deluded but harmless and that oh yeah, they do take care of the widows and orphans and occasionally pick up trash along the highway." I dosed my coffee liberally with cream and sugar. "I don't know what those men in gray died for, but it wasn't so these idiots could have a gift shop with KKK tote bags."

Trey watched me. He didn't say anything. The city lay below us, cobblestones and tabby warmed by the dusty light of sunrise. It was easy to forget that we were in the twenty-first century, that we'd made any progress at all.

I went to the window and stood by him. "Fifty years ago they'd have lynched me as a race traitor, right after I watched them hang Rico from a tree. But it's all whitewashed now. Literally. Like it never happened."

Trey still stood quietly. I took a sip of coffee, my hands trembling. Trey made it weaker than I usually did, but it would be a start. He was right—I knew all about the Klan. But I'd forgotten too, as deliberately as they had. I'd stowed this baggage down here in the pluff mud and made haste for Atlanta. The city too busy to hate, it called itself. Or remember.

"It all comes together," I said. "My stuff, your stuff, the entire Civil War. It all flows down and gets lost in the end."

Trey watched and listened. Any other man would have put a hand on my shoulder or pulled me into his arms. But Trey waited, as always, for me to make the first move. And maybe for the first time, I understood what a powerful gesture that was. *I will always show up,* he'd promised. Not save the day. Not make everything better. But he would always be there, for as long as I wanted him to.

So I put down the coffee and leaned against him. And he took my weight, all of it. He didn't say anything for five minutes. But when I eventually buried my face in his chest, he put his arms around me and held me close.

"Do you still want to go through with your plan?" he said.

I nodded against his shirt.

"Do you still want me to come and help?"

I nodded again.

He exhaled. "Okay then. I'll get dressed. You should too."

And then—tentatively, tenderly—he patted my back. Without any prompting from me whatsoever.

◇◇◇

Skidaway Island State Park felt like the very pivot between past and future. In the parking lot, the twenty-first century held sway—farm trucks with pull-behind trailers, motorcycles, muscle cars—but on the other side of the palmetto ridge, time blurred and dissolved. I could glimpse the reenactors' camp through the morning mist, dozens of white A-frame tents and larger walled ones, all of them set up the previous night.

The public area teemed with activity. Spectators toted plastic coolers to the shade of the picnic pavilions. A few vendors stayed in character and manned tables filled with circa-1860 wares, but most of my fellow Expo participants reclined in the shade, lemonade and hot dogs in hand, fully grounded in contemporary America.

Emmy Simmons wasn't among them, however. Neither was her son, the Rock. The rest of his biker buddies were out in full force, clustered around their Harleys in the parking lot, shooting belligerent glares in my direction.

I ignored them and headed for the spectator area. The low breeze felt heavy and dense and ancient, stirred up from some prehistoric cave. Beyond the barrier rope, deep in those cool fronded depths, hundreds of men gathered, preparing for a battle. For those in the audience, however, it was bird song and crowd murmur.

Dee Lynn met me halfway. "I got a picnic blanket set up over yonder." She frowned. "What's that?"

She pointed at the document tube I carried. It was a professional-looking thing, like an architect might tote fancy papers in.

"You mean this?" I said. "It's bait."

Her hands went to her hips. "You'd better explain."

I did. As I gave her the gist of things, Trey came to stand beside me. Every eye that wasn't already on me swiveled our way. We made quite the pair—me the disreputable map seller and him… well, nobody really knew what he was, but he looked exotic and official, and that was good enough to get tongues wagging.

"Reynolds is checking in," he said.

"So he decided to participate after all."

"He did. I double-checked all his weaponry this morning. Everything was in working order." Trey reconsidered his words. "Or nonworking order."

"In other words, no real bullets, black powder only."

"Yes." He examined the field, the fog-shrouded stands of trees and the vast green meadow opening between. "I wish I could say the same for the rest of the reenactors."

"You're not happy about this."

He shook his head. "In many ways, this will function like a real battle. And real battles are chaotic and unpredictable, with multiple failure points."

Reynolds joined us from the check-in tent. Twin rows of gold buttons gleamed on the front of his dove-colored coat. Bright

yellow piping accented his cuffs and neckline, complemented
by a gold brocade sash, a feather projecting from the sweeping
officer's hat on his head. He even sported a sword, a slender presentation model in a leather scabbard festooned with flashing gilt.

He doffed the hat and bowed low in front of Dee Lynn.
"M'lady," he intoned, then snapped back to attention.

Dee Lynn gave him the up and down. "Who are you supposed to be?"

"I am my own creation, madam."

I laughed. "With some flourishes borrowed from General
Jeb Stuart perhaps."

"Maybe a few. The gentleman had style." He popped the hat
back on his head, tilting it at a rakish angle. "I have received my
orders and will be joining my regiment."

He waggled a little index card at me—his instructions for
the day's action, delivered by the reenactment coordinator. How
he was to fight, if he was to fall. The battle this day wasn't a
recreation of any actual moment in the War. Savannah's defeat
had been incremental and relatively bloodless. They'd lost the
forts along the ocean early in the war, and had existed with
Union battleships visible offshore for years. Today's fight—
with its charging cavalry, massed regiments, and hand-to-hand
combat—was more educational demonstration than historic
representation.

"Do you die today?" I said.

He tucked the index card in his boot. "That's between me
and my maker." Then he spotted the container and moved in
close. "Is that what I think it is?"

I nodded and dropped my voice. "But you can't tell anybody.
You can't even look this direction. The FBI is on its way to pick
it up, and they're pretty sure they can figure out who killed the
old man from it."

"Really?"

"Yeah. Fancy CSI stuff. Way over my head."

He looked left and right. "I thought the map was fake."

"That doesn't matter. They said it's the evidence they need to put someone away."

"Who?"

I put a finger to my lips. Reynolds nodded.

"The secret is safe with me, m'dear. Now if you'll excuse me, I'd like to get into a martial frame of mind."

We watched him saunter toward the sutler's area, the part of the field reserved for sales. Several soldiers both blue and gray mingled there. Trey stood beside me, sizing up the scene.

"Do you think that was wise?" he said.

As we watched, Reynolds chatted up a sutler behind a table of games appropriate to the era—playing cards, chess, checkers. As they talked, the clerk's eyes drifted our way, taking in the document tube.

"Oh yes," I said. "That was the smartest thing I've done yet. Nothing spreads information like trying to keep it secret."

"Are you sure this is necessary?"

"I've got a reputation to salvage and an ATF audit coming up. I've got to do something to bring this fiasco to an end, and quick."

Trey didn't look convinced. "So now what?"

"Now we see what happens."

"That's not a plan."

"Sure it is."

"No, it's a…I'm not sure what it is, but it isn't a plan."

Across the field, a women in a hoop skirt eyed us and then averted her gaze. Behind her, two young boys walked a little closer to us than necessary, eyes on the document tube. They looked like central casting for Huck Finn, both dressed in beige cotton long shirts and trousers held up with suspenders, mock rifles on their shoulders.

I handed the tube to Dee Lynn. "My friend Kendrick will be at the main entrance in a patrol car. He's officially on KKK watch, but he said to call if anybody made a grab for this. Trey will set up surveillance in the parking lot."

She tucked the tube under her arm. "And where will you be?"

I pointed to the open green meadow between stands of trees. "Watching from over there."

"But the reenactment will be coming through soon. The horses, foot soldiers, the whole crashing bunch of them."

I shook my head. "I won't be in the field. I'll be behind the campground. It's deserted now, so I'll be out of the way of both the battle and the vendors. All you have to do is leave that tube unattended so that our guilty party can try to snatch it."

Dee Lynn didn't seem convinced. "Your friend Kendrick approved this plan?"

"He said it was worth a shot. It's not something he can use in court, but it will give him a reason to take in a likely suspect. And he said that's the big secret of police work—most cases get solved because one of the crooks spills the beans."

Dee Lynn snorted. "That part makes sense. So what do we do now?"

"We take our positions and wait for the fireworks."

◇◇◇

Men. So many men. The womenfolk were shoved to the sidelines in war both real and pretend—only the smattering of females willing to cross-dress ever saw the battlefield. During the war, the elite gave cotillions and raised money for bandages, while the poor gutted hogs and scrubbed clothes and did without, every single night. Very little evidence documented their valor—there was no romance in survival, unlike its flamboyant second cousin, triumph.

But for now, the men occupied the deep recesses of Skidaway Island's maritime forest, and I could slip among the tents and cast iron cooking pots unnoticed. I could still smell the remnants of breakfast—coffee perked in the fires, sausages on the griddles—and feel the heat coming from banked ashes. The morning fog had lifted somewhat, giving me a clearer view of the spectator area.

I saw Dee Lynn on her picnic blanket surrounded by the audience, the document tube at her side. The KKK was present now, weaving through the crowd, polite and smug in their clean white shirts. A woman joined them this morning—friendly, low-key, approachable. I remembered the photos from my night of research—the swinging corpses and the row of white robes, men's dress shoes and women's dainty heels peeking under the hems.

I stuffed down the anger and lifted my binoculars. Across the field, I got my first glimpse of the cavalry through the foliage, already on their horses, massing at the far end of the theatre. They would fight on horseback today, carrying carbines and pistols, even though most actual units during the war fought as mounted infantry, arriving on horseback, then dismounting for hand-to-hand combat. I knew they'd come through first in today's scenario—the better to avoid trampling the reenactors who'd pour onto the scene on foot.

I turned around and checked out the parking lot. I couldn't see Kendrick and Trey, but I knew they were there, waiting.

A flash of movement in the officers' tents caught my eye. As in actual wartime, these tents were set away from the enlisted men's, and with only a few minutes before showtime, they should have been deserted.

But they weren't.

I scanned the area, finally spotting the lurker. He was a small skinny guy, dressed in the simple trousers and white shirt of the civilian, the pants held up with suspenders, a dark gray slouch hat pulled low over his face. He skulked at the edges of the campground, hovering, waiting.

Beyond the trees, I heard the first noises of the coming armies—the bugle calls, the dull huzzah of a hundred voices. I crossed my fingers, hoping that nobody in the spectator area could see me, then jogged from the A-frames to the larger walled tents, which were tall enough to hide me from view.

I peeked around the corner. Nothing. The ivory cloth flapped in the breeze, row upon row of deserted squares.

Suddenly I heard a female voice behind me. "Hey, Tai. How's tricks?"

I spun around. The mysterious stranger stood there, gun pulled. Not a he. A she. And not a stranger.

"Hope," I said.

She raised the gun higher, a short-barreled revolver, and from the way she hoisted it, I knew she knew what she was doing. "Hands up. Don't go for that phone, or anything else you might be packing. Unlike every other weapon out here, mine has real bullets in it. Nobody will notice you're really shot until it's too late."

She pulled her hat off, and I gaped in astonishment. She'd dyed her hair to match mine and styled it in a tumble of curls. Her tresses were lighter, though, a honey blond.

I was so mad I could have strangled her. "You've been pretending to be me!"

She tossed her head. "You like? I had to pad my rump to get the full effect, but—"

"What are you doing here?"

"Same thing as you. Business."

"Bob Simmons is dead because of you."

Her mouth twitched. "Nobody was supposed to die."

"But people did. They always do. Then people like you act all surprised."

"You're wrong. People like me expect things to go haywire. We plan for it." She shoved the hat back on her head without lowering the gun. "But I didn't expect anybody to die."

"It's still your fault. He was following the map you sold him."

"I'm not responsible for other people's bad choices." She kept her mouth in a straight hard line. "You want to blame somebody, blame Winston. That map was all his idea, the double-crossing son of a bitch. All I wanted to do was make the sale and split, but no, he decided to complicate things."

"How? Why?"

"Why don't you ask Winston?"

"Why don't I call the cops and let them sort it out?"

"You could. But they won't find any evidence he did a damn thing, not yet anyway. But if you wait…"

"Wait for what?"

The thunder of hoof beats grew louder, like the edge of an approaching storm. Hope glanced over her shoulder, the gun never wavering.

She took two steps backward. "Uh oh. Time to go."

"The offer's still on the table. Turn over the materials, including the Bible, you and John split whatever profit comes of it, and he doesn't file charges."

"John should know there's no profit in a fake Bible."

I stared at her. "What? Then why—"

"I'll be in contact. Later. Once I'm done with Winston."

Behind her, the war cries intensified, and I saw the first smatterings of blue and gray uniforms, the Union Jack and the Stars and Bars rippling like jungle beasts through the undergrowth.

And then she bolted for the meadow.

"Don't!" I screamed. But I was running after her before the words were out of my mouth.

She hit the tree line and vanished. I plunged in after her. Spanish moss tangled my hair. Palm fronds slapped my face. The interior was all shifting gray light and dappled green, dripping wet, shadow and movement and sogginess. I grabbed a palm tree for support, caught a glimpse of white ducking behind a palmetto. I lunged in that direction…

But then battle was upon us.

Chapter Twenty-eight

The Union horses arrived first—sweaty, dusty, surging—their riders bellowing commands, brandishing curved sabers. I hit the ground at the base of a live oak and scrambled against the trunk, pulling my legs up tight, covering my head with my hands. The cavalry flowed around me in a tide of horseflesh, mud and debris flying from their hooves.

One of the riders saw me huddled there and pulled his mount to a halt. He threw a hand toward the tents.

"Get off the field, you idiot!" he yelled. "The artillery's coming!"

Too late. The infantry troops charged to meet the riders in the open. The cannons went off with a deafening roar, and a cloud of blue-white smoke rolled over me, opaque and dense. My eyes burned, and I covered my mouth with my shirt, choking on grit and ash.

The rider snapped the reins and dashed for the field. I hunkered down as the battle raged around me, men in gray massing in the meadow. The Confederates sent up the rebel yell, that infamous unholy whooping cry. It surrounded me, hundreds of men passing it from tongue to tongue, and for a second, I understood the terror of the front line, your own death coming for you with bared teeth.

The wind whipped the smoke into a column, then as the troops dispersed, thinned it into a haze. I tried to spot Hope, but I knew she was gone. And there was nothing I could do about it except wait until it was safe to move.

Eventually, the cavalry thundered to the secondary theatre, where a fresh set of cannons and muskets resounded. I waited to make sure everything was clear, then stomped to the sidelines, muttering curses. My phone started ringing as I reached the picnic pavilions.

I stuck it to my ear, coughing. "Trey! Omigod—"

"We have the suspect in custody."

I coughed some more. "You got her?"

"Her?"

"I know she looks like a guy, but—"

"Who looks like a guy?"

"Hope!"

"Hope?"

I hacked and spit, squinting toward the entrance. Even with my eyes watering, I could see the flicker and spin of blue police lights.

"I'll explain in a second. Put her in handcuffs until I get there."

A pause. "It's not Hope."

"Of course it is!"

Another confused pause at his end. "Come to the parking lot."

I pushed through the thick fascinated crowd to see Kendrick leading away a handcuffed and protesting figure in bike leathers. Lank black hair fell about the man's face as he spewed curses.

Not Hope.

They intercepted me at the orange-ribboned perimeter. "Tai—"

"Wait a sec, I know that guy. He's a member of the bike gang that was at Mrs. Simmons' table. One of her son's friends."

"Earl, I'm told. Dee Lynn caught him stealing the document tube, so she called Sergeant Underwood."

"Who?"

"Your friend Kendrick." He noticed my disheveled appearance. "What happened? Are you okay?"

I coughed into my sleeve. "Hope pulled a gun on me and vanished into the woods, and then I almost got trampled by a herd of horses, but other than that, totally fine."

Trey looked befuddled. "What?"

"Hope. Don't bother sending anyone after her. She's long gone."

"I don't understand."

I gave him the condensed version. Earl argued throughout the reading of his rights. I watched as Kendrick shoved him against the side of the cruiser, patting him down quickly and expertly.

"So Earl's the thief?"

"And the killer. He said it was an accident, of course. He admitted he took Simmons to Wassaw, at Simmons' request. He said there was a fight between them."

"And then what? He dumped the old man's body in the channel, made it look like a drowning?"

"I don't know. But that seems probable."

I spat out a bug of some kind and wiped my mouth. Earl saw me and started wrestling in his restraints. Spittle flecked his mustache.

"Arrest that bitch over there!" he yelled. "She's the one who sold him the map!"

"I am not!" I yelled back.

I could hear Earl still bellowing as they shoved him in the police car. The door slammed and the vehicle moved out. Behind us the battle still raged, but it was in its death throes. Soon the doomed would succumb, and the victors would raise their guns in triumph. Soon the trampled grass would straighten and grow toward the sun again.

Kendrick came over. He looked exhausted and apologetic and way too official.

"Tai?"

I sighed. "I know. Time to go downtown. Again."

◇◇◇

Trey came with me to the station, but wasn't allowed into the interview room. Kendrick was polite but firm. Fortunately, as he explained, there was no evidence that I'd done anything illegal. And since I'd been such a good citizen—my connection to Boone notwithstanding—there was no reason to make an arrest or even treat me with anything less than courtesy.

They had fine coffee at Savannah metro headquarters. I even got a cruller. So far it was better than the Atlanta PD in every way, even if my attempts to convince Kendrick of something nefarious still in the works were not working.

"The case is done, Tai. He confessed."

"To the murder. He's still accusing me of selling Simmons the fake map."

"So? I'm not charging you. What's the big deal?"

"My reputation is the big deal!"

"We got the story, and a confession. Case closed."

Apparently, once Simmons had figured out the code word and the latitude-longitude markers, he'd decided to head to Wassaw. He didn't have a boat, however, so he called his son's friend—that would be Earl—and asked him to take him there and wait on the beach for him to return. Unfortunately, Earl got curious and followed the old man's trail. When he saw the gold…

Kendrick scrubbed his face with his hands. "It's the usual story with the usual protests—didn't mean to do it, blah blah blah—but he's sticking to it. Which means we can close this case."

"But how did the map get in the tree?"

"Simmons must've heard Earl coming and stashed it there. According to what Earl told us, Simmons swung at him with the shovel. Earl took the shovel away and swung right back—one blow, ka-bang to the side of the head—then panicked when he figured out the old man was dead. So he dragged the body back to the boat, dumped it in the sound on the way back home. He's claiming self defense."

"I'll bet he is. But this doesn't explain why Hope—"

"He says he doesn't know Hope."

"But she and Winston—"

"—are small potatoes, Tai. Off the radar. That whole mess is a domestic dispute, plain and simple. If your boy John wants to file charges against her, he has to do it in Duval County, Florida, where the crime occurred."

I stared at him. "So she's gonna get away with everything? Creating a forgery? Stealing my identity?"

Kendrick sat back in his chair. "Identity theft is a crime we can prosecute."

"So we can keep chasing Hope?"

"Chasing her, no. Collecting evidence that she's the one who stole your identity, yes. And as for trying to link her to the murder, or linking her to this other guy you mentioned—"

"DiSilva. The original old dead guy. In Florida. The forger."

"Yeah. Him. He was a petty criminal, but he died of natural causes. No murder. No crime."

"So what about Winston? Hope implied he was up to something. So did this other source of mine."

"You mean Skippy who has skipped town?"

I licked cruller glaze off my fingers. "How'd you know about Skippy?"

"I'm a cop. I know shit."

For a second he reminded me of Garrity, all gruff talk and grumpy professionalism. They were the same kind of cop, that was for sure. Suddenly I missed Garrity. I would have given my whole box of nicotine patches for a chance to sit down with a beer and hash the case out with him.

I took another sip of coffee. "So haul Winston in here and ask him some tough questions."

"We did. He denied everything. And since we've got no proof he's involved in either death, if we keep pestering him, he can sue us for harassment and probably win."

"But—"

"It's open and shut, Tai. We got a confession. And I like those, very very much."

"But—"

"Go home. Get some rest. Comb the sticks out of your hair and wash your face. Nice to see you again and all, but I mean it. Go home."

◇◇◇

Trey took me by Café Gelatohhh on the way back to the hotel. We sat at a tiny table in the City Market courtyard, under the spreading branches of a massive live oak, and he watched while I ate a large helping of panna cotta, slowly and methodically. The sweet coolness salved both my raw throat and my ravaged ego.

"Are you okay?" he said.

"That's the third time you've asked me that. I'm fine. Here. Eat gelato. It's organic and locally-sourced."

He shook his head. I'd finished explaining everything Kendrick had told me and then dumped my tote bag full of notes on the table for him to read. He was halfway through, already sorting things into piles.

"I'm not seeing the connection," he said.

"But there has to be one! The Bible, the map, the two old dead guys. Something links them together."

"Hope and Winston."

"I mean motive-wise. There's a story here that connects all these events, I know there is."

Trey paged through the notes, the folders. He got out his pen and drew asterisks in the margins, created flow charts. I ate gelato and watched him draw circles on the notepad. Information maps, one of his tools for organizing data into a spatial perspective.

I shoved a large spoonful of gelato into my mouth. "I have squeezed every clue I can out of this. John said Winston was involved, so I went to Winston, which got me stalked by parties unknown and you stalked by Hope. And then Reynolds hinted the KKK was involved, so I went to Boone, and he said to watch the Expo, so I did. And sure enough, there was the Klan, but they weren't doing anything but being obnoxious."

Trey turned his yellow pad sideways and frowned at it. Then he reached for his little leather notebook. Didn't look up, didn't say one word.

"But then I learned about the damned map and the missing old guy, so I chased *that* trail to Wassaw Island. And then Gabriella said it was a fake, and Dee Lynn said it was a fake, so I went back to Winston, which led me to Skip, which led me *back* to Winston—and Hope—and then to the reenactment—and Hope—and freaking Earl the homicidal biker for crissakes, but I still haven't seen the damn Bible, which Hope says is fake too, which could be another lie, or which could be the God's honest truth for all I know. It's been nothing but dead ends and false leads and—"

"Tai?"

"Yeah?"

"I need some quiet, if you don't mind."

I stuck my spoon in my mouth, listened to the clop-clop-clop of the horse-drawn carriages, the babble of tourists, the buzz of traffic. The wind wound through the high green leaves above us, scattering sunlight in dappled pinwheels on the ground. Trey drew more circles, connected them with lines.

And then he cocked his head. "Tai?"

"Yeah?"

"What if the sequence of events isn't linear?"

I put down the gelato. "What do you mean?"

"You're looking at it like this." He drew three circles, labeled them A and B and C, then drew lines from A to B, and then B to C. "Causal sequencing. One action leading to the next."

"Okay. So?"

"So what if it's this instead?"

Then he drew another circle, labeled it A, then below it drew two more circles, one labeled B1 and the other labeled B2.

"See?" he pronounced. "Branching divergence."

He tapped the diagram. All the incidents related to Simmons and the treasure map split onto their own path separate from the main series of events, which started with DiSilva the old forger guy's death in Florida, proceeded to Hope and John buying the materials from his niece, Hope sneaking off with the Bible, John consulting me, and then…the split.

Trey tapped the secondary trail. "The inciting incident here is a deliberate attempt to trick Simmons."

"Which he fell for."

"Yes. But why?"

"Because he was greedy and foolish?"

Trey shook his head, tapped the B1 circle again. "No, I'm not asking why Simmons did what he did. I'm asking why Hope did what she did. Why take him the fake map? Why blame you? Why create this entire sequence of events?"

"Is this you being rhetorical? Because I'm not used to that either."

He exhaled in frustration. "It's not rhetorical. You know motives aren't my strong point. What possible reason could Hope have for setting this particular sequence of events into play? Because when you discover that, you can extrapolate this second sequence, perhaps predict her next move."

I stared at the paper. "She did it for the same reason she came to our hotel—distraction. It's all a ruse to throw us off the real trail."

"The trail to what?"

"I don't know. The real trail is invisible. We only know it exists because of the distraction."

"So what could she—"

"Omigod!" I grabbed Trey's arm. "That's why she came to the hotel and got herself on the surveillance camera—long dark hair, slim build—because now she looks like me! Blond and… not slim."

Trey's eyes sharpened. "She was setting up a false description."

"And we helped her do it." I turned the paper around and stabbed at the circle with my finger. "She took the map to Simmons because she knew he'd be at the Expo with me. She knew I'd hear about his treasure hunt because she'd set me up to take the heat for it. And she knew I'd run after that lead like a dog after a squirrel."

"All part of the same plan."

"Yep. And I fell for it."

"We fell for it."

I was surprised to hear him use the word "we," but it applied. She'd outfoxed, outsmarted, and out-connived both of us. Again. Which could only mean one thing—whatever she was trying to distract us from was very very big.

I spooned up the last bit of gelato. "Winston is the key, I know he is. Hope said as much. And his desk calendar suggests he has something huge and secret happening tonight."

"His calendar? How—"

"Unfortunately, as Kendrick explained, Winston hasn't done anything illegal. Not yet anyway."

Trey didn't reply. *Easy now*, I reminded myself. Baiting Trey was a delicate maneuver, hooking him even trickier. One false move, and he'd cut and run.

"It's police business, that's for sure," I said. "And we should definitely let them handle it."

Trey nodded. This was a plan he could support.

I licked the spoon clean. "But can't we do both?"

"Both what?"

"Let the cops handle it and investigate ourselves? I mean, I can't actually investigate Winston. I don't have a security professional's license. According to the law, I'm just a potential stalker subject to fines and imprisonment." I tried to sound nonchalant and reasonable. "But you *are* a licensed security professional, are you not?"

His expression remained bland. "I am."

"So you could see what Winston's up to tonight, say around seven?"

"I could, but—"

"And since the Harringtons are all about finding that Bible, this could even count as billable hours."

"Hope said the Bible was a fake."

"And I trust her about as much as I trust a wharf rat." I licked the final drop of gelato from my spoon. "So what do you say? Wanna do a little surveillance?"

He examined the paperwork one more time. I watched the wheels turn in his head.

"I'll have to fill out the 302 ahead of time," he said.

I stifled the grin. "I wouldn't have it any other way."

Chapter Twenty-nine

I licked salted butter from my fingers. "So this is a stakeout?"

Trey thought about it. "I suppose so."

"I thought it would be more exciting."

He didn't reply. We were parked in a lot next to the river watching Winston's shop. The Lincoln had all the comfort of a luxury suite on wheels—all it needed was a mini-fridge. I had popcorn and a Coke. Trey had tea. Lapsang souchong. Decaffeinated. No sugar, no honey, no milk.

He kept his eyes on the pavement. Winston hadn't left his shop, not even for one second. We knew he was in there, but the door remained shut with the CLOSED sign out. It was extremely weird behavior for a late Friday evening, when normally he'd be on the stoop, hawking pamphlets and coupons.

I stirred my coffee. "Is this typical for a stakeout? Sitting around for hours?"

"We've been here thirty-five minutes."

"You know what I mean."

He took another sip of his tea. The crowd moved in a river of alcohol and high spirits, and the sun set behind the bridge in sluicing orange light. One couple stopped at the sweetgrass weaver to buy a rose. The man presented it to the woman with a courtly flourish, and she pressed it to her nose, even though it had no scent.

They were on a date. We were on a stakeout. I tried to remember our last date-date, and couldn't. It had been dinner, I supposed, or sex. Did sex count as a date? Not that Trey ever actually asked me out. I usually made the plans, and he showed up. Unless he was working. Or running. Or off kicking things. Or it was past nine o'clock.

I looked over at him, so capable and efficient, eyes riveted on the tour shop. "Trey? Do you ever wonder how we ended up together?"

"Your brother hired me for a personal protection detail."

"No, I mean romantically."

"You propositioned me."

"No, I...I mean yes, but...you're messing with me, aren't you?"

He kept his eyes on Winston's door. "What exactly are you asking?"

"I'm asking why you're with me. You know. Like a couple."

His forehead creased, and he looked thoughtful. One finger tapped the dashboard, but his eyes remained on our target.

"Can we talk about this later?"

"You're sticking a lot of conversation on that later plate, Trey. If I didn't know better, I'd think—"

"Because Winston's leaving the shop now."

I snatched up my binoculars. Sure enough, Winston was locking his door, a briefcase in hand. He looked left, then looked right, then left again, the epitome of paranoia. He didn't spot us, however, and started walking briskly, one hand shoved in his pocket.

Trey put down his tea. "Come on."

He got out of the car, and I scrambled after him. We walked along the water's edge, next to the concrete barrier. Pedestrians wandered in intoxicated flocks, gazing into shop windows, clotting around maps.

Winston was an easy tail, however, despite his rather sedate non-Hawaiian shirt. He stayed on the sidewalk next to the shops and moved with purpose, the briefcase close to his body. Trey knew how to keep distance, but it didn't matter—Winston was oblivious to us.

"He's definitely up to something," I whispered.

Trey put a finger to his lips. *Shhh.*

I shushed.

Winston sat abruptly at a table for two in front of one of the smaller cafés. Almost as abruptly, a man moved out of the alley and sat opposite him. I didn't recognize the two men who remained standing at his shoulders, but I recognized the man at the table with Winston. There was no mistaking that hatchet nose and high forehead.

"Oh shit."

"What?"

"That's Gerard Dupre. He's the Grand Wizard. Remember his picture? On those pamphlets the KKK's been passing around? High level Klan, a much bigger deal than those morons at the booth."

Trey pulled out a simple tri-fold map and opened it in front of us. He pointed to Forsythe Park.

"Look," he said.

"At what?"

"At the map."

"Why?"

"Because Hope's here."

I got a chill. "Where?"

"Eyes on the map."

"I am!"

"She's at a table—don't look—on the rooftop bar, two hundred and fifty feet to the right."

I fought the urge to search the rooftops. "What's she doing?"

"Watching Winston and Dupre."

He kept his head bent over the map, but I knew he had her locked in his peripheral vision. I tried to do the same, but couldn't. I chanced a quick look at the roof. Sure enough, Hope sat at the corner table, her attention riveted on the street.

Trey's voice was annoyed. "Tai!"

I snapped my eyes back to the map. "Sorry. Does she see us?"

"I don't know."

A wild thought occurred to me. "Trey, what if this is a set-up? What if she's—"

"Shhh." Trey didn't move his head at all, but his eyes tracked the street. "Something's wrong."

"What?"

He shook his head, his brow furrowed. "The crowd flow isn't right. There's something—"

He froze, dropped the map, and then before I could take another breath, tackled me. He moved with the blinding speed of lighting, fierce and total, and I hit the pavement hard, the full weight of him landing on top of me. In the distance, I heard screaming.

"Trey!"

His hand covered my mouth. "Be quiet and stay down!"

"What happened?"

"Quiet!"

He shifted his weight so that I could breathe easier. Then he shoved me backwards against the concrete barrier, his body a shield. I couldn't see anything, but I could hear the panic. The stampede. The screaming.

I twisted my head, craned my neck. One brief glimpse—Winston sprawled on the cobblestone, the café table overturned. I started shaking.

Trey took a deep breath in and out, his face expressionless, his eyes flat blue. He rolled off me in one swift tumble, pulling his gun as he did. Then he lay on his back, the H&K on his belly. He pushed himself to sitting, back against the concrete.

"Call 911," he said. "And stay down. Don't move from this spot."

He was in the program now, not an ounce of shake in him. I closed my eyes. I wanted my boyfriend back, somebody to hold me against the rising hysteria, to tell me everything would be fine. That was the Trey I wanted. But this was the Trey I needed, this one with the clipped words and the cold eyes. He would be the one to get me out of this, not my boyfriend. He was the one I had to trust.

And so I did.

Chapter Thirty

Somewhere behind the crime scene tape and pulsing blue lights, I knew that Winston's body was being processed. There were no more sirens anymore, no crowds, no honey-colored sunlight. Only the wind remained. It rippled up and down the empty sidewalk, riding across the rocks and the water, colder than before.

Trey and I sat in a booth inside the deserted café, cleared of customers and employees now. Kendrick sat opposite us, in uniform, a wall of official irritation.

"What the hell where you doing stalking Winston Cargill?" he said.

"I tried to tell you—"

"And I told you to drop it."

"You told me to drop the murder, and I did. This was about figuring out why Winston and Hope set me up so that I could clear my name."

"Yeah?" His expression was fierce. "How's that working out for you?"

I shivered and pulled my jacket tighter. "What happened?"

He shook his head. But Trey answered for him.

"The shot came from behind us, probably from Hutchinson Island. That's a long-range hit, even more difficult with the crosswinds, but possible." Trey turned to Kendrick. "Head or body shot?"

Kendrick hesitated. He was watching Trey very carefully.

"Head," he said.

"One bullet?"

"Right in the T-zone."

"I thought so. Most likely police-trained, although I'm certain he used a suppressor system, which is more of a military strategy." Trey turned and pointed. "I'd check the undeveloped lot next to the conference center. It's a good set-up for a hide site—superior concealment in the underbrush, clear angle of sight, easy access to the highway."

Kendrick examined Trey with new eyes. "Where'd you train?"

"SWAT. Eight years with the APD dignitary protection unit, four of them with the urban tac team."

Kendrick leaned back. "So you know."

"Know what?" I said.

Trey took a sip of water and looked out over the river. "That was an expert shot. You and I presented even easier targets. And yet we're still alive."

I looked to where we'd been standing by the water. The concrete barrier was only three feet high. We'd had our backs to Hutchinson Island, the soft vulnerable spot at the base of the skull exposed.

Kendrick nodded. "One shot, one kill. Sniper's creed. If the shooter had been aiming for you…" He shrugged and looked at Trey. That cop thing passed between them.

"We would be dead," Trey said.

I huddled deeper in my jacket, a sudden chill scraping my spine. Not from the coming night. Not even from my close call with a bullet.

I turned to Trey. "I didn't know you were a sniper."

He didn't look at me or answer the question. His eyes were on Hutchinson Island, across the turgid water, debris floating downriver under the bridge.

His phone rang, and he pulled it out. "It's Marisa. I have to take it."

He got up and moved to a secluded spot next to the bar, away from the windows. Despite the workout clothes and running shoes, he carried himself in Armani mode. Precise. Proficient. Cool.

Like a sniper.

Kendrick watched him. "You didn't know?"

I shook my head. "I knew he was on the SWAT team. The dignitary protection unit. I guess I never really pushed that idea to its logical conclusion."

"He never told you?"

I shook my head again. I remembered Marisa's words, her implication of the dark things lying in his psychological profile. His denial of such. I shook off the apprehension and got back to business.

"Did you find the briefcase?"

Kendrick shook his head. "Any idea what was in it?"

"I'd guess our infamous Bible. Except that every piece of evidence I've run across suggests it's a fake."

"Any idea who might be behind this?"

"The KKK is a good start. So is Hope Lyle. Trey can give you a 302 on her. We saw her on the rooftop right before the shooting, so if Trey's analysis is correct, that the bullet came from behind us, she wasn't the shooter. But she's involved."

Kendrick sat back, arms folded. I remembered riding home with him in the back of someone's truck once, both of us young and beer-filled and happy. Now his eyes were black and serious.

"So are you," he said.

A uniformed officer approached, a quietly authoritative young woman with close-cropped hair and dark eyes. "Excuse me, Sergeant, but they need you in the tour shop." Then, to my surprise, she looked at me. "You too, Ms. Randolph."

"Me?"

"They have some questions."

I got a prickle of apprehension. "About what?"

Kendrick stood. "Let's go find out."

◇◇◇

Winston's shop was a swarm of uniforms and radio chatter. The officer took us the back way, down the alley and into the storage room. Brightly lit now, stark, the colorful posters lurid. Jezebel the parrot was gone. I wondered who had her, what would happen to the disreputable scrap of feathers.

The officer looked at me. "They say you know something about antiques."

"Depends what kind."

"Do you know what this is?"

She showed me the paper box under Winston's counter. I peered inside and saw dozens of tiny glass bottles. Old books too, probably with the front pages ripped out, an old forger's trick I'd read about. Stacks of fine ivory paper that I knew better than to touch, but that I recognized instantly. I'd held a piece of that paper in my hands only a few nights before.

"It's a forger's kit. See?" I pointed. "That's the same paper used to make the fake treasure map."

Kendrick turned to me. "You sure?"

"Reasonably." But then I looked closer. "Except for one thing. This paper is longer and has a letterhead. It's from the Marshall House."

The officer scratched her head. "That's right up the street, on Broughton."

"Oldest hotel in Savannah," I said. "Built in the 1850s. During the Civil War, it was a hangout for rebels of the more genteel stripe, eventually seeing duty as a military hospital. It's also quite haunted."

None of the officers were up for a ghost story, however. Kendrick got right to the point.

"So the paper's valuable?"

"All by itself, yes, but it's even more valuable as raw material. To a forger, this stuff is gold. Cut off the identifying letterhead, and you've got a properly aged piece of blank paper. You could turn it into a letter, a certificate—"

"A treasure map?"

"Absolutely. Old pens, old inks, a little hydrogen peroxide, maybe a few passes with a hot iron to age the thing. That box contains almost everything you need to make an impressive forgery."

Kendrick caught the word. "Almost?"

"Yeah." I sighed. "You need a forger to put everything together correctly, otherwise you've got a mishmash. And the forger who owned this kit keeled over from a heart attack three weeks ago."

Chapter Thirty-one

Trey drove us back to the hotel without a word. It was fully dark now, the bridge silver-white against a clear black sky. Marisa wanted a meeting, he said. I wasn't one bit surprised at that. What did surprise me, however, was that she wanted me in on it too.

I kept my eyes on the water below us. "You never told me you were a sniper."

"No. I didn't."

"Why not?"

He thought about that, then shook his head. "I don't know."

"Is this what Marisa was hinting at? In your files?"

"No. Maybe. I don't know. I resigned from the sniper team two months before the accident, so I didn't include that part of my service in my Phoenix application. Marisa is a thorough researcher, however. She probably pulled the records."

"But you said there was nothing in those files!"

"I didn't know there was!"

I didn't reply. Trey rarely raised his voice. When he did, I knew to back off and let him get a rein on things. I knew this, but didn't always do it. This time I did.

He took a deep breath. "I want to tell you about this. But I can't right now. I know I'm saying that a lot, but it's true. Things are closer to the surface now. Your words. And it's hard…it's very difficult…"

He shook his head again, this time with agitation. "After the meeting with Marisa. I'll tell you about it then. All of it. I promise."

◇◇◇

Trey went up to the room without me. I told him I'd be in the bar for a few minutes, that I needed a second to get my head together. This was almost true. What I really needed was Garrity.

So I sat in a corner booth, phone in hand, hesitating. Garrity was my go-to guy for anything involving pre-accident Trey, but he'd nail me to the wall the second he heard the story. Amateur, he'd say. Come back to Atlanta and let the professionals handle it.

And he was right—I was an amateur. Not like a sniper. They were the ultimate professionals. I understood people getting mad enough to kill each other. You get angry, your vision goes red, soon enough the bat or pistol or switchblade finds it way into your hand. And then, bam. You're a murderer.

Snipers were different. Snipers killed only after a cold, calculated analysis. For them, putting a bullet between someone's eyes was logical, the end result of an equation. It was a job, one that didn't get their hands dirty.

And I had two of them in my life at the present moment. One taking shots in my general direction, the other in my bed. And the worst thing was, I wasn't sure which one was the most dangerous.

I took a deep breath and punched in Garrity's number. He was not sympathetic.

"Of course he was a sniper. What else did you think he did?"

"I don't know, busted up heads, knocked down doors."

"Well, yeah, that's how everybody starts in SWAT. But that gets boring, especially if you're as smart as Trey." His voice went suspicious. "Why are you asking?"

So I explained. He reacted entirely as I expected.

"Sweet Jesus, Tai! What the fuck?"

So I explained some more. He listened. At some point in the conversation, he stopped being obnoxiously bossy and started being concerned.

His voice softened. "You really didn't know he was a sniper?"

"How was I supposed to know? He's never said one word. I knew all the other stuff—dignitary protection, SWAT, marksmanship awards—but that did not add up to sniper."

"I forget you're a civilian sometimes. The signs are obvious. The way he handles physical space, always measuring distances and calculating angles. The way he controls his breathing and heart rate. The running, the decaf tea, the patience, the detachment. Textbook sniper."

"If he's so textbook, why'd he resign?"

Garrity made a noise. "Because his car slammed into a concrete embankment and he scrambled the judgment-making part of his brain! You don't hand somebody like that a sniper rifle and say hey, go get some bad guys."

"But he resigned *before* the accident."

A pause. "What?"

"Two months before. Didn't you know?"

"No, I…Before? Are you sure?"

"That's what he said."

There was silence at the other end of the line. I stared out the window over the river. I'd spent so much time this week on the edge of it. It was an unpredictable body of water, changeable in its eddies and currents, salt and fresh mixing in a brackish chaos.

Garrity's voice sounded far away. "Did you say two months before the accident?"

"Yeah." I hesitated. "You know what happened, don't you?"

"I got a good guess. But that's his story to tell, not mine."

"He killed somebody, didn't he? Somebody he shouldn't have."

Garrity sighed. "The exact opposite actually."

It was too much at that moment. I knew Trey and Marisa were upstairs, waiting. Or not waiting. Regardless, I had to go up there eventually. I couldn't stay in the bar forever.

Before I could ask Garrity any more questions, however, a familiar figure caught my eye, out of place in his camo pants and hunting jacket. Jefferson. He stood at the entrance to the bar, waiting for me to notice him.

"I gotta go," I told Garrity.

"Call me tomorrow. I'll be in-field, but I want to know what happens, you hear?"

I assured him I would. As I set the phone down, Jefferson came and sat across from me. His eyes were calm and concerned.

"Daddy told me I was to come check on you," he said.

"Tell him I'm fine."

Jefferson stretched one arm along the back of the booth. His sleeve rode up, and I saw the triple tau tattoo on the inside of his forearm. One of the selectmen council, Billie had said. I also saw his wedding ring, and knew that he probably had pictures of his kids in his wallet. Two little girls, one seven and one three.

"Your cross-burning social club know you're here?" I said.

"This is a family visit, not business."

"Oh, that's right. Business is your Grand Wizard meeting Winston on the sidewalk and then snatching his briefcase from his dead hands."

"That shooting was none of ours. Neither was the stealing. We trade and trade fair, so I suggest you stop mouthing off about things you don't understand."

He had Boone's eyes, cold green-gray, but like his brother Jasper, he'd gotten his build from my mama's people. Husky, broad-shouldered, sturdy.

I shook my head. "Boone must be proud, you being a KKK officer and all. They give you an extra pointy hood for that?"

He ignored the jibe. "Daddy says each man has to choose his own path. He made his choice ten years ago, and he hasn't strayed from it. But he doesn't see what's happening, what me and Jasper see, how the white race has become the government's kicking dog, how we are denied our heritage and our culture in the name of political correctness."

I clenched my teeth to keep from spewing obscenities. "I'm not drinking that poison."

"We're not the ones spreading poison! It's the—"

"Say that word and I will slap it out of your mouth, I swear I will."

Jefferson leaned forward, eyes blazing now. "There's a war coming, and it's coming fast. You better choose the right side while you still can."

I shoved my drink away, gathered my things, and stood. "I chose my side a long time ago. Tell Boone I said thank you for checking on me. But tell him I won't be troubling any of you again."

And then I turned around and left him sitting in the booth, the lights on the river burning and rippling behind him.

Chapter Thirty-two

I went by the ice machine on the way in, then by the front desk to have a bottle of Jack sent up, a full-size one to replace the teensy bottle that wasn't going to cut it this night. When I got back to the room, I found Marisa and Trey deep in discussion. He sat on the edge of the sofa, hands clasped, elbows to knees. She stood before him in her red suit, the one she wore when she was feeling optimistic. It clashed with her mood now, like a fever.

She turned my way. "Are you okay?"

"I'm fine."

"Good." She returned her attention to Trey. "You're the expert, so correct me if I'm wrong, but snipers and muggings don't usually go together, do they?"

"Not this caliber of sniper, no."

"And you're sure that you and Tai weren't the target?"

"I'm sure."

Marisa gestured toward the window. Her voice was almost gentle. "Then why do you have every shade in this room pulled?"

He didn't even try to answer her question. He kept his eyes on the carpet. I sat beside him. He didn't seem to notice I was there.

Marisa continued. "I talked to Audrina. I told her you and I would have a meeting in the morning and then make a decision about whether or not to continue with the tournament planning."

I felt a surge of temper. "What's to continue? The Bible is gone. An elite sniper team took it. Only an idiot would go chasing it now, especially since chances are good it's a forgery."

"It's not about the Bible."

"What is it then?"

Marisa went to the mini-bar and got a highball glass. "Let's lay the cards on the table, shall we? It's tough times out there, despite our summer reconfiguration. Phoenix weathered the storm, but we're barely breaking even. And in this business, that's the beginning of the end. We need clients like the Harringtons or in six months, we're finished."

Trey kept his eyes down. "What are you proposing?"

She scooped ice into her glass. "Reynolds wants to continue with the plans for the golf tournament. He says the Black and White Ball is an important part of making that happen, so he's still willing to attend."

"It's not cancelled?"

"At this point, no. The metro PD is not releasing a single press release with the word 'sniper' on it, which is an eminently sensible decision. No sense causing panic in the streets."

Trey did some mental calculations. "What about the special event assessment rating?"

"They'll probably bump the entrance protocols to SEAR 4, maybe double-down on the credentialing, but since the shooting appears to be an isolated incident, I doubt there will be further changes."

"What about the Expo?"

"Same story. Look, Trey, those decisions aren't ours to make. We have only one decision, and it concerns the continued involvement of our clients, nothing more." She gave him a level look. "Reynolds wants to proceed. But only if you say it's safe for him to do so, and only if he can engage you as his personal protection during the Black and White."

Trey closed his eyes. He'd seen this coming.

Marisa sloshed a finger of gin into the glass. "I don't know why you avoid protection assignments. It's what you do."

"It's what I did."

"Whatever. You worked dignitary protection. You have the perfect credentials."

His voice was flat. "I suppose I do."

"So stick with Reynolds until the ball is over. See him safely back to Fulton County and save Phoenix for another billing period." She drained her glass, smoothed down her skirt. "That's what I'm asking you to do. The decision whether or not to do it, however, is all yours."

He looked at her for the first time. "It is?"

"It is. You say you're tired of my making decisions without consulting you. Fine. This decision belongs to you and you alone."

He read her face, and she let him do it. Even in a room with the shades pulled, in the half circle of lamplight, he could see a lie as clearly as other people saw colors. And as he examined Marisa—her eyes tight, her mouth straight and narrow—he evidently saw truth.

He rubbed between his eyes. "I'm not sure I want this decision."

"It's yours regardless."

He thought about it, then nodded. "When do I need to tell you?"

"Nine a.m. Will that be enough time?"

He did the math. "I can do that."

◇◇◇

When she'd gone, I took a long shower and changed into sweatpants and a t-shirt, then wrapped up in a hotel bathrobe. Trey was still at the desk. It was unusual to see him there in casual clothes, working past his bedtime. But he had a decision to make in the morning, and Trey did not do instant decisions. They only came at the end of a complex and comprehensive process.

I came up behind him and put my hands on his shoulders. "So what do you think you'll decide?"

"That depends on what this program says."

"What program?"

"Something I was working on with a professor at Georgia Tech, a sniper preference model."

I peered at his computer. "What does it do?"

"It uses crime scene information and geospatial criteria to predict the next incident. We've only got one shooting to input, but snipers working outside of law enforcement or military assignments operate according to patterns. Higher preference for multiple escape routes, for example."

"You think this one is police-trained?"

"The data suggest so. Which makes him predictable in certain ways, even if he's operating asymmetrically."

I knew that had broken him a little, the thought that one of his fellow peace officers could have turned into a murderer. I ran my thumbs along his trapezius, taut like power cables.

"Are you ready to talk about it?" I said.

He didn't ask what I meant. Which meant it was already on his mind.

"It's hard to talk about."

"Do you want to?"

"No." He kept typing, eyes on the computer. "But I'll try. If you want me to. Because it wasn't something I was hiding. I wasn't lying to you. It's something...different."

I massaged slow deep circles over the middle of his back, the lats and obliques, hard and knotted now, resisting the pressure.

"I'm listening."

He stopped typing and sat very still. "There was barricaded shooter scenario in a motel near I-85. I'd been on the scene for only a few minutes, not long enough to get a full briefing, but long enough to know that the negotiation team was in play. Their best analysis was that we were dealing with a potential suicide, possibly an SBC."

"A what?"

"Sorry. Suicide by cop."

He'd slipped into the vocabulary of the SWAT team leader. Even his sentences changed when he talked about that time in his life—surer, more fluid. I applied steady pressure across his shoulders, easy and sustained, so the hardened muscles wouldn't fight me.

"It was a tricky set-up—nighttime, close range, multiple civilians, scene not completely secured. Even the .338s would have over-penetrated, and we hadn't cleared the area fully. We were still gathering intel."

I could envision the scene. I could see him screwing the scope on a rifle, calculating wind speed, humidity, ambient temperature. He'd have been in black urban tac gear, blending into the darkness.

"The negotiation team thought they could talk him down. They said the risk of collateral damage was high, and that he hadn't yet demonstrated imminent threat. No hyper-vigilance, no antecedent behaviors." Trey stared at the computer. "But none of us knew."

"Knew what?"

"He had a hostage. His ex-wife. She was out of sight, tied to a chair, gagged. There never was a chance for negotiation. He was waiting for the TV news crew to arrive. When they did, he shot her once—point blank range to the chest—then turned the gun on himself."

Trey stopped talking. I could feel the rise and fall of his respiration through my hands. I pictured him waiting outside the motel with the suspect in the crosshairs, his breath like a metronome, his heart rate stabilized. A study in practiced patience, poised for the signal, the clue, the moment. And then suddenly, spraying blood and panic and confusion.

"I had the shot, but not the orders," he said. "So I waited. She died at the ER. He died on the scene."

"Your bullet?"

"No. I could have taken the shot, but until the moment he shot her, the negotiation team thought a peaceful resolution was possible. I'd seen nothing to contradict that assessment." He shook his head. "It wasn't a bad call. It was just the wrong one."

I pulled his face around so I could look him in the eyes. I'd never seen them haunted before. It was startling and disconcerting.

"You followed orders. Based on what anybody knew, they were good orders."

"Yes. That wasn't the problem. The problem was the next call. And the next." He exhaled slowly. "It got harder."

"What did?"

He didn't drop his eyes. "Waiting."

I bit my lip. He didn't need to explain any further. Of course he'd resigned. I would have expected nothing less of him. I put my arms around him slowly, then rested my head in the crook of his shoulder. He didn't resist, but he didn't respond either.

"This is where you hold me," I said.

"Tai—"

"Deal with it and do what I said. I told you before, I'm not going anywhere. Get used to it."

He did as instructed, solid and reliable. He was calm, yet I could sense the Under-Trey, the one that functioned simultaneously and in parallel with his more carefully-constructed counterpart. And they were somehow intertwined in one man. A man who was holding me very close, and who wasn't letting go until I told him to do so.

Which I didn't do for a very long time.

◇◇◇

He reached for me in the night—wordless, raw, insistent, more submission than seduction. There was need in him, a deep well of it, and I slaked it as best I could with everything I had to offer.

Afterward, I lay on his chest, feeling his heart throb beneath my cheek. Not steady, not controlled. Fierce. Like an animal beating itself bloody against the bars of a cage.

Chapter Thirty-three

A little before seven in the morning, I rolled over to find his side of the bed cold and empty. I squinted into gray light—the bedroom was still, but not silent. In the next room, I could hear the soft tap-tap-tap of keystrokes, the dry-leaf rustle of paper.

I dragged on my robe and went in. Trey sat at his desk in his white shirt and black slacks, his jacket on the back of the chair.

I yawned. "What are you doing?"

"Inputting the final data."

"What data?"

He handed me a piece of paper without looking up from the computer. It was the crime scene report from the shooting.

"How'd you get your hands on this?" I said.

"Sergeant Underwood sent it."

"Who's…Oh yeah. Kendrick."

He nodded. The brotherhood code. Once a cop, always a cop, always privy to cop information. I examined the report. The preliminary findings were not surprising—gunshot wound to the head—but seeing the diagrams of Winston's sprawled body, the black and white specificity of his murder, was sobering.

I handed the report back. "When did you get up?"

"Five-thirty."

His desk was its usual patchwork of diagrams and graphs. I recognized familiar names and places—Savannah's parks and fields, squares and streets.

"So what's your decision?" I said.

"I don't know."

"Marisa wants something in two hours."

"I know." He rubbed his eyes and leaned back in his seat. "I'm sorry. This is difficult."

"Of course it is. You're running on four hours of sleep."

"That's not what I mean. The algorithms run themselves. The roadways, terrain, the specifics of the crime itself. Input those and the conclusion is clear."

I waited for him to share said conclusion, but he kept staring at the computer screen. He had a pot of tea at his elbow, cool and half empty.

"Trey?"

He exhaled sharply. "The conference center is a low probability strike zone. So is the ballroom. I ran the data set twice to make sure. Limited access, well-controlled population density, high probability of video recording."

"So it's safe for me to go to the Expo? For Reynolds to go to the ball?"

"There's no such thing at one hundred percent safe. But the Expo and ball pose no greater than average risk."

And yet the shades were still drawn. His desk was a study in black and white, but the room was a palette of gray and shadow, shifting and insubstantial. He put his head back and stared at the ceiling.

I sat on the edge of the desk. "If that's the case, why are you still bothered?"

"Because it's not about the equations." He got to his feet abruptly and started pacing. "The synthesis of the data is clear. The risk is negligible. And yet I can't think of you walking out that door without...and it's not rational, it's not logical, it's not...but I can't."

I moved to stand in front of him, and he stopped pacing, hands on hips. I pressed my fingers against his temples, gently but firmly. He closed his eyes. I kept my voice low and calm.

"Listen to me, Trey. That's not a box you can live in. The lid locks behind you."

"But—"

"Shhh." I pulled his jacket off the back of the chair. I slipped his arms into the sleeves, easing it over his shoulders, smoothing it neatly across his back. "It's all an illusion, you know. Control. We pretend we have it, and it gets us out of bed in the morning. But it's not real."

His eyes were piercingly bright. "I don't know how to do this."

"Of course you do." I buttoned his jacket, then kissed him lightly. He tasted of Darjeeling. "I'll get a shower and get dressed. Then we'll find Marisa and tell her your decision."

"But I don't know what that is."

"Of course you do. You're going to make the logical and rational and sensible one, the one supported by your data. Everyone will be pleased—Marisa, the Harringtons. And then afterward, we'll go to the Expo, you and me."

He looked puzzled. "That wouldn't be overprotective?"

"Not if I ask you."

I straightened his tie as best I could. He regarded me warily, like I was springing another trap. And in a way, I was. Common ground and compromise, negotiation and ambiguity. I was asking him to stand with me on that uncertain territory, if only for a few hours.

Finally he nodded. "Okay. If you say so. Of course I'll come."

I gave up on the tie, patted his lapels. "Good. You can stand in the corner and glower menacingly. The whole thing's over at five, plus an hour for takedown, which will give us an hour to change for the ball."

"The ball? But you said—"

"If you can mingle with a bunch of unreconstructed rebels for eight hours, I can manage a hoop skirt for one evening. If you'd like."

He let out the breath he'd been holding. "I would."

"You think Gabriella can hook me up with something antebellum on short notice?"

"I'm sure she can."

"Then it's settled." I put my hands on my hips, smiled at him. "We go to the Expo, then we go to the ball, then we go back to Atlanta, and nowhere in there do I investigate a damn thing. The tournament gets planned, the Bible goes into the wind, and the adventure is over. Deal?"

"Deal. Once we go over this, of course."

He reached behind him and picked up a set of papers stapled into a booklet. I looked at the cover. *Sniper Evasionary Tactics: A Primer.*

I sighed. "Oh joy. A manual."

"I printed it out from the SWAT site. You can read it over breakfast."

I accepted it and pressed it to my chest. "I will."

He regarded me, eyes unreadable. He'd have to fix his Windsor knot properly before we met Marisa. The room remained in thin half-light, but I knew that on the other side of the heavy shades, the clear new dawn was sneaking into the sky.

"Thank you," he said.

"You're welcome." I patted his chest, right above his heart. "Come hell or high water, boyfriend, I'm with you all the way."

Chapter Thirty-four

We got to the Expo thirty minutes before the doors opened. The parking lot was even worse than before—picketers, news crews, a seething crowd massed at the entrance. I threaded my way inside, Trey at my heels.

"I guess they got the permit," I said.

"Who?"

"The Klan."

Inside the cavernous pristine space of the conference center, the rows of tables displayed more artifacts for sale than I would have guessed existed. Revolvers, carbines, bullets, caps, belt buckles, canteens, photographs, newspapers, jewelry, toys. If Walmart had existed in 1865, it would have looked like the Expo.

The Klan had a display too. The same man from the first day sat behind a table, the prim woman beside him, both of them wearing blinding white camp shirts with the triple tau on the front pockets. Booklets and pamphlets covered the table, bumper stickers too.

I looked back at Trey. "So what now?"

He did a quick check of the security cameras, scanned for hidden spaces, located the exits. "Now I find a vantage point where I can see the entire floor. What do you do now?"

"Now I find Dee Lynn—who is waving at me from the table, I see—and I try my hardest to sell some underwear and t-shirts."

"Okay."

"Okay."

He squared his shoulders and wove his way through the crowd, headed for a corner to put his back against. I pushed my sleeves up and headed for the table. Dee Lynn waved when she saw me coming, practically frothing at the mouth.

"It was a sniper, wasn't it?" she said.

I put down my coffee. "Jeez. Let me sit already."

She leaned closer. "The cops aren't saying so, but I heard people talking."

"Dee Lynn—"

"They say the shot came from across the river."

"Dee—"

"They say it was a gang hit."

"It wasn't. And I'm done talking about it. I'm here to sell stuff, not gossip."

I sat down behind my table. Trey was already on the job. I'd watched him enough to recognize the process—first, he'd pace off the building's perimeter. Then he'd double-check the fire alarms. Soon he'd take up position in a corner, his back to the wall, his eyes sweeping the room.

I scanned the crowd. "I'm still getting suspicious looks."

"Blame the sniper you refuse to talk about."

"I'm serious. You know as well as I do that reputation makes or breaks you in this game. And if I—"

"Uh oh, darlin'. Speaking of your reputation."

She pointed. I saw him across the room standing at his mother's table—Rock the grieving biker. He was more mountain than rock this morning, a six-four craggy blockage flanked by dozens of sympathetic fellow retailers and his motorcycle crew. Except for Earl the homicidal sneak thief, of course. Mrs. Simmons was nowhere to be seen, but Rock had spotted me. Suddenly the crowd parted, and the mountain was coming my way.

My stomach sank. "Aw shit."

"You wanna make a run for it?"

"No. I braved a damn sniper to come to this thing, I can brave a mad-ass biker."

I lifted my chin and met his eyes. Up close, his grief showed in stark relief, his eyes red-rimmed, his mouth straight.

He put his hands on my table. "I came to apologize."

I almost dropped my coffee. "What?"

"To say I'm sorry. We're sorry. I talked Mama into dropping that restraining order. Weren't no call for that, especially not after Earl confessed." His expression hardened. "You won't have any more trouble from me and mine. I wanted to tell you that face to face."

I smiled, a little dumbfounded. "Thank you."

"No, thank you. I know you were doing it to clear your name. But I also know you've been right respectful, even when Mama pulled a Dirty Harry on you."

"Grief is hard. We all deserve a little slack then."

He held out his hand. I took it. We shook solemnly, me and the mountain. And then he went back to his table. When he did, dozens of eyes swiveled in my direction. Curious and sharp, but not as suspicious anymore.

I sat behind the table, straightened my stack of long johns. Across the room, I saw Trey. He'd found a spot in the corner near the snack counter with an unobstructed view of my table and was making a quick notation in his leather notebook, eyes locked on me.

I shot him a thumbs up. He inclined his head in acknowledgement, tucked the notebook into his jacket. The doors at the front swung open.

Dee Lynn grinned. "And they're off!"

◇◇◇

The next hours galloped by in a headlong rush. I smiled. I shook hands. People showed me old photographs of Dexter. I helped Dee Lynn protect her shark tooth fossils from a handsy toddler, then identified a LeFaucheux pinfire revolver and pronounced its value with only a tiny hint from Dee Lynn. I took a request from a woman seeking a cavalry saber like her great-great-grandfather wore at the Battle of Bull Run, then discussed the intricacies of rolling your own black powder charges.

And I sold hell out of that underwear, the handmade socks and t-shirts too. By the time lunch was over, I had twenty new orders. My cousin in Alabama would be very busy for the next few weeks.

The hours passed quickly, and I fell into the rhythm. When four-thirty came around, I did a quick tally of my receipt book. Lo and behold, it looked pretty full. I closed the book with a satisfied snap as my next customer stepped to the table.

I smiled and looked up. "How can I help you?"

But this was no customer—it was Jasper. He held himself aloof from the rest of the milling crowd, a thick menacing presence in camo and heavy boots. Built strong and solid like his older brother, but edgier, less stable. From the way his jacket bunched, I guessed he was in violation of the "no loaded firearms" rule.

He fingered my samples. "We need to talk."

"About what?"

"Not here." He pointed toward the vendor's private area. "Over there looks good."

"Sorry. I've got customers."

Jasper leaned forward. "I don't have time for this. I've got a message."

"Then deliver it." I leaned forward too. "But you'd best drop the threatening mannerisms or my boyfriend will have you up against that wall in three seconds."

Jasper looked Trey's way, and Trey looked back. Hard. Jasper did a quick calculation, then cut his eyes back at me. They were Boone's eyes, but callous and humorless.

His mouth twisted. "How fast you think he can get over here?"

"Lay a hand on me and you'll find out."

He laughed. "You always let your man fight your battles?"

"He fights everybody's battles. It's who he is. Now say what you came to say. I've got work to do."

Jasper put his hands on his hips. He stood with his feet spread wide, taking up room. Alpha male posturing. And though it was stunt behavior, Jasper was capable of delivering. I crossed my fingers and prayed he wouldn't.

"You made a mistake yesterday," he said. "You thought you saw Winston meeting Gerard Dupre, but you didn't."

"Yes, I did. I told the cops all about it."

"I know. They've been in contact with Mr. Dupre, who explained that he was sitting at his own table at that café, with his own associates. He was not meeting Winston Cargill there because he had no business with that individual, and he has no idea who shot him. So the next time you make an official statement, that's what you need to say."

Jasper's words had all the precise delivery of a memorized speech. I was trying hard to keep my emotions in check. Anger warred with caution, disgust and curiosity mingled like oil and water.

"I told them what I saw," I replied. "That's what I'll tell them again. Take that to your associates. Tell them burning crosses and grown men playing dress-up don't scare me."

I kept my voice steady. Across the room, Trey stood at attention, shoulders dropped, hands loose. Not turning a blind eye, but not barging over and slamming Jasper into the suspect prone position either. Occupying the middle ground.

Jasper was also calm. "I'll tell them you said exactly that. But you'd best reconsider. Lots of things burn besides crosses."

He gave me a twisted smile and headed for the exit. Trey watched him leave, then raised one eyebrow at me. I shook my head, my brain buzzing. So the KKK had something to hide too—they didn't want it known that their Grand Wizard was meeting Winston, and they especially didn't want that briefcase being associated with them.

I reached for my Coke, and noticed for the first time that my hands were shaking violently, and not from fear. From anger. I wanted nothing more than to march over to the KKK's table and wipe it clean with a swipe of my arm. I imagined I wasn't alone in that. But I also knew the Klan wasn't alone either. They had their numbers in any crowd—cops and lawyers, teachers and politicians, CEOs and ministers. They were invisible but ever-present, like hatred itself.

So I stayed at my table until closing time. I filled my last thirty minutes debating the morals of battlefield excavations with one of Dee Lynn's customers. I sold the last pair of my underwear and took the contact information of a man who claimed he had a real pair to sell. Through it all, I smiled, and smiled some more.

I did not look at the KKK table. I did not move from my seat. And I did not investigate. Not one bit.

Chapter Thirty-five

Back at the hotel, we sent the boxes up with the bellhop and took the elevator to our room. I was exhausted, but Trey remained insistent that I tell him everything about my encounter with Jasper.

"Did he say anything else?"

"No, just that one threatening message."

Trey was on full seethe. "I'm filling out a 302 on him as soon as we get to the room. If he shows up at the ball tonight, I'm calling in the authorities."

"Here's the thing," I said as the elevator rose. "Why would the KKK be interested in a Bible signed by Lincoln and Sherman, the two biggest enemies of the Confederate cause, especially if every piece of evidence is demonstrating it's a forgery? It makes no sense."

Trey didn't reply. His ears were listening, but his eyes were scanning every corner with paranoid intensity. He was also snippy and noncommunicative and getting on my last nerve. I took a deep breath. All we had to do was get through the ball, and we could go back to Atlanta.

I checked the time. "When do you have to fetch Reynolds?"

"I don't. Marisa is escorting him there."

I got a little twitch of vengeful satisfaction at the thought of seeing Marisa in antebellum fashion. The woman would do anything for Phoenix, even pull a Scarlett O'Hara and make a ball gown out of the curtains if necessary.

The elevator dinged, and we stepped into the hall. I shook out my ponytail. "You shower, I've got to—"

"Stop." Trey froze, one hand on my stomach. "There's someone outside our room."

I peered toward the end of the hall. Sure enough, I saw a flicker of movement. Someone—dark-clothed, furtive—hid behind the cart of shampoo and towels parked near our door.

"Housekeeping?" I suggested.

"No." Trey's hand moved toward the H&K. "Get back in the elevator."

"But—"

"Now."

I pushed the button, but the elevator had already moved to another floor. I pushed it again, spread my hands in frustration. *Now what?*

He flattened his palm and pushed it down. *Stay here.* Then he took two steps forward, hand hovering at his beltline.

"You behind the cart," he said. "Move into the open. Hands in the air. Slowly."

After only a second's hesitation, a man stepped into the open. Instead of staying put, however, he hurried in our direction. Trey's hand went under this jacket. At that moment, I recognized our visitor, even if his navy suit was disheveled and his white-capped grin nowhere to be seen.

"Whoa whoa whoa!" I grabbed Trey's elbow. "It's that guy, what's-his-name, the Harrington's authenticator!"

"Who?"

"David Fitzhugh. I met him at Audrina's tea."

Fitzhugh, oblivious to the danger, kept walking until he was standing two feet away. He was sweaty and wild-eyed, his complexion waxy, like a man on the verge of fainting.

"Do you have it?" he blurted. "Because if you do, for the love of God give it to them before they kill me too!"

Trey looked at me, puzzled. He put his hands on his hips, and I relaxed a little. I stepped between him and Fitzhugh and walked to our door.

I fished in my tote bag for the keycard. "You'd better come inside, Mr. Fitzhugh, before you get ventilated. Then we can have a talk about why you're lurking outside our hotel room."

◇◇◇

Fitzhugh and I sat on the sofa. I had Jack on ice. He took his straight. Trey stuck with Pellegrino, and hung out near the curtained window.

"First off," I said, "we don't have the Bible. It was stolen by an elite sniper team. Didn't you see the news?"

"Of course I did! But somebody seems to think I have it. I got back to my hotel room this afternoon, and it had been searched. Suitcases dumped out, drawers emptied."

"But how do you know it was the Bible they were looking for?"

"Because they called me later and said so! They said I had twenty-four hours, or I'd get a bullet in the brain, just like Winston!"

I looked at Trey. He nodded. That was the truth.

This was making no sense. The bad guys had the Bible, after all. They killed Winston and snatched it. Why would they be searching for it in Fitzhugh's room?

I poured myself another shot. "Let's start at the beginning. You're in Savannah chasing that Bible, correct?"

"Among other things, yes."

"But in Atlanta, you called it a wild goose chase."

"I thought it was. But then Winston contacted me, the day after you came to Miss Harrington's. He'd seen me on television too, and he wanted to know if I had a client with the funds to afford something really special. Then he told me about the Bible. Two people, same story? That made me reconsider my assessment. So I arranged a meeting with him, here in Savannah." He stared at his drink. "I told him you were looking for it as well, to claim it for John Wilde."

I frowned. "Now why did you do that?"

"I thought that might incline him toward selling it more quickly." Fitzhugh's expression grew canny. "I had the feeling he had other buyers lined up, and I needed to remind him that I could outbid you and anyone else, easily, should the item prove to be authentic."

I cursed. So that was how Winston and Hope had known Trey and I were at the Westin. Fitzhugh had spilled everything.

"So you've seen it?"

"More than that. I've actually held it in my hands." He swirled his drink, staring into the amber liquid. "Unfortunately, it wasn't worth my time."

"It's not real, is it?"

He shook his head, and I felt a stab of disappointment. All this time and energy chasing a phantom, and it turned out to be another special effect. Like the villains in sheets and roller skates on Scooby Doo.

"The Bible itself is authentic," he continued, "a fine example of an Oxford King James. Slightly foxed but in otherwise excellent condition. However, the handwriting on the inscription isn't representative of Mr. Lincoln's, and the aging is suspicious, probably enhanced. I declined to buy it and told him why."

I looked at Trey. Trey nodded. So this much was true too.

"When was this?"

"Monday."

Then it hit me. "It was you, wasn't it? You were the one following me on River Street when I went to see Winston for the first time. I almost caught you, but you ducked into the alley and escaped."

He shook his head. "That was me, yes, but I was there for the Bible, not you. I'd left Winston's shop and was trying to get back to my hotel unseen. I was avoiding you, not following you."

I sipped my Jack, thinking hard. "So explain this to me. If that Bible is fake, then why are you still here and not back in Atlanta?"

Another hesitation. "I had further business here."

"Doing what?"

"What I always do—searching for artifacts to enhance Miss Harrington's collection."

"I didn't see you at the Expo."

His lips tightened in a supercilious line. "I prefer private transactions with individuals, not dealers."

"Oh, you mean those people who bring you...what was it you said? Deliberate fakes and sentimental slop?"

"I prefer that to over-priced trinkets from dubious sales-people."

Fitzhugh was firmly back in know-it-all land. But I knew why he avoided other dealers—they were harder to cheat. Audrina Harrington's collection had probably been purchased for pennies on the dollar from folks who didn't know better.

I'd opened my mouth to explain what I thought of this when I noticed Trey's expression. He'd tilted his head to the left, and then to the right. Recalibrating. I knew what that meant. I'd triggered that response a hundred times.

I tsk-tsked at Mr. Fitzhugh. "Technically true, but deliberately evasive."

His forehead wrinkled. "What?"

"It's a common trick habitual liars use, telling the truth but not the whole truth. Trey can peg it every time." I leaned forward. "So tell me, Mr. Fitzhugh, what are you hiding?"

"Nothing!"

I looked at Trey. Trey shook his head.

"And that," I said, "was a downright lie."

Fitzhugh stared at him, baffled, which was what most people did when faced with Trey's cranial lie detector. Some bluffed. Some blustered. But most went baffled.

"But I've told you everything!" Fitzhugh said, his voice pitched with fear again.

Trey stepped forward. "No, you haven't. We don't have the Bible, which means that you're still in danger, and will be as long as it's missing. If you want our help, you need to tell us everything, right now."

Fitzhugh stared at him, outrage written on his features. He said nothing.

Trey remained firm. "In that case, there's nothing more I can do for you. Now if you'll excuse me, I have to get ready for the ball."

He went into the bedroom without another word. Fitzhugh watched him go like a man watching the cavalry ride over someone else's hill. The bourbon in his glass trembled. Nonetheless, he stood and buttoned his jacket.

I stood too. "You really should come clean, you know. These people don't play, and if they think you're holding out, which you obviously are, you're in serious trouble."

He ignored the warning. I saw fear and stubbornness in his eyes, and also determination.

"I'll take care of this situation myself," he said.

"How?"

"That doesn't concern you."

I pulled one of my business cards from my pocket and slid it into his jacket. "When you come to your senses, call me. Until then, I suggest you find a copy of the *Sniper Evasionary Manual.* And avoid open spaces."

Chapter Thirty-six

Once I shut the door on Fitzhugh, I joined Trey in the bedroom. He was already in the shower. I noticed a garment bag lying in state on the bed, a froth of white showing through the plastic—my dress for the ball. I pulled it from the bag and laid it on the bedspread. It was bride-white, with black satin trim at the hem and bodice. A laced corset underpinned the whole gig, which included a massive pouf of crinoline skirting ribbed with assorted hoops.

I kicked my shoes into the corner. Then I opened the bathroom door and got a face full of steam.

"Fitzhugh's gone," I said loudly.

"I heard." Trey's voice echoed in the shower stall.

"He's decided to go it alone since we turned out to be less pliable than he thought. But he must have been desperate to ask for help in the first place."

"He thought we had the Bible."

"He thought wrong."

I returned to the bedroom, picked up my dress, and groaned. Two dozen hook and eye fasteners ran up the back in an intricate track. I sighed and got busy undoing them.

"But all that stuff about Winston and the Bible being a fake was true, right?"

"Those parts, yes," Trey called back. "And the part about someone searching his room and then calling him afterward."

"But who could that be? Not the people who did the snipe and grab—they have the Bible, fake as it may be."

"Perhaps someone has taken it from them."

"Competing criminal interests? Really?"

"It's one possibility. Graph it and you'll see."

I pulled my shirt over my head and threw it in the corner with the shoes. The jeans followed next, the bra too. I heard the shower stop, then the sound of the curtain being pulled back. I picked up the corset, a tangle of lace and underwiring as complex as a time bomb.

I stepped into the thing. "Okay, let's say you're right. Say somebody wanted the Bible enough to steal it from our sniper team." I shimmied the corset up over my hips. "What if they got it before Winston went to the meeting with the Grand Wizard? What if our sniper team clipped Winston and snatched the briefcase, only to get back to Bad Guy Headquarters and find it empty? That would put them on the prowl for it in a big way."

I heard the sound of a garment bag being unzipped in the bathroom, followed by the rustle of heavy cloth. "I hadn't considered that."

"Why would you? This is the first we're hearing that people are still looking for that damn Bible. Factor in Jasper's warning about the Grand Wizard wanting to hush up his involvement, and things get even more confusing."

I sucked in a breath and yanked the corset over my heaving bosom. The hose went next, seamed thigh-highs topped with white lace. I fumbled them up my legs and snapped them to the garter straps, wondering for the life of me what men found so sexy about this particular contraption.

"So maybe this is how Hope fits in," I said. "Maybe she's the one. Maybe she took the Bible from Winston before he could make the trade with the Grand Dragon. Maybe that's why she was there, to watch him get humiliated when the briefcase turned up empty. Unfortunately, somebody shot him between the eyes first."

"Unfortunately."

"And I'll bet Hope stuck that forger's kit back under the counter too, so that when the cops came looking, they'd find it in Winston's possession. Hope doesn't do things by halves. If she was going to set up Winston, she was going to do it all the way."

There was no reply from the bathroom.

"Trey?"

"I'm listening. It's just…" He exhaled in annoyance. "Go on."

"Hope was at the scene when Winston was killed, so everybody assumed she was a part of the sniping. But what if she wasn't?" I picked the dress up in a heap and dumped it over my head. It spilled around me in a waterfall of taffeta and fluff like a collapsed circus tent. "What if she was there to watch Winston open up an empty briefcase? That would mean *she's* the one with the Bible, not the snipers."

The hooks tangled in my hair. I tried to pull free, which only complicated things further. I cursed and snatched harder.

"Stop," Trey said, his voice close now. "Let me help."

I felt one hand maneuver under the massive skirts and pull my right arm gently through the gauzy sleeve. Then I felt his fingers in my hair—patient, dexterous, working the hooks free from the frizzed ringlets.

"And what the hell is the KKK up to?" I said, my voice muffled under layers of fabric. "Why are they trying to erase their involvement with Winston? Is it because they were responsible for his death?"

"That seems the most likely motive."

"Except for one thing—what would the KKK want with that particular Bible? It makes no sense ideology-wise."

"Perhaps they saw it as an investment."

"Perhaps. But it still feels wrong to me."

The dress fell heavily about me in a cascade, and I poked my head through the neck hole. Trey stood behind me, fastening the hooks.

I held my hair out of the way. "So maybe the KKK is afraid too, of whoever shot Winston."

"Maybe."

"Regardless, somebody's got the Bible and somebody else wants it, and these somebodies don't play nice. That leaves two questions. One, what is Fitzhugh hiding that's worth risking his neck over? And two…"

I turned around. And completely lost my train of thought.

Trey wore a black cutaway tailcoat and trousers, sharply creased, his snow-white linen shirt and matching cravat secured with a tiny silver pin. A sword dangled at his hip, etched silver with a foiled scabbard. He was utterly discombobulated and devastatingly handsome.

I stared. "Omigod."

He raised an eyebrow. "Well?"

"Well what?"

"What was the second question?"

"Oh." I swished my skirts into place. "Why are people dying over a Bible that isn't real?"

"Those are good questions."

"I know." I put my arms around his neck, his skin still hot and moist from the shower. "But they don't change the fact that I'm not chasing that Bible anymore."

"You're not?"

"Nope. Done with that. My goal now is to get us back to Atlanta in one piece."

He was a study in chivalrous gentility, except for the outlines of the holster under his jacket. I reached down and ran a finger along the shiny blade at his hip. A very nice reproduction of an officer's presentation sword.

I smiled up at him. "Remember the night we met? How I held a sword to your throat and called you a lying son of a bitch?"

He ignored my reminiscence and glared hotly at the scabbard. "It's utterly unworkable for either offense or defense, especially with this jacket." He rotated his shoulder. "The sleeves are too tight. I can barely raise my arm."

"It's not cut for concealed carry. And the sword is a status symbol, not a weapon."

"Nonetheless—"

"Trey." I reached up and rubbed the spot between his eyes. "It's four hours of discomfort. We'll deal with it. And then we're done."

He looked me in the eye, his expression serious. "Stay close tonight. I can't look out for you and watch Reynolds at the same time. I need you where I can see you, at all times."

I stood on tiptoe and kissed him. "I'll be as close as your shadow. Now fetch the hairpins. I gotta get this mess into something resembling a hairdo."

Chapter Thirty-seven

The key to replicating a nineteenth-century ball appeared to be lots and lots of swag—white draperies, tablecloths in black linen, ribbons and garlands and hundreds of carnations. Small tables clustered on the perimeter of the ballroom, candlelit and cozy, with the larger inner space kept clear for dancing. And there would be dancing—reels and waltzes and polkas—the music provided by a five-piece band already filling the air with fiddle and dulcimer.

Trey surveyed the scene. The row of windows on the far wall overlooked the water. Even from where we stood, I could see the luminous sparks of River Street and the white dots of boats pulled up to the dock.

Trey eyed the room critically. "They didn't close the curtains."

"Didn't your data proclaim this a low-risk zone?"

"No greater than average risk, yes. The dock is problematic, however, not enough on-site surveillance." He frowned. "The interior perimeter should minimize any difficulties, however."

"So everything looks good?"

"Everything looks acceptable."

He still hadn't reconciled his data and his gut. He might have been assigned only one asset—Reynolds—but some part of him still felt the urge to protect everyone in the room. He stood too close to me. A true Victorian chaperone would have swatted him by now.

I took his arm. "You're nervous."

"I know."

"Can you go off the clock? Maybe have a drink, take a spin on the floor?"

"I don't…" He looked across the ballroom and relaxed the tiniest degree. "Good, they're here."

I followed his gaze. Reynolds and Marisa stood next to the punchbowl. She wore all black, including a French mantilla veil over her sleekly styled up-do. I'd never seen her work a room before, but her eyes swept back and forth like Trey's, cataloging every detail. For the first time it occurred to me that she was as well-armed as Trey, and as potentially dangerous.

Reynolds spotted us and bustled his way over. He looked like a daguerreotype come to life, his white beard trimmed, his stocky body in a black frock coat, this time with a white sash across his chest. He had a sword too, the same one he'd worn to the reenactment.

"Good evening!" He grinned at Trey. "You're looking all the dash, young man. Marisa wants to see you for a quick yoo-hoo." Then he turned to me. "May I ask the lady for a dance in your absence?"

Trey looked at me, puzzled. I tapped him with my fan. "He's supposed to ask you, and you're supposed to say yes, and then I'm supposed to dance."

"Oh. Yes. I suppose."

I took Reynolds' elbow and moved onto the dance floor as Trey went over to talk to Marisa. The band began a lilting waltz, all strings and harpsichord.

Reynolds swiveled me into position. "You're looking exceedingly lovely, m'dear."

"Really? I feel like a top-heavy wedding cake."

"Nonsense."

I put one hand on his shoulder, and he gathered the other in his gloved fingers. He smelled of aftershave and warm wool. In his time, he'd been a heartbreaker, I was certain of it. We mingled with the sweeping circle, in the timeless one-two-three. Reynolds was a fine dancer—assured, natural, easy.

He laughed. "You're trying to lead."

"You're surprised?"

He laughed some more. I tried to follow. Things worked easier when I let the pressure of his hand guide me, when I countered his movement not with resistance, but with response. I caught glimpses of Trey over his shoulder, he and Marisa in a close confab.

Reynolds smiled. "You like the sword?"

"It's very suave."

"Look closer."

I glanced down again. For the first time, I saw the cross-hatching on the scabbard, the dings and discolorations on the grip, and most telling of all, the floating C. S. casting on the hilt.

"Omigod, that's a genuine Leech and Rigdon!"

Reynolds grinned. "Yes, ma'am."

"That thing's worth fifty thousand dollars!"

"And then some," he agreed pleasantly.

"How in the hell—"

"Easy." He bent his head closer to my ear, not once dropping the beat. "I smuggled it out of Audrina's safe room."

"Won't she notice the sword-shaped hole?"

"Not if there's a sword in it."

I stopped dancing. "Are you telling me you stuck a fake sword in your sister's collection and stole the real one?"

He made a hurt face and swirled me back into step. "Not stole. Borrowed."

"I'm not sure Audrina will see it that way."

"Bah. She'll never know."

"She will if she opens up that display case."

He made a scoffing noise. "Like she ever breaks the seal on that glass. Besides, even if she did, she can't tell the difference. The only person who can is Fitzhugh, and I'll have it back before he notices a thing."

"I noticed!"

"Not at the reenactment, you didn't."

I gaped at him, then smacked him with my fan. "You cannot go waltzing around—literally—with a fifty-thousand-dollar sword on your hip!"

"People don't see what's there, m'dear, they see what they think is there, and they think they see a prop sword worth maybe a hundred bucks." He moved me into step again. "Let the poor old sword have a night on the town. It'll be trapped in the museum soon enough."

"There are snipers!" I hissed. "Also on the town. Also looking for something exactly like that to snatch!"

"Trey said it was safe here."

"His actual words were 'no greater than average risk' which is not the same thing!"

Reynolds rolled his eyes. "Now you sound like him, all tedious and stick-in-the-mud."

I planted my feet and glared at him. "Trey came here tonight for one reason—to protect you—so for you to go flaunting—"

"You're overreacting. Smile and dance."

I smacked him again as the orchestra brought the dance to a close. Reynolds bowed and backed away, leaving me standing on the dance floor, my brain whirling. The fiddles kicked into high gear as a reel unspooled, but I wasn't sticking around for it. I hiked my skirts and headed for Trey, who waited beside the punchbowl.

"You're not gonna believe this."

He frowned. I explained. On the dance floor, Reynolds spun some giggly young thing in a circle. Trey watched him, astonished.

"You can't be serious," he said.

"Of course I'm serious!"

"But I explained the risk factors involved—"

"I know! He told me I was overreacting!"

Trey stared after him. "I need to tell Marisa. Stay here."

He hurried over to where Marisa stood, then bent his head to her ear. Her eyes widened. She whispered something back to him and marched onto the dance floor, where she snagged Reynolds by the elbow and hauled him off the floor. He shot me a look as he passed, like a naughty boy being dragged to the woodshed.

Trey came back and stood beside me. "She's taking him back to the room. She'll be putting the sword into the safe and calling Audrina next."

"Who is gonna be seriously pissed."

"I suspect so. But it's the necessary response."

The ball swirled around us, glamour and illusion weaving itself into a tapestry. Appearances deceived, half-revealed, half-revealing. Real swords, fake uniforms, the sheen of the surface. Nobody ever looked below the surface. Nobody ever wanted to.

People don't see what's there, they see what they think is there.

The realization struck me so hard I gasped. "Omigod, I know what Fitzhugh's hiding!"

Chapter Thirty-eight

The reel flowed, and new dancers joined the circle in a flurry of black and white. I grabbed Trey's elbow and pulled him close.

"Reynolds told me he thought Audrina was trying to kill him by sending him on all those dangerous trips. But Audrina lets Fitzhugh make all her decisions, right?"

Trey frowned. "Fitzhugh is trying to kill Reynolds?"

"No, it's not the danger that matters, it's the distance! Fitzhugh's trying to keep Reynolds as far away from Audrina as possible."

"Why?"

"Because Reynolds is persuading her to open the museum, and Fitzhugh can't have that. Because dollars to donuts, if a museum curator ever gets their hands on Audrina's collection, they'll discover it's full of fakes."

Trey's eyes narrowed. "Explain."

"Authentication is a tricky business. It takes smarts and study and practice, none of which Audrina is willing to invest. Which means that when it comes to antiques, she doesn't know a verso from a recto. Reynolds doesn't either. They rely on Fitzhugh. But what if he's been doing the same thing with Audrina's collection that Reynolds did with that sword?"

Trey was catching on. "Taking pieces and replacing them with duplicates?"

"Exactly. Only unlike Reynolds, he's stealing, not borrowing, so that he can sell the real stuff to someone else. It's brilliantly simple—unless your reclusive mark suddenly starts listening to her brother and decides to open a museum." I grabbed Trey's arm tighter. "Omigod, that's what Fitzhugh's been doing here all week—making private purchases to try to fill the holes in the collection!"

Trey cocked his head. "That explains the conversation in the hotel room."

"Technically true but deliberately evasive, I know! And I figured it out all by myself!"

"Stop bouncing." He disentangled his arm from my fingers. "We need to find Marisa. Now."

He turned on his heel and headed for the exit. I grabbed my skirts and followed after, only to hear the buzz of my cell phone. I snatched it from my reticule and held it to my ear.

"This isn't the best time," I said, "so—"

"Do you want the document?"

I stopped and gripped the phone a little tighter. "Hope?"

"Do you want it or not?"

I shot a baffled look at Trey. He raised one eyebrow. *Hope*, I mouthed at him. *She wants to hand over the Bible!*

"Where are you?" I said.

"Look out the window over the courtyard."

I hurried to the window, Trey right behind me. Sure enough, Hope stood at the threshold of the dock, near the courtyard. She was dressed in a simple black sheath dress, her hair once again dark and cut as short as a boy's.

"Why now?"

"I watched the top of Winston's head get blown off! You think I'm gonna fuck around after seeing that? All I need from you is an answer—do you want it or not?"

"Why would I want a fake Bible?"

"This isn't about the Bible anymore. This is much, much bigger."

Trey watched me through this exchange, his expression alert. *Not the Bible*, I mouthed. He whipped his eyes down to where Hope stood, her face hard in the angled light.

I made my voice calm. "We need to know—"

"You've got ten minutes to decide. No cops, no security guards. I see a single uniform, I'm outta here."

"But—"

"Ten minutes."

She hung up on me. I looked at Trey. "Game change."

I gave him the summary. He listened. He pulled out his phone and called Marisa, explaining in succinct no-nonsense language. Then the conversation became one-sided.

"Yes, I realize that, but…yes, I'm willing, but this isn't a decision I…Very well. I understand."

He tucked the phone in his pocket and didn't say anything.

"She told you to go, didn't she?"

He shook his head, baffled. "She said it's my decision."

"What?"

"She said I'm on the ground, not her. She said it's my call because she's up to her elbows with Audrina and Reynolds right now. Her words."

I was a little stunned. Leave it to Marisa to pick the worse possible time to start treating Trey as a partner. Because Trey didn't do instant decisions. His decisions required hours of sifting, sorting, integrating, charting.

I peeked at his watch. Eight minutes.

"So what do we do?" I said.

"I don't know."

He moved to the window and stood to the side, pulling the sheer curtain back slightly. The courtyard lay below, square and golden and rimmed with tiny pearl-toned lights, tossing in the rain-spiked gusts. A dozen yachts bobbed in the inky water. It had all looked so innocent from our balcony. Now it glared like ground zero. Hope tapped her foot, checked her watch.

Seven minutes.

Trey went into assessment mode. "It's relatively protected as a meet point. Two access zones—one from the courtyard, a second from the dock. The dock is unsecured, no doubt why she chose it, but the rain has kept the foot traffic down. There's one problem."

"What?"

He pointed to the left, beyond the trellis. "Limited sight range. There's a blind spot just past the dock entrance. Someone could be waiting on the other side of that wall, concealed by the foliage."

I saw the danger zone exactly as he described. "Shit."

"Exactly."

I stomped my foot. "Damn it, Trey, this isn't about some artifact anymore. That bitch needs to be behind bars."

"I don't have that authority."

"But you could detain her, right?"

"Not unless she presents imminent danger to others. Which she doesn't."

He stared down at Hope. I stopped talking and started considering my words very carefully. I was treading on the edge of the phrase that would decide for him—life or death. Once that clause was evoked, there was no going back. Trey was a straight line to action, all his rules flying out the window.

"That woman is wreaking havoc wherever she goes. If we can put an end to it by getting whatever she has away from her, then we should, before she gets me in any more trouble, or worse, gets another innocent person killed. But it's not worth doing anything stupid. And from what I heard you say, going down there with a blind spot is stupid."

He examined the courtyard again. "There is one solution."

"What?"

He pointed. "Our suite is there—corner window, seventh floor balcony. From that perspective, I could see the entire area. If you stayed here while I went there, I could surveil the blind spot before proceeding to the meet point."

I followed his finger. "Then you could go down to the dock entrance using the back stairwell, staying under cover the whole way."

"Concealment."

"Whatever. With all those trellises and ivy, there's no way for a sniper to get a sight line."

He blinked in surprise. "You read the manual."

"Of course I did."

"Good. Very good." Then he checked his watch. "Six minutes."

I cursed again. I knew he'd do whatever I told him. If I said stand down, he'd stand down. If I said go, he'd go. Damn Marisa.

He looked at me, waiting. I shook my head.

"You have to decide, Trey."

"I can't."

"You have to."

He blew out a breath. "Tell me what to do."

"Trey—"

"Please."

I took a deep breath. I was going to ream Marisa out when this was over. "Fine. We go. But only if you think it's safe."

"It has an acceptably low level of risk. Nonetheless." He slipped the H&K out of his holster and pressed it into my hand. "Take this. I'll get the spare in the room."

I held his gun, warm from his body. Suddenly everything seemed real. Too real. Suddenly I wanted to crawl into that metaphorical box I'd warned him against.

He scanned the courtyard once more. "You wait here at the window, but keep an eye on the ballroom. This could be a diversion. Let me know if you notice anything out of the ordinary."

"Okay."

"But don't leave this spot." Trey looked me in the eye. "We stick to the plan. No deviations. You do not move from this window until I call you. Do you understand?"

I hid the gun in the folds of my dress. "I understand."

He wasn't even pretending to be trusting. He analyzed my mouth, my eyes, the tic of each facial muscle. I let him read the truth lying on my face. There wasn't anything that could get me away from that window until he called.

I turned my attention to the courtyard. "Go. And be careful."

He left me standing alone in a hotel ballroom surrounded by men and women pretending to be dead sympathizers to an armed rebellion. I was among the doomed and blinkered and blind, deliberately unaware of the crashing violence roaring down on them, holding onto their illusion even as it dragged them to the bottom of the river.

I called Hope back. "Trey's coming to get whatever the hell you have. Stay where I can see you. And if this is a trick, I will spit and roast you, you hear me?"

She hung up. And I took my spot at the window, the gun in one hand, the cell phone in the other.

Chapter Thirty-nine

The ball swirled around me. I watched the window of our suite, waiting for the light to go on. And then I realized it wouldn't. Trey would find his way in the dark. Behind me a polka roared to life, pierced by a shriek of feminine laughter. I scanned the ballroom quickly. Nothing unusual, only the dancers in a black and white blur. I looked back at the courtyard.

Hope had vanished.

My stomach lurched. I punched in Trey's number. He answered on the first ring.

"Don't do it," I said. "It's a trap. Or a ruse. Whatever it is, she's gone."

"No sight of her?"

"None."

"Stay where you are. I'm on my way back to the ballroom. Let me know if you see her."

"Where are you now?"

"At the hotel room. I'll get my spare gun and be right down."

He hung up, and I saw the light go on in our suite. He'd been two minutes from the courtyard. I took a deep breath of relief, feeling my ribs strain against the corset. I was done. Forget Hope. Forget Savannah. I was ready to be back in Fulton County.

The lights on the dock flickered with the rising wind, and the light in our room went out. Hope did not appear, and I didn't budge from my vantage point. *Don't leave the window, not for any reason.* I held my breath, waiting for a scream, a cry, the crack of a rifle. But nothing happened. The only sound was the band behind me and the voices of the guests.

No Trey. I scanned the ballroom again. Still no Trey. I called his phone. No answer. I looked down into the courtyard. Nothing.

"All right, Trey," I muttered, "what are you up to?"

I gave him sixty more seconds. I counted them off in my head one by one, willing him to appear. When he still wasn't back in the ballroom, I hiked up my skirts, hid the gun in the folds of my skirt, and made for the hotel room, instructions be damned.

◇◇◇

The lights were off when I opened the door. "Trey?"

No answer. I bustled to the window and pulled the curtains back. The courtyard remained deserted. I reached for the desk lamp with one hand, still holding Trey's gun with the other. Damn it, why wasn't he answering his phone?

I examined the desktop. Nothing seemed to be missing, but the pens clustered in a pile like loose kindling, and the edges of the folders were skewed and uneven. Not how Trey left his desk, ever.

Our room had been searched.

I cursed and called him again, cursing louder when it went straight to voice mail. "I don't know what you're doing," I said, "but we've got a bigger problem than Hope. Someone's gone through your files. Call me back ASAP."

I turned on the floor lamp. And my stomach plummeted.

I saw the sofa cushion on the floor in front of the bar, the crooked chair. I went into the bedroom. The search had gotten sloppier in here. My suitcase lay like a gutted fish. The comforter crumpled at the foot of the bed. I reached to turn on the bedside lamp, but I couldn't find it.

Then my foot crunched broken glass. Not just a search. There had been violence here.

I took a deep breath and willed myself calm. I called Trey again. And standing there in the darkened room, I heard a soft vibration. I got down on all fours on the broken glass and followed the sound under the bed.

Trey's phone.

My heart stopped, then hammered. I reached under the bed and pulled it out with a trembling hand. I was going to be sick, pass out, scream, cry. I breathed until the worst of it passed, then stared at the phone. How had it gotten under the bed? Where was he? *Slow down*, I told myself. *Think*. There was a way to figure out what had happened. He'd shown me himself, the two of us in bed, the rain lashing the window.

I pulled up the password sign-in with shaking fingers. What was the formula? Okay, it was Saturday, Saturday was the seventh day. No, the sixth. What was the date? The fifteenth. I typed in the words, then fed that into matrix six. I hit enter, got a nine digit code. I entered that.

Access approved.

I sobbed once in relief. I was in. I scrolled down the library until I saw the file. I clicked it.

It began with the door opening. "Find it," a voice said. Male. Monotone. "Start with the safe, then the bedroom. I'll post up at the elevator."

The door closing, the sounds of searching. Then something muffled and unintelligible. A radio? A different voice suddenly. "Who? Fuck." An electronic crackle. "Seaver's on his way. Go to Plan B."

And then twenty seconds later, Trey was in the room. I heard the door open and close. Heard the last snatches of our phone conversation. Silence. Then there was only the sound of blows, and grunts, the whiplash of flesh colliding with flesh, the hard reverberation of bodies.

Trey's voice next, strained from exertion, but calm. "Who are you?"

Not people he recognized. The first clue. They didn't answer.

Trey again. "You're law enforcement, both of you. Savannah metro uniformed patrol."

"Not tonight, we're not. Now you gonna come easy, or you gonna make it hard?"

No response. A shuffle of footsteps, more fighting. The golf clubs tumbling, the thunk of metal on flesh.

Somebody hissed in fury and pain. "Goddamn fucker broke my arm!"

Satisfaction jolted me. Trey could hurt people, and I wanted him to hurt *these* people, I wanted to hear him break every one of them. But I knew that wasn't how things had ended. My stomach clenched, knowing what was eventually coming, ordained by the empty room.

There were two of them, one of him. They were cops. They had guns, and he hadn't made it to his weapon yet.

Something unintelligible, then Trey again. "What do you want?"

"You."

"Why?"

"Because that's the order."

"Whose order?"

A shuffle of feet. More meaty blows. Another sound, a hard slap against the wall, muttered curses, another crash. More grappling, the hotel door opening and slamming shut. A new sound, a muffled rapid clicking. The thump of a body hitting the floor. Silence.

I started shaking.

The first voice again, still monotone. "Get him in the cart. Now."

More noises, frantic and hurried. Dragging, muttering, a curse from the man with the broken arm.

Anger burned in my chest. I would kill them. I wanted it more than I'd wanted anything in my life.

"Tape him tight."

More muffled sounds, banging and clattering. The rip of duct tape, the door shutting, the hiss of silence. I shut off the recording.

They had Trey. I'd sent him right to them.

I rocked back and forth on the floor. In all that uproar, he'd found a way to leave me the phone—a key and a clue and a warning, all rolled into one. He needed to leave it so that they wouldn't take it from him later. He needed me to know that the bad guys were Savannah metro cops, in uniform. Cops he didn't know. Three of them.

A noise then, my own cell phone, ringing. I knew who it would be before I put it to my ear. I swallowed hard and willed myself calm.

"What do you want?" I said.

The monotone voice was unemotional. "You have the document?"

"I don't have anything. We—"

"Then find it. You have two hours, if you want him back. Don't call the cops. Don't call your detective friends. Don't call 911, or we take him apart piece by piece, understand?"

I closed my eyes. Focus. Think. Listen.

The voice grew firmer. "I said, do you understand?"

"Yes."

"Good." The voice softened, calm, persuasive. "There's no reason he has to die, not if we keep things simple. Can you do that?"

"Yes. Please let me—"

"We'll be in touch."

The line went dead.

I sat in the rumpled wreck of my dress, phone in hand. Two hours, they'd said. I had two hours to find Hope and convince her to give me whatever it was she had.

My phone vibrated in my hand again. I stared at it for a moment, lost, dazed. I put it to my ear.

Hope's voice was angry. "I told you not to call the cops!"

A bright fury rose. "We didn't!"

"Liar! They were there, I saw them, the same ones. I told you—"

"You know them?"

"What?"

I licked my lips and spoke as calmly as I could. "Listen to me. We didn't call those cops. They were already there. And they took Trey. So if you know who those men are, you'd better tell me and tell me quick."

Her voice wavered. "I don't know who they are, but I know…I know…"

"What?"

"They're cops, bad ones. One of them shot Winston. You can't—"

"I need that Bible, Hope."

"It's not the Bible they want."

"Whatever it is. Give it to me. Now."

"I can't, they'll—"

"I don't goddamn care! I need it or they'll kill him, and I swear to God, if they hurt him, I will track you down and I will end you!"

"This isn't my fault! I needed money, that's all!"

I closed my eyes. This was an opening. "I'll get you money, however much you need. Just give me—"

"I can't! It's all the leverage I have now! If they come for me—"

"Hope—"

"They're dangerous!"

"So am I. You have no idea."

"I can't!"

I took a deep steadying breath. "Hope, I will give you enough money to vanish. You don't ever have to show your face around here again. But I need whatever it is you have, or they'll kill us all. Me, Trey, you. You have to give it to me."

A muffled sob at her end, then her voice, almost a whisper. "Meet me at our old break spot behind the tattoo shop. One hour. Bring ten thousand dollars."

Then she hung up. I wanted to throw the phone against the wall, but I couldn't. I closed my eyes and willed down the sick creeping horror. No official channels. No Phoenix. No best friends, no reluctant helpmeets. Not even Garrity could save me this time.

Because the bad guys were cops. Trey had made sure I knew that, and Hope had confirmed it. I examined my phone. Could they be listening? Did rogue cops have access to that kind of technology?

I didn't know. I got angry then at all the things I didn't know, at the situations I found myself in. Hope's refrain was my refrain—I hadn't meant for any of this to happen—and like Hope, I was in way over my head.

But I knew where I needed to start. There was only one person who could help me now, and I was willing to pay whatever price he asked.

I stood up and shucked the ridiculous dress, kicked it in the corner. I peeled the corset off, tossed it on the heap. I got jeans and a t-shirt. I went to the safe for my gun, but it was empty. Ransacked too. Luckily, I had Trey's H&K with me, and a fresh mag.

I dressed quickly, then pulled Trey's new leather jacket from the closet. I put the ammo in one pocket, the nine-millimeter in the other. The jacket didn't fit well, but it was tangible and comforting and smelled like Trey.

I practiced a draw in front of the mirror. It was awkward and slow, and I knew I'd have to do better in the real world. I barely recognized myself—my eyes dark with smudged make-up, my hair tumbling from its bobby pins in tangles and tendrils. I looked haunted and strung out, wild and desperate.

Like a woman capable of anything.

Chapter Forty

Boone's place lay on a peninsula between Talahi and Whitemarsh Islands, at the end of a winding path that looked nothing like a driveway and everything like a dent in the underbrush. But the road was true, and it had only one destination once you were on it. The cat briars tangled thick at the edges, every foot I drove taking me deeper and deeper into the untamed.

The rain came down harder, and the wind rose with it, thrashing the slender branches of the water oaks into a frenzy. I clutched the wheel, barely able to see six feet in front of me. Finally, I rounded the first curve and saw the dock stretching into the water. Another curve and the house came into view, a two-story Lowcountry, built on pilings so that the underneath was open to the marsh. Unlike most such houses, however, Boone's was surrounded by a high stone gate with razor wire along the top.

I drove the Camaro right up to it, got out, and banged on the doors with my fist. "Boone! Let me in!"

The security camera to my right swiveled back and forth. I stood under it and looked directly into the lens. "I swear I will stand here screaming until someone opens this gate!"

The side door opened, and Jefferson stood there. "Goddamn it, Tai, what—"

"I need to see Boone."

"It's too late, he—"

"Now!"

Jefferson pulled out his phone and turned away from me. A hushed conversation ensued, then he held the door open. "Hurry up. Leave your weapons here."

"No." I pulled Trey's jacket tighter around me. "I'm family. I keep my gun. Now let me see him."

◇◇◇

Jefferson took me through the house to Boone, who was sitting on his back porch, watching the storm roll in over the marsh. The interior was low-lit, but I caught the details—the IV pole next to the armchair, the rows of medicine bottles on the kitchen sink—and I knew like a punch in the gut why he didn't receive visitors anymore.

He was stretched out on a wooden lounge chair, a blanket at his feet. An oxygen tank stood sentry beside him, and although he wasn't using it, I could still see the indentations against his nose where the clip had been. He looked yellow-gray in the dim porch light. In the shadows beyond that small illuminated circle, I saw a tall dark shape in the corner. Jasper. I ignored him and went right to Boone.

"They took Trey," I said.

"They who?"

"I don't know. It doesn't matter. I need money, and weapons, and I need them fast."

"Slow down, girl—"

"I don't have time for slow! Trey's been kidnapped, and I have to get this document from Hope so that I can get him back, and to do that I need money! You have to help me!"

Jasper didn't like any of this. He hovered in his corner of the screened porch, antsy and combustible. Jefferson maintained his position, calmer. They both looked ready to shoot me and be done with it.

Boone took the toothpick he was chewing from his mouth. "Were you followed?"

"Of course not."

He pointed at the ottoman. "Sit down."

"There's no time—"

"Sit!"

I glared at him, not sitting.

He swore softly. "I need you calm, girl, because right now, you're just meanness talking. You wanna hurt these people, I can see it in your eyes, and I can't work with that. So sit."

"Boone!"

"This is the place where we commit. And we'd better get that part goddamn right because we don't get another chance. Now sit!"

I sat, unable to fight the tears any longer. "They're cops. The ones who took him. That's all I know."

Boone blew out a breath. "Shit."

He swung his legs to the side, his face clean of all emotion. I knew the look. I'd seen it on Trey, when he'd close his eyes and count to three and then open them with that look, as fathomless and impassive as the ocean.

I met it head on. Sink or swim.

"Tell me what happened," Boone said, "start to finish."

I did. He listened. I tried to include the details he needed, leave out the ones he didn't.

I wiped my eyes. "That's all I know. Hope's going to meet me in the alley behind the tattoo shop in one hour. I'll get the document, give her the money, and then the kidnappers will call back with the location to make the trade."

"Tai—"

"Don't argue with me, I can do this. It's a swap, one-two, that's all. I'm not scared."

"Ain't about scared or not scared. Look at me."

I did. His voice stayed steady.

"I need you to listen, and listen good. This ain't a ransom, probably never was. There won't be any trade. You show up planning on that, and he's already a dead man, you hear me?" He took me by the shoulders. "They'll kill you too, on the spot. That's why they want you to come. Because it's a trap."

Tears pricked my eyes again, blurring the swaying palmettos, the porch light. "No." I shook my head. "No, that's not—"

"Look at me, Tai. Don't quit on me." Boone took my hands in his. "Tell me true, girl. Are you willing to do whatever it takes?"

I raised my eyes to his. "I would burn down the world for that man."

He squeezed my fingers, and I felt it swell in me, the deep power of saying yes to whatever it takes. I squeezed back. His grip was still strong, and it sealed a pact as solid as any ever made at any midnight crossroad.

I took a deep breath, blinked the last of the tears away. "Okay. What do I do?"

He stood. "Whatever I tell you to."

He motioned for Jefferson and Jasper, and they met him in the corner. They talked, their voices low and urgent. I watched, numb. My hands were cold and wet. I resisted the urge to wipe them on my jeans. I resisted the urge to scream. Boone motioned me over, and I went to his side.

"Jasper will take you to the dockhouse," he said. "You go inside, lock the door, and stay there. That leaves you alone, which I don't like, but I need all hands on deck. He'll leave the boat keys with you. Take it if you need it, but if it comes down to that, get the hell away and don't come back to the house, got it?"

I nodded.

"And you stay there until I come get you myself, understand?"

"But…" I gestured toward the ankle cuff.

"Jefferson can cut it off in five minutes, but not until it's time. No sense letting them know what's up until we have to." Boone touched the side of my face. "I'll come for you myself, or I won't be coming at all, you hear me?"

I nodded. I could feel the beginning of tears again. If I let them, they'd ambush me. But I wasn't giving them an inch.

Boone moved closer. Something young and vital sparked in him despite the pallor and shortness of breath. His eyes gleamed bright like the mouth of a spring.

"I won't come back without him," he said. "One way or another. I promise."

I stared at him, this killer and thief and smuggler, the rawboned rebel, this man who was my kith and kin, all the history I'd tried to whitewash. Who was fighting for me. Who was showing up.

"Whatever it takes," I said. I didn't recognize my voice. But I knew it was me talking.

Chapter Forty-one

I followed Jasper out toward the dock. He was all business, and angry to the point of fury. "Daddy shouldn't be messed up in this thing. I told Jefferson that, but does he ever listen to me. No."

He moved quickly down the trail. I was having a hard time keeping up. I'd known this land once, a long time ago. But Jasper moved fast, without any consideration. The rain didn't help either. It beat a steady tattoo on the ground, on the wide palm leaves, on the two of us.

"What's the plan?" I said.

Jasper pulled his rain hood lower over his face and kept walking. "Make the meet with that Hope woman. Get the document and give her the money. Wait for the kidnappers to call back. Then Boone makes the trade while me and Jefferson make sure they deliver their end."

"What if they just take the document?"

"They won't."

"What if Hope doesn't show?"

"She will."

"But—"

Jasper spun around and faced me, flinging raindrops. "You act like we ain't never done this before. That's why you're in the dockhouse, and we're dealing with the hard stuff. Now shut up and keep moving."

He wasn't happy to be mustered on my behalf, but he'd soldiered up. He'd always been clever in a mercenary way, and

I suspected he saw an opportunity to move up in his father's ranks, usurp Jefferson even. I fell in beside him, huddled inside Trey's jacket.

"They're cops, you know. Bad ones."

"I know."

"Why would cops want an old Civil War document?"

"There's paper worth killing for. Dying for too." His voice dripped with contempt. "You wouldn't know, though, would you?"

"What's that supposed to mean?"

"You abandoned your people. Now you want back in when things get tough. It don't work that way, cuz."

I didn't take the bait. He could dangle that KKK propaganda all he wanted. He was helping get Trey back; the rest didn't matter. But there was no way in hell I was standing around waiting while Trey's life hung in the balance. And it was time Jasper knew that.

I stopped. "I'm not gonna do it, you know."

"Do what?"

"Stay locked up in that dockhouse."

Jasper kept walking. "Daddy said—"

"Boone thinks I'm still twelve. But you know better. You know what I can do."

Jasper stopped. He examined me over his shoulder. "I reckon I do."

"I can drive, I can play lookout, I can shoot, I can fight. Let me help get him back because I swear to God, Jasper, nothing means as much to me as that man. Nothing."

He didn't reply at first. I couldn't see his expression in the dark, but I saw him nod.

"Sure, cuz. Whatever you say." He started walking. "Come on. But you gotta do what I tell you to do, you hear me? None of this go-your-own-way bullshit."

"Whatever you say."

As we neared the next clearing, a group of Boone's other men were coming up the path from the dock. They were ready for action too—dark rain slickers covering a multitude of weapons, heavy boots, gloves.

Jasper held out a hand. "Wait here. I've got to get some things straightened out."

The three men met Jasper in a huddle under the single light. Two were brawny hard men, but one was small and slim. Unlike the others, his face was pale and tight, and he looked sweaty, maybe even sick. Jasper talked, they listened. They nodded, agreeing to do what he told them. They did it resenting the hell out of me, but they did it.

They continued on to the house, leaving Jasper and me to head for the dock alone. I turned to watch them walk up the narrow path. The biggest one was laughing, but his friend was serious. The pale one shot one last look over his shoulder, glaring at me with more than resentment, more than hate even.

Satisfaction.

"Come on," Jasper said.

He hurried down the path into the woods, out of the light. I followed, Jasper's shape indistinct in the diffuse darkness. He moved swiftly and surely, accustomed to being in charge.

The realization came like a jolt of electricity. It left me heady, dizzy, almost paralyzed.

I stopped. "Wait."

Jasper turned around. "What's wrong?"

I put a finger to my lips, Trey's gun heavy at my side. The night and the wind and the rain played tricks. Half-light and half dark, shifting and impossible to trust. I moved closer to Jasper.

But not too close.

I lowered my voice. "Did you hear that?"

He froze. "Hear what?"

"Somebody's coming." I pointed. "Over there."

He peered into the dark marsh, his face obscured by the rain hood. I took one deep breath and slammed my heel sideways into his knee. He screamed and went down, one hand going for his gun, the other grabbing at me.

I snatched free. And I ran.

Chapter Forty-two

I ducked into the dark woods, branches slapping me, Spanish moss sloppy and wet in my face. I tripped and wrenched my ankle, dragged myself up, kept running. I heard Jasper behind me. The first shots rang out, and I ran harder, trying to get my bearings.

The dockhouse lay ahead, the main house behind, my car outside its gates. But the three men were there too, and Jefferson. And Boone, I admitted, whose allegiance I could no longer trust.

So I ran for the dock, lungs burning, chest tight. Behind me, Jasper crashed through the thickets.

The woods opened into the cove, and I saw the dock, Boone's sport fisher tied up at the end. I bolted for it, my footsteps pounding the wooden slats, just as Jasper cleared the woods. More bullets, two of them at my heels.

Too late for the boat. I ran for the dockhouse instead, yanked open the door and threw myself inside. I slammed the door shut, dead-bolted it. The dark loomed thick and heavy, and I crashed to the left, into the gear room. I heard Jasper's boots on the dock, his footsteps uneven from the injury, but leisurely now, no hurry.

I had to move quickly. I slid open the outside window and squeezed through the spider webs and dust, scraping my skin. I couldn't jump—the splash would have been a dead giveaway—so I shimmied down the piling into the dark water. It was high tide, but still the splintered wood and oyster shells tore the flesh of my hands.

I lowered myself into the water as lightning flicked cloud to cloud downriver. A few strokes took me under the dockhouse, then under the dock, where I surfaced beneath the slatted wood. Here it was shallow enough to stand, submerged up to my nose, the river bottom sucking at my sneakers.

Jasper limped down the dock. "I know you're in there, cuz." He reloaded, racked the slide. "And when I find you, you're dead, you hear me?"

Shaking violently, I put one hand on the butt of Trey's gun. I remembered the cell phones, both of them ruined now, and tears welled again. I prayed Jasper wouldn't look down.

He remained calm, relaxed. Boone's boat bobbed in the fractured waves, a thirty-footer with enough space to hold fishing gear for ten or marijuana for a hundred. Weapons too, guns and ammo and knives. And Jasper had the keys.

His voice echoed on the lake. "You run and your boyfriend dies, you know that?"

A crack of lightning, a roll of thunder, the rising wind, bladed and cold. The boat's bumpers rubbed against the dock, and I heard the slap-slap of water against its hull, the ticking of its engine.

"He's still alive, you know. For now. We had to hurt him pretty bad. And if you don't get your ass out here right now, we'll do worse." Jasper raised his voice against the wind. "I will make him die so hard, cuz."

The shivering intensified. I kept my hand on the gun.

Jasper moved from shadow to shadow, letting the darkness provide concealment. So he remembered I had a gun. He kept his own gun in low ready, like Trey did. Like professionals did.

"And it's not like you're going anywhere without the boat keys." He examined the dockhouse, then plinked one shot into it, shattering a window. Trying to flush me out.

I wanted to hurt him, kill him, over and over and over. I fingered the semi-automatic. It would be smooth and accurate, even wet. I could kill Jasper, take the keys and head for…where? Until I knew where Trey was, shooting Jasper was his death sentence. But we were already dead, it seemed, both of us. The rush to the inevitable, one agonizing second at a time.

Jasper kicked in the dockhouse door, punching the light on as he did. He disappeared inside, confident now that he could get the drop on me. He kicked the door to the gear room open next.

I swam silently to the swim ladder and hauled myself up with my mangled burning hands. My sneakers squished as I took my stance with Trey's gun—arms straight, chest forward, feet apart. I waited, dripping.

Jasper came out, framed for a second in the backlight. I squeezed the cocking mechanism, and he froze.

He gave me a twisted smile. "I knew you were around somewhere, cuz."

I waved the H&K at him. "Drop your guns, both of them. Right in the water."

He did, still smiling.

"Now the knife."

"I don't—"

"I know you got a knife. Drop it."

He reached for his ankle. I held the gun on him, cocked and ready, finger on the trigger. Trey's gun was like him—reliable and obedient and relentless. It would not fail me.

Jasper pulled out a hunting knife and dropped it in the water, where it disappeared with a soft plunk. He was being too submissive. Something was wrong.

"All this for a little old book," he said.

He opened his jacket. I caught a glimpse of burgundy velvet peeking from the interior pocket. He pulled it out with two fingers, carefully, its gilt-edge dull in the night. He tossed it on the dock. It made a thump as it hit the boards.

"There," he said. "All yours. You happy?"

I didn't reply.

He kept his eyes on me. "It's a piece of desecration. That old man in Florida took the Good Book and ruined it with the names of those traitors."

"You've had it all along."

"Only since my boys took it off of Winston's dead body. Found it in the briefcase instead of what we were looking for. I had plans for it, but not anymore. Not since your friend Hope called you."

He kicked it into the river. It splashed and hung at the surface, slowly soaking up the dark water, soon to sink and be gone forever.

"It's a fake," I said.

"I know. It would've been worth something, though, to somebody who didn't know better. But this ain't about money, cuz. That's what you've been missing all along."

"What's it about then?"

"Honor. Justice. By any means necessary."

"You're quoting Malcolm X."

The insult didn't hit home. "He knew that much of the truth. The races must be separate because they are not equal. And I will no longer swear allegiance to those who have abandoned the fight for the white man's rightful place."

"You mean the Klan?"

Jasper's eyes blazed. "Traitors. Prostitutes. Selling our name for profit, hiding behind the ACLU." He spat the words out like bitter poison. "They'll see. Judgment is coming."

"Oh it's coming, all right." I held the gun on him with both hands. "Right in your face unless you tell me where Trey is."

I squeezed the handle, and the cocking mechanism responded. Jasper shook his head, that infuriating half-smile twisting his mouth.

"You shoot me, and your boyfriend's dead."

"So you'll be telling me where he is now. And handing over your cell phone and boat keys."

Jasper pulled the phone and keys from his pocket. Before I could take a step, he dropped them, and the black water swallowed them whole.

"Doesn't matter where he is now," he said, "you can't get to him."

My vision reddened at the edges. I leveled the gun at his chest. He shook his head.

"You got a choice, cuz. We can go back to the house, get the car, and go get your boyfriend. Or you can kill me here, and he dies alone."

I tightened my grip. Here at least it was one-on-one, and until I figured out where Trey was…

And then I knew. I knew it as clearly as I'd known anything in my life. The dropped keys, the ticking engine, the three men coming from the dock. Jasper's calmness, Trey's explanation of the one security hole at the ball.

I steadied the gun. "Get in the dock box."

"What?"

"I said, get in the dock box."

Jasper didn't move. I put one bullet into the board in front of his feet and leveled the gun at his chest again.

"Don't fuck with me, cuz. I'm not that girl anymore."

He opened the lid of the coffin-shaped box and climbed in. Mounted at the end of the dock, it was a tight space, crammed with tackle and netting, smelling of brackish water and bait. I slammed the lid on top of him and shoved a fishing pole through the latch to hold it closed. Jasper spewed obscenities the whole time, kicking at the sides, his voice muffled through the plastic.

"He's dead now, bitch! And it's all your fucking fault!"

I aimed the gun at the box. I wanted to empty the magazine, give him a reason to scream. It seemed so right, so easy.

Instead, I put another bullet into the dock, inches from the box. "Shut up, Jasper, before I kill you here and now. I'm not that girl yet, but I might become her any second."

He shut up. I shoved an anchor of top of the box for good measure. He'd eventually kick his way out, but his crew would find him first most likely. Still, it would buy me enough time to get a head start.

I jumped on the deck of the boat, shoes squishing, ears ringing from the gun's blast. I put both hands to my mouth. "Trey!"

Chapter Forty-three

I did a quick survey—twenty feet of deck space, a head, the engine compartment, the pilot station. Fish cleaning area, gear boxes. Lots of hidden places too, for stashing contraband and weapons.

"Trey! Where are you?"

No answer. So I started with the engine compartment, dark and dank and smelling of oil. I pulled out my phone, and Trey's. Both were soaked and ruined, as I expected.

"Trey!" I yelled again.

I almost didn't hear it. One thump, then another, coming from the head. I yanked at the door. Deadbolted.

"Hang on, I'm coming!"

I took a quick inventory—oil cans, boxes, ropes. Then I saw the gaff hook. I hoisted it, and beat at the lock until it snapped. I snatched open the door, hit the light.

Trey raised his head. He was bound in the corner, back against the wall, hands behind his back. He was barefoot, his ankles duct-taped. They'd taped his mouth too, but his eyes blazed in the dingy light

I scrambled down the steps and fell to my knees in front of him. "Oh God, are you okay?"

He nodded. But he wasn't okay. He was in bad shape, his face mottled with blood. I steadied myself against the rising shock.

"Hang on." I reached for him. "I'm gonna get your mouth."

I grabbed the tape and tried to peel it off easy. Trey glared at me and stamped his feet. So I ripped it off in one slash. He exhaled sharply, his eyes watering as he coughed.

"Where's Jasper?" he said.

"Locked in the dock box."

"And the other three?"

"Up at the house. Are you okay?"

"Get a knife."

I scrambled back up the stairs to the fish cleaning station. I yanked open the drawer and pulled out a serrated knife, then clambered back down the steps and fell at his feet once more. I sawed at the tape, trying not to see the bruises, the slicing wounds.

His voice was raw. "They're Savannah metro, all three. One's the sniper."

"I know." I moved behind him with the knife only to see handcuffs. "Oh shit. Now what?"

"Give me a bobby pin."

It took me a second to make the connection. I sank my fingers into my tangled hair and pulled out a pin.

"Put it in my hands," he said.

I did as he asked. He stayed calm, his brow furrowed in concentration, but his eyes were electric.

He looked up at me. "Boone isn't a part of this. He doesn't know."

In the distance, I heard the pop-pop of gunfire, muffled yelling. My stomach dropped.

"He knows now."

Trey brought his hands forward and shook them out. His wrists were bloody and raw. He tried to stand, toppling as his legs gave way beneath him. I grabbed his shoulder to catch him, and he sucked in a jagged breath of pain.

"Trey?"

"Broken rib. We need to—"

The sputter of the radio on the bridge interrupted him. I heard Boone's voice, crackling and urgent. "Tai! Answer me, girl!"

I ran up the steps and snatched the radio. "Boone! Are you okay?"

"I'm fine. Where are you?"

"At the dock, with Trey. I—"

"Get the hell out. Me and Jefferson got one, but the other two are headed your way. Where's Jasper?"

"Locked in the dock box."

"You kill him?"

"No."

"Why not?"

"I don't know."

"He's a dead man anyway." Boone coughed, then spat, his voice rough. "Get to open water. And don't call for help. These guys are cops. They have friends we don't know about. If they hear a call go out…"

"I know. Can you get to the dock?"

Trey limped to the wheel, breathing hard, listening. The rain hissed, and another fork of lightning split the darkness.

Boone coughed again. "No, but we got things under control here. Go!"

"But—"

"Go, I said!"

In the distance I heard shouting and more gunfire. I shoved past Trey and hit the dock. I unhitched the dock line and threw it into the boat. Then I went to the console, remembering Jasper's smug expression as he'd dropped the keys into the water. He'd always underestimated me, the chauvinistic pig.

I pulled open the access panel. Reached in and snatched the wires off the back of the keyswitch, twisted the power wires together and touched them to the starter. The motor sputtered, and I moved to the wheel. I slid it into gear then threw open the throttle, and the boat roared into the dark river. Behind me, I heard Trey slam into the rail.

I looked over my shoulder. "Are you okay?"

"I'm fine!"

He pulled himself upright, then lurched for the cleaning station. He yanked at the drawer, tumbling silverware all over the
floor. Another thump, heavy, flesh against wood.

I picked up the radio again. "Boone! You there?"

"Still here. You on the water?"

"Good and gone. What the hell is going on?"

"Jasper decided to have himself a little armed rebellion against
the Klan. Jeff's here with me. He says this is about some speech,
that the selectmen council—"

I heard gunshots at Boone's end, Jefferson yelling.

"Boone!"

"It's okay, they can't get in here."

"Call for help, Boone."

"Like hell! He's got the cops in on this, the ignorant—"

"You got a cell phone?"

"Yeah."

"Look up Kendrick Underwood. He's Savannah metro,
straight and narrow. Call his home phone and tell him what's
going on. Use my name. Tell him to keep it QT."

I got no answer. I cursed and tried to call him up two more
times before I gave up. Behind me, I heard the metallic clash of
another drawer being dumped on the floor. Then Trey kicked
the cabinets. Hard. I heard other words, bad words.

"What's wrong?" I hollered.

"Drive the boat!"

"I'm just—"

"Goddamn it, Tai, drive the fucking boat!"

I hit the throttle. Behind me, the carnage continued.

"Sit down!" I yelled.

"I'm looking for the weapons cache!"

"Can't you—"

The first bullet pinged the hull. I dropped to my knees, hands
still on the wheel.

"Get down!" Trey yelled. "Now!"

"I am down!"

Behind me, I heard the buzz of a motor. One look revealed exactly what I didn't want to see—two of Jasper's men on a flat fishing skiff, right behind us and gaining fast. Another bullet shattered the left windshield. I cursed and tried to stay low.

"Trey!"

"I found the guns! Keep the boat steady!"

He jammed a mag into a semi-automatic .45, a gun like a cannon. I turned my attention back to the water as he dropped to one knee behind the leaning post.

"Damn it!" he said. "I can't get a shot!"

I stayed low. "Wait until we're through the next curve. You can get a side shot, take out the motor."

"I can't see them!"

"Hang on!"

I hit the docking lights, and the bright white beams illuminated the water behind us, including the skiff. It also made us a much easier target. Another shot pinged the canopy. Another flood of adrenalin as I slung the boat around the steep turn.

"Keep it steady!" Trey said.

"I'm trying!"

I wrenched the wheel. The boat heaved, heavy. The skiff followed. I kept my eyes forward, even when I heard Trey's gun, four quick staccato shots. I heard yelling behind me and risked another look. The skiff floundered in the water. I saw one man swimming for shore, the other staying on the boat. As I switched off the lights, another bullet zipped by, then another, but we took the next curve and moved out of range.

Trey limped to stand beside me, busy reloading. His left eye was a welter of blood, his lip split. Dried blood caked his collar, his shirtsleeves.

"They're down," he said.

He grabbed a spare mag and proceeded to fill it with ammo. We were alone on the waves, ten minutes from River Street, the rain a pummeling wall of water, the wind a banshee.

Trey kept his eyes on the gun. "There were two of them. There's a third man, smaller."

I switched on the running lights. "Boone said he and Jefferson took care of him."

"What does that mean?"

"I don't know." We hit the curve just past the bridge. Close now, very close. "How'd they manage to take you down?"

"The one posted in the hall had a stun gun."

I winced. "Damn. You can't fight a stun gun."

Trey slammed the mag into the chamber. "They put me in a laundry cart, taped and handcuffed. Then they locked me down below on the boat, at least one of them always standing guard."

"It's how they bypassed the security detail at the gate, isn't it? It's how they got into our room so easily. Fitzhugh's room too. They're cops, in uniform. Safety protocols don't work against the people who are supposed to protect you."

He reached for a new gun, a SIG Sauer nine-millimeter. "It wasn't supposed to be a kidnapping. They were looking for...I don't know what it is."

"Boone said something about a speech."

"They did too. But I don't know what that means."

I hauled the boat around a curve. "Neither do I."

He finished loading the nine and picked up a new gun. "I surprised them as they were searching. But Jasper—"

"Jasper was there?"

"No, he was with Boone on the island. They called him when I arrived. He decided I would make good leverage, so he told them to take me. I didn't know it was Jasper on the other end of the line, of course—"

"Or you would have told me. I know."

"Right." Another sharp glance. "How did you know where to find me?"

"Because you said the dock was the weak point in the security plan. Plus the boat's motor was still hot when I got there, with a quick and messy tie-up. But it wasn't until Jasper dropped the keys in the marsh that everything clicked."

He gave me another look. "I didn't know you could hotwire a boat."

"Are you kidding? Someone who loses keys as much as I do learns to hotwire all kinds of things." I sent him a look too. "I didn't know you could pick handcuffs."

"Garrity taught me. He also taught me to keep a spare cuff key in my shoe. Which they took, along with my wallet."

He was skipping the part of the story where he got bloodied and beaten. I couldn't see his eyes in the low light, but I knew they'd gone flat blue, steely and opaque.

"Where is Hope meeting you?" he said.

"In the alley behind the tattoo shop."

"Head that way."

He kept jamming bullets into magazines with machinelike efficiency. It took that long for me to realize what was happening. In the relief of finding him, of making the getaway, of hearing Boone's voice and knowing he was safe and on my side, I'd forgotten Hope. She was still in danger. And we were on a direct course for her location.

I felt sick to my stomach. "We're going to save her, aren't we?"

Trey opened another box of ammo. "I'll need to get as close as possible to the meet point. Where can you dock?"

I stared at him, the water peeling away in front of me. The men would have let Jasper out of the dock box, but he wasn't on that skiff. I knew what Trey had figured out. Jasper was headed for Hope, probably by car, the faster route. And when he found her, he would not negotiate or hesitate.

Did I care if Hope died? Not at that moment. Would I care later? No answer came.

"Trey?"

He didn't look up. "What?"

"Why are we doing this?"

"Because it's…because she's…"

I saw the confusion in his face. He wasn't a cop anymore. No more vows to protect and serve, no more wading into the fray. He could put the gun away and stand down and let the consequences play out. *I'm not responsible for other people's bad choices*, Hope had said. Maybe she was absolutely right.

"Boone's calling Kendrick," I said. "He'll respond."

"If he gets the message. If he gets there in time. If not, Jasper will kill her."

"That's not our problem."

"Nonetheless." Trey pocketed the mag, reached for another. "You stay on the boat, I'll—"

"You're not serious."

"Of course I am. You can't—"

"No, Trey, *you* can't. You can't do shit right now!"

He swallowed, eyes on his weapon. "But I have to."

And he did. This wasn't a choice for him, not like going down to the courtyard or not. This was Life or Death. He was trapped in the web of the right thing to do, and he could not get out, not even if he tried.

I licked my lips. "What if I told you not to?"

"Tai—"

"What if I begged?"

He flinched, his expression unreadable. "Please don't do that."

I wanted to scream. He'd stop if I told him to. He'd crawl into the box and close the lid, and I'd crawl in with him and we'd be safe forever and ever. There were lots of ways to die, and suffocating on your own safety was a slow but sure one.

I kicked the console, then kicked it again. "Aw, fuck."

"Tai?"

I exhaled sharply, then pointed to the map above us. "I'll dock here. The meeting place is a few hundred yards from there, down the side alley. I can make that pretty quick even lugging all this hardware."

"But—"

"We're in this together, Trey, or we're not in it at all. You know this."

He almost toppled, caught himself. Then he got his footing, and after only a second's hesitation, he handed me the SIG. "It's loaded, extra mags here."

He was all resolve suddenly, all plan and organization. He was saving someone in need, someone who didn't deserve it, but who would die otherwise. This was what he did. And it was the truest, realest part of him.

I shoved the gun into my empty pocket. "Thanks. Now hang on."

We were taking the curves as fast as the boat could go. The wind and rain combined into a gray-sharded onslaught.

Trey peered at the speedometer. "Can you go faster?"

"This thing draws four feet. This is the best we can do."

"Will we get there ahead of Jasper?"

"It'll be close. The road's faster, but we had the head start."

"When we get there, you go find Hope. I'll secure the boat and follow as quickly as I can. If there are authorities on the scene, don't engage. If it's Jasper, same response. If it's clear, then get Hope and bring her back to the boat."

This was the plan, and there wasn't an ounce of give in it. Things were simple for Trey now—no moral quandaries, no confusion, no competing priorities. He wasn't my boyfriend anymore. That guy wasn't showing up for a while. Which was just as well—we didn't have any room for him.

I grabbed the wheel. *Drive, Tai, drive the fucking boat.*

Chapter Forty-four

We pulled up to River Street, next to the floating dock. The storm had emptied the area, especially the west end where the tattoo shop was. I searched for cops. None, not even a patrol car.

I threw the line over the cleat. "Finish that for me, the other line too. Nothing finicky. We have to be able to untie quick." Then I handed Trey his familiar H&K. "Here. It's two bullets down."

"I've got spares." Lacking a holster, he jammed it in his waistband at the small of his back. "Go. I'm right behind you."

The boat bucked in the water, almost pitching me into the river. I jumped onto the dock, then scrambled into a run, my sneakers slipping when I hit the treacherous stone and concrete. River Street felt post-apocalyptic. Blurred lights, the ponderous rain-chilled darkness, the wind's unbroken yowling.

I ran for the tattoo shop, for the alley beside it. I stopped at the entrance and peered into the darkness, wiped my hair from my face, shielding my eyes with my hands. But I could see nothing at the other end, only shadows.

I looked behind me. No Trey, not yet.

I took the alley at a slow jog, my brain throwing horrors at me. Jasper waiting, gun pulled. Hope dead already, her blood a cooling puddle on the cobblestones. I reached the larger connecting passageway, open to the right and left, blocked in front by a sheer limestone wall.

And then I spotted Hope huddled under the shop's awning. She wore a gray sweatshirt over her dress, the hood pulled over her head, her bare white legs ghostly in the dim light.

I ran up and grabbed her arm. "We have to leave! Now!"

She snatched free. "I'm not going anywhere with you!"

"Jasper's coming. We have to get back to the boat!"

"What boat?"

"The one on at the floating dock. I—"

She looked over my shoulder and screamed. I spun around.

Jasper stepped from the shadows of the passageway. His gun glinted oily black even in the darkness, and he was wet and mud-pocked and lacerated from his tumble in the oyster beds.

He pointed the gun at me. "Stop right there, both of you. Hands in the air."

I did as he said. I thought of running, but there was nowhere to go. I thought of screaming, but he'd kill me where I stood.

"Take whatever you want and go," I said. "We won't stop you."

He shook his head. "Too late."

"You don't need us. All you need is that document, right? So take it and go!"

Jasper took two steps closer. I saw his next move coming, and I knew I'd have only one shot. I opened my hands, trying to remember the rules—eyes on Jasper, not the gun, don't give away the move—but I couldn't stop the tremors, everything spastic and surreal.

And then, in the mouth of the alley to Jasper's right, I saw the shadow materialize. I saw it in the corner of my eye, smooth and silent and inevitable, an assassin's shadow. I didn't look, though. I kept my eyes on Jasper. I didn't give a single thing away.

Trey's voice came from the threshold, soft and full of authority. "Jasper."

Jasper whirled, and the gun whirled with him. "Stop right there, or I'll—"

Trey fired, one-two-three. The first bullet hit Jasper's wrist, the second his shoulder. The gun flew from his hand as the third took out his left knee. He pitched to the ground, screaming. It was over before I could hit the cobblestones, but I hit them anyway, hands over my ears.

Trey closed the space in five steps and kicked Jasper's gun behind a stairwell. Then he pressed his own gun into the back of Jasper's neck and pushed him on his stomach.

Jasper went down. His bloody hand snaked toward Trey's ankle, but Trey slammed his bare heel down on Jasper's shredded wrist and twisted, hard, all of his weight behind it. Jasper screamed and tried to roll to his back, but Trey kicked him in the head, one solid strike that spun him on his back. He didn't move after that.

I lifted my head, but kept my belly against the ground. "Trey?"

He didn't answer. He was breathing hard, his gun trained on Jasper's chest. He cocked his head, evaluating, examining. I stood up and went to him. Hope remained slumped under the awning, sobbing, incoherent.

Trey looked my way. "Are you okay?"

"Yeah. Are you?"

"No."

Trey turned back to Jasper, who was sprawled unconscious on the cobblestones. He kept his hands wrapped around the gun.

I put a hand on his shoulder. "Trey?"

"Do you have your gun?"

"Yes."

"Good." He placed his own on the ground. "Keep him in your sights, finger off the trigger. And call an ambulance. Jasper needs an ambulance. I probably do too."

He dropped into a sitting position on the wet cobblestones, legs bent, arms folded across his knees. He looked on the verge of passing out—shivering, pale, eyes closed.

I knelt beside him. "I'll do it. You take it easy."

His voice was weak. "And call Garrity, please. Would you do that?"

"Of course. Now be quiet."

"Where's Hope?"

I looked. She'd vanished. I cursed. In the distance, I heard a wail of sirens. Police and ambulance and maybe even a fire truck from the sound of it. *Please let that be Kendrick coming to the rescue*, I thought. *Please let Boone have called a cop this one time in his life.*

I returned my attention to Trey. "Hope's run. Again."

"Oh."

"But help is on the way."

I lifted his head and pushed the hair from his face. His skin was ashen, and he shook like he had a fever. I put two fingers to the side of his neck. His pulse beat fast but steady.

"Tai? I'm going to lie down now. Is that okay?"

I stroked his forehead. "Lie down, boyfriend. I've got everything under control."

Chapter Forty-five

The next hour passed in a blur of official activity. The EMTs did a load and roll on Jasper, transporting him immediately to Memorial where a police team waited at the ER. The rest of us weathered the storm in Train's empty tattoo shop—the remaining EMTs, plus police, plus all the lawyers Marisa could drag out of bed at one a.m. on a Saturday night.

She'd arrived not long after the cops, still in her ball gown. She'd carried Trey's medical files under her arm, the thick documentation of all his now-normal abnormalities. Eventually she joined me in a relatively quiet corner of the shop, next to the stained glass window. Out back, we could see crime scene techs working under a white tent. Across the room, Trey sat on one of the leather stools, hidden from our view by a cluster of uniforms.

"He insists he doesn't need the ER," I said.

"I know."

"He wants to finish his interview with the detectives. He says he's fine, that he knows a non-displaced rib fracture when he feels one, and that all he needs is some pain medication and an incentive spirometer, whatever the hell that is."

"I don't care, he's going. As soon as the police get finished with him, that is. And they're taking their own sweet time."

"He's their best evidence now that the crime scene's a lake."

"I don't care about that either. We need to establish self-defense, which means we need to get him to the hospital ASAP and get his injuries documented."

"He's got a different priority for the time being."

Marisa blew out a breath of frustration and checked her phone. Back in Atlanta, she had Phoenix's tech support guy accessing Trey's phone records and doing a forensic reconstruction of the surveillance audio from the hotel room. She'd also contacted the company monitoring the surveillance cameras in the alleyway and had the footage being sent over by courier. She'd probably get her copy before the police did.

I'd told her what the video would show. She'd nodded in approval, then told the responding officers all about it. She'd used the phrase "former law enforcement officer" seven times, the words "highly decorated" three.

She shook her head in his direction. "He can't resist being a part of the investigation, can he?"

"He absolutely cannot. The men who did this to him are racist, murdering rogue cops. He's not going anywhere until he's shared every pertinent detail."

"But they have them all in custody! They caught two on the river, and there's one in the ER with Jasper, the one your uncle shot."

"Doesn't matter. In Trey's mind, it's the worst kind of betrayal, and he's going to help until he can't help anymore."

"God, I wish he'd stop thinking like a cop." She checked her phone again, texted a quick response, a frown on her face. "Speaking of, I heard Detective Garrity is on the way."

"He is."

"Good. Maybe he can talk some sense into him."

For the first time, I glimpsed the woman underneath the make-up, which was splotchy, and the perfect hair, which was falling in straggling wisps about her forehead. Her real face showed through the crumbling layers—plain, hard, weary. But she was a fighter, pragmatic, as unsentimental as gunmetal. And she was on Trey's side.

"Thank you," I said.

She didn't look up from her phone. "No problem."

The crime scene techs had already put him through the official gauntlet, right down to testing his hands for powder residue. I'd gotten the same treatment.

Marisa put the phone away. "I need to get ready for the press. You keep an eye on him, okay?"

I managed a small smile. "Like anybody could stop me."

◇◇◇

Thirty minutes later, Garrity blew into the shop, looking more official than I'd ever seen him. His hair was a wet red mess, but the rest of him was suit-and-tie. He had a similarly dressed companion, a wholesome-looking young man, brisk and bureaucratic. Garrity flashed his badge at the officer manning the perimeter, and the two came over.

I looked up at him. "I can explain."

"Shut up." He took me by the chin and examined my bruises. "Are you okay?"

I pulled away. "I'm fine, but I swear to God, Garrity, if you yell at me—"

"I'm not going to yell at you."

"—I will start bawling and fall to pieces in this floor, and I can't do that. Not yet." I squinted at him. "How did you get here so fast? Atlanta's four hours away."

"I was in the neighborhood."

"What neighborhood?"

"Brunswick. Now hush and let me look at you."

He examined me critically, cataloging every bruise and scrape. Behind him, the newcomer pulled out a fancy phone. He had the wide-eyed earnestness of a puppy, tempered by the service piece on his hip.

"Agent Garrity?" he said.

Garrity jerked a thumb over his shoulder. "Check in with the officer in charge. I'll be there in a second."

The young man did as he was told. Garrity turned back to me. The shield clipped to his belt said Atlanta PD, but the spanking new suit told a different story. As did his being in Brunswick, headquarters of the Federal Law Enforcement Training Center.

I widened my eyes. "*Agent* Garrity?"

"A courtesy title."

"So you're a feeb now?"

"No, a liaison to the feebs. That's Bryan, my new partner. He's a little eager-beaver, but smart as a firecracker. Plus he does whatever I tell him."

"Does this mean—"

"I'll explain later. Where's Trey?"

I pointed, and saw Garrity stiffen. "Sweet Jesus."

"Broken rib, cuts and bruises. He took several hits with a stun gun. The EMTs pronounced him concussion-free, however."

"What happened?"

I gave him the quick and dirty. Marisa's legal assistant moved in circles around Trey, who let her snap photos without complaint, his gashes and contusions lurid in the bright camera flashes.

"Marisa says Phoenix needs to document his injuries," I explained.

"She's right. He needs all the protection she can give him right now."

My temper flared. "Are you serious? Trey could get in trouble for this?"

"He's already in trouble."

"But—"

"He's not a cop, Tai, he's a civilian, so yes, he's in trouble. Which is why we're going to let Marisa get him out of it. She's covering her ass, which means Trey's ass gets covered too. And I may not like the woman, but she's fierce, smart, and thorough."

The camera flashed. Trey winced. When the assistant pulled his head around, he blew out an abrupt exhale of pain. I bit my lip to stop the tears.

"There's security footage. It will prove he's telling the truth."

"Good. But I wish we had another eyewitness."

"There's only Hope, and she's long gone. And good thing too, or I'd kill her myself. And I don't think even Marisa's team could acquit me."

Across the room, an EMT wrapped a bandage around Trey's forearm while the second held a stethoscope to his chest. Trey ignored them; he was explaining something to a uniformed officer, who was taking copious notes. Trey eventually took the clipboard from him and sketched a quick precise diagram, emphasizing some pertinent detail by tapping the pen against the paper.

"How is he otherwise?" Garrity said.

"I don't know. He seems calm now, but I swear, Garrity, I've never seen such…"

"What?"

"Fury. Kicking things, cussing, screaming at me. He said the 'fuck' word."

"He knows worse words."

"It's not that."

"What is it then?"

I shook my head against the memory. The anger burning out and cooling into efficient ruthless purpose. Trey's utter lack of hesitation, three bullets like a trip hammer, bam-bam-bam. Then the cracking open, the collapse.

"He shot Jasper three times—once in the knee, once in the shoulder, once in the wrist."

Garrity considered. "That could be either bad aim or expert accuracy."

"He had a lethal shot, the…what do you call it?" I rubbed my finger between my eyes. "The T-zone. Jasper was looking right at him. He could have gone for the heart too, clear shot at center mass. But he didn't."

"Not exactly a SWAT response."

"Not a vigilante one either."

We looked at Trey, exhausted but surprisingly alert. He was shirtless, his hair sticking up, a plastic ice pack pressed against the swollen rawness of his eye. He looked our way and cocked his head.

I turned to Garrity. "He asked for you, you know."

"He did?"

"Yes. When it was over. He said to call you. He said 'please.'"

Garrity froze. I saw the diamond flash of tears in his eyes, but he blinked it away fast. He started moving in Trey's direction.

"Come on," he said. "It's time for you to see him."

"But they won't—"

"They will for this badge."

I followed him across the room. It wasn't until he stood in front of Trey that his composure crumbled.

"Damn, my friend, you look like you stepped into a meat grinder." Garrity shook his head, his eyes bright again. "Heard you got one of them with a golf club."

"The seven iron, yes. Good concentrated force, excellent reach."

"Tai told me you had a sword."

"A very dull flimsy one that stuck in the scabbard. Utterly useless." He looked my way. "Is Boone okay?"

"That old fox?" I managed a laugh. "When he saw that one of Jasper's guys had a broken arm, he figured out what had happened and locked himself in the safe room with Jefferson." I shook my head. "I didn't even know he had a safe room."

Trey nodded in approval. "That's how safe rooms are supposed to work."

"He bolted it tight, then called Kendrick. I think it's the first time in his life he ever voluntarily called a cop." I stepped closer to Trey. "Are you okay? For real?"

I watched him do a quick evaluation. Blood pressure, pulse, respiration—check. Vision and hearing—check. All bloodthirsty impulses smoothed and tamed—check.

"I'm fine," he said.

But I remembered watching him step on Jasper's wrist, the fine bones shattering beneath his heel. I remembered him on the boat—brutal, efficient, powerful. He'd never been more dangerous, or more virile. My response was pure chemistry, the ruthless surge of hormones, all tangled up in flight and fight and…other f-words. I knew it worked that way for him too, that the twin currents of violence and arousal ran parallel, so close they opened into each other at the slightest rendering, flowing in a single artery.

But now? Now he was calm. He'd sublimated it again, like a trick of the light. I moved closer to him and took his hands. He turned mine palm-up and examined the damage, my fingertips pocked with splinters, bandages covering the nail gouges.

I reached for him, and he stiffened, the muscles hardening against my touch. I wrapped my arms around him anyway. Maybe his dangerous part was more dangerous than most people's. I didn't care.

"I'd have done anything to get you back," I whispered against his neck. "Anything."

I held him even tighter then. I knew it had to hurt, but he let me anyway. And we stayed that way until Marisa tapped me on the arm. She'd changed back into her black power suit, white-bloused, hair and make-up once again impeccable.

"You have a visitor," she said. "Two actually."

I looked behind her to see Kendrick standing in the doorway in beat-up jeans and a t-shirt, his badge pinned to his waistband. He held Hope tightly by the elbow. She was wet and dirty and handcuffed, and she looked both resigned and combative, like a polecat in a cage.

"Found somebody trying to steal your uncle's boat," Kendrick said. "ID says Tai Randolph. I'm thinking it's fake."

Chapter Forty-six

Hope glared at Kendrick. "I told you, I wasn't stealing the damn boat! Tai told me to get on it!"

"I suppose she told you to rip off the top of the console and try to hotwire it too."

"That wasn't me!"

"Right."

I stepped forward. "She's telling the truth, Kendrick. I told her to go there. And I hot-wired the boat."

Hope turned the glare on me. I saw no more glimpses of the smooth operator. Her hair was a clump of tangles, and blood streaked her sweatshirt. I realized with a start it was Jasper's, the spray from Trey's bullets.

Kendrick pulled something from under his jacket. "I suppose you can explain this too?"

He handed me a roll of papers the color of watery parchment. I took them to the counter and unrolled them gingerly. They were old, rain-dappled, the writing penned in looping old-fashioned lines.

I read the first few words, then stared at Hope. "Is it real?"

She stared back. "Winston went behind my back to get a bidding war started between Fitzhugh and the KKK for it. So yeah, I'd say it's real."

"You set him up."

"He deserved it." She wiped her cheek on her shoulder, leaving a stripe of mud on the sweatshirt. "When I found out he was trying to cheat me, I took that from his briefcase and left the Bible in there. I moved the forger's kit back under the counter where the cops could find it. And then I went to watch Winston try to explain himself to the Klan. But I didn't kill him. I had nothing to do with that."

I ran my finger along the powdery surface of the papers. They looked too decrepit to have inspired such mayhem and blood, and not just Winston's. Centuries of blood.

Trey rose, steadying himself with a hand on the counter. He examined the papers. "It's letterhead stationery. From the Marshall House."

"Yep. Exactly the same paper the police found in the forger's kit, which was the same paper used to make the fake treasure map, only that particular piece had its letterhead lopped off."

He tilted his head and peered closer. "It looks like notes for an essay."

"For a speech, actually, an infamous one. One that wasn't supposed to exist in any written form."

Marisa popped her hands on her hips. "Enough with the drawing room nonsense, what the hell is it?"

"It's the Cornerstone Speech."

"The what?"

I took a deep breath. "A speech presented by the vice president of the Confederacy, Alexander Stephens, in 1861. He delivered it a few blocks from here, on Wright Square, declaring clearly and specifically that the foundation of the Confederate nation was the superiority of the white race and its divine right to subjugate lesser races."

I'd lapsed easily into the smooth patter of the tour guide, the details drawn verbatim from my memory banks. I saw Wright Square in my head, green with spring. During Stephen's speech, it had been thronged with cheering white people, too many to fit in the building, all of them delighted to hear their superior nature championed by this officer of the Confederacy.

I stared at the paper, so genteel and innocent in appearance, so vile in its declarations. "Afterwards Stephens recanted most of it, said the press misquoted him. He said this from a Federal prison. During his visit to Savannah, he stayed at a private residence, but apparently, he spent some time at the Marshall House too, hanging out with other well-heeled rebels. And he made these notes while he was there."

Marisa shook her head. "But where have they been all this time?"

"Probably stuck in storage with other old papers when the Union converted the hotel to a hospital, eventually offered as a lot to anyone willing to haul them away. I'm betting our forger down in Florida picked everything up for cheap. It was only a bunch of old paper, after all. Except that to a forger, it was a gold mine of raw materials."

Marisa joined Trey and me at the counter. "That's it? Two people dead, multiple felonies on the tab, for…that?"

Every eye in the room went to the document. Not gold, not jewels. Four crumbling pieces of paper, hardly worth a second glance.

I handed the papers back to Kendrick. "Jasper was right about one thing—it wasn't about money."

Trey frowned. "What possible motive could he have had for stealing this from his own organization except to sell it and make money?"

"He thought it was his duty. He knew the Klan didn't want to honor the speech—they wanted to hide it."

The silence in the room thickened. Everybody stared at me, baffled. Except for Hope. She knew the score as well as I did.

I sat on the edge of the counter. "We're talking about the new Klan, a bunch of pamphlet-pushing revisionists. They've put a spin job on the entire Confederacy—it wasn't about slavery, they say, it was about state's rights, and they're not anti-black, they're pro-white." I pointed. "That piece of paper? It undoes every bit of propaganda they've created. Jasper started his own militia group within the KKK, remember? Something like the Cornerstone Speech may be inconvenient for the new Klan, but for people like Jasper? It's holy writ."

I remembered his words on the dock, the glow of the fanatic. He believed in the words on the old paper, had been willing to kill for them. By any means necessary, he'd said.

"Jasper was on the selectmen council," I said. "He was one of the few who knew the Grand Wizard was purchasing the Cornerstone Speech from Winston, and he knew what would happen to it if they did. So he and his militia buddies killed Winston and stole the briefcase before he could make the exchange."

I pointed to Hope. "Only the document wasn't in there, thanks to Hope here. So they started looking for it, thinking that if Winston didn't have it, Fitzhugh probably did. But Fitzhugh didn't—he was too busy trying to cover his own lying, thieving tracks. Next, they decided Phoenix had it. So they broke into Trey's hotel room. Hope saw them, in uniform, headed into the hotel from the dock. She thought I'd squealed on her and ran."

Hope didn't argue. A lot of the spit and vinegar had gone out of her, but her cunning remained. I could sense her juggling her options, trying to find an escape clause.

I moved to stand in front of her. "I still don't get it. You're smart. You knew what kind of evil bastards you were dealing with. Why didn't you drop this a long time ago?"

"I told you, I needed the money. The business is going under because John's an idiot, so the IRS is coming after me. Winston told me the Bible was a forgery, but insisted we could probably still find a buyer." Her eyes hardened. "He didn't mention the real document he'd found, oh no, he didn't breathe a word about that."

So that was the story—greed, revenge, stubbornness. Nothing new under the sun. I turned to Kendrick. "So now what?"

He shrugged. "Now we take her in."

"What?" Hope struggled in his grasp. "You can't stick me in jail! What if Jasper's got men in there?"

I folded my arms. "I have a hard time caring."

She was panting now, desperate. We'd been friends once. She'd been exactly this person then—charismatic and adventurous, selfish and devious—and she'd be this person forever. John too. Neither of them had changed one bit.

I looked over at Trey. Stalwart, patient, honest. Again and again he showed up for me, and again and again he would. John really was an idiot, but he had one thing right—my taste in men really had changed.

Hope noticed me looking in Trey's direction. "You can't put me in jail. You need me to testify." She licked her lips. "You help me, I'll say Trey saved my life."

My temper finally snapped its leash. "Damn straight you will. It's the only hope you have for a shred of leniency." I stepped closer, right in her face. "But we don't need you, we've got real-time footage. So let me put this in terms you'll understand. It's *your* neck on the line if you don't cooperate, not Trey's, so you'd best spill the truth, sister, every drop of it. You hear me?"

She froze, the reality of her situation finally knocking the perverse hard-headedness right out of her. She nodded, and Kendrick pulled her uncomplaining into the hall. I felt a surge of relief. Finally, somebody besides me was getting hauled downtown.

Trey watched them leave. "Marisa says I have to go to the ER now."

"I know."

"Will you come with me?"

I knew I'd spend hours in the waiting room chewing my nails, that I'd end up bumming a cigarette from some orderly before it was over, sucking it down behind some dumpster. I knew I'd drink too much bad coffee and fill out paperwork while the real action played out here with Marisa and Sergeant Kendrick and Federal Agent Garrity.

I patted his shoulder. "Of course, Trey. Whatever you need."

Chapter Forty-seven

I didn't sleep that night. I lay in bed beside Trey until Marisa came for him at nine to fly back to Atlanta. I helped him dress, biting my lip every time he sucked in a breath. He'd insisted on doing his job, however, on seeing it through until the end, and I couldn't deny him that.

I stayed behind to pack. I ignored my phone—most of the calls were from John, and I'd had enough of him. The hotel room became a revolving door of concerned friends and relatives and hotel staff. First Billie, who cried and hugged me, then Dee Lynn, who cussed and hugged me, followed by housekeeping with some complimentary room service and a delivery person with a pot of flowers.

Marigolds. No card.

So when I heard knocking yet again, I answered the door with a mite more attitude than I should have. "What now?"

Trey stood there. "I'm sorry. I turned my key in when I left."

"What the…get in here." I took his hand and pulled him inside. "I thought you were on a plane to Atlanta."

"I was. But then Garrity and his new partner showed up to handle things from there."

"Officially?"

Trey nodded. He was moving even more stiffly than when he'd left, and his eyes were glazed with pain. I led him to the sofa, and he sat.

"Garrity met me on the tarmac and told me he'd escort the flight back to the city limits. He told me I wasn't to argue." Trey leaned back gingerly. "He also said there are APD and FBI officers waiting to interview Reynolds."

"About the sword? Really?"

"Not about the sword. The fire."

I did a doubletake. "What fire?"

"The one in Audrina Harrington's collection room."

"Reynolds is an arsonist?"

"No, not Reynolds. Fitzhugh."

My memory flashed—Fitzhugh getting on the elevator, head high, saying that he'd take care of his problem himself. "Are you telling me Fitzhugh set her safe room on fire?"

Trey shot me a sharp look. "He tried to. But that room is protected by a liquid-to-gas fire suppression system. He panicked when the alarm tripped, inhaled the fluorochemical spray and went into shock. Audrina called 911. The EMTs called the police."

Trey related this story with an edge of satisfaction in his voice and the tiniest hint of a smile at the corner of his mouth. I suppressed my own grin.

"Is he okay?"

"Of course. The gas has a no-effect level of ten percent. Practically non-toxic."

"And the Harrington's collection?"

"Unharmed."

"Also full of fakes, isn't it?"

He considered how much he could tell me. "That's being determined by the Harrington's insurance adjustor. Which is why Reynolds is being interviewed, not because he's being charged with a crime."

"And Fitzhugh?"

"No charges filed, not yet. But Garrity says there will be, probably with RICO statutes since it's a multi-state investigation."

"So this is his first case as Agent Garrity?"

Trey nodded.

"You don't seem happy about this."

His forehead wrinkled. "In the past decade, there have been three Major Crime Liaisons with the FBI. The first went to prison for extortion. The second was gunned down in his driveway. The third resigned and moved to Los Angeles."

I winced. "Oh. That's not good."

"No, it's not. Garrity will be good. But the job is…"

"Problematic?"

He nodded. "Very problematic."

As was Garrity's first case, this stew of pride and greed and domestic terrorism. "So what will happen to the Cornerstone Speech?"

"It will stay in evidence until its rightful owner is decided."

"Which will most likely be the state of Georgia."

"Most likely, yes."

I felt a twinge of regret. So much for my fifteen percent finder's fee.

Trey pulled out his phone. "I'm officially on duty until the plane lands. Garrity said he'd let me know when that happened." The phone chirped at him, a text coming in. "Which should be about now."

Sure enough, it was Garrity, reporting that everyone was safely back on Fulton County turf. Trey loosened his tie and pulled it off. Another text came in. He cocked one eye at it and then stuck the phone in his pocket without response.

"Marisa?" I said.

He nodded.

"You're not taking it?"

"I'm off duty now." He shrugged out of his jacket, wincing as he did so. The shoulder holster went next, then the Phoenix ID. "Where did you put the codeine?"

I finished untucking his shirt. "You rest. I'll get it."

◇◇◇

We set out a little past noon, after some time on the couch for Trey and more sorting and packing for me. I'd run some quick numbers, and it looked like my hand-sewn underwear had fetched me a tiny profit, a fact I put in the win column. I'd tried to get Trey to go to sleep while I loaded the car, but he refused. Instead he'd watched the river. Quiet, deep in thought.

Now, he stretched out in the Camaro and tilted his head back against the passenger seat. I slammed the trunk and slid behind the wheel, noticing once again his little leather notebook open in his lap, a mechanical pencil stuck behind his ear.

"You're off duty, remember?"

"This isn't work."

"What is it then?"

"Not work."

He offered no further explanation. As I cranked up the Camaro, I slid a surreptitious glance at the pages. A list of some kind, neatly lettered. Trey saw me looking and closed the book, but he didn't put it away.

"Better not be work," I said.

Trey shook his head. I pulled out of the parking space, the morning-after sunshine as clean and shiny as a new penny. Trey faced the window, but I thought I saw that almost-smile at the corner of his mouth.

Instead of taking the interstate back to Atlanta, I crested the bridge and took Highway 80 instead, passing liquor stores and cotton fields and farms with giant Confederate flags as big as swimming pools. Trey watched the landscape pass. We had the windows down. His hair blew and tousled, but he didn't seem to mind. He closed his eyes and turned his face into the breeze.

Driving north to Atlanta felt like moving forwards in time. Despite the deepening autumn color, the air was temperate, with a satin-soft breeze, almost like spring. I knew better, though. Winter lay ahead of us, the fallow and the fallen time. Ashes to ashes, dust to dust.

From where I sat, I couldn't see the scrape along Trey's neck, or the swelling bruise at the back of his head. I could see the black eye, however, and the bandages along his forearm, covering the raw skin around his wrists. He was a map of pain and spilled blood.

But he was alive, and safe, and sitting next to me. And we'd been so close to some other ending.

The tears came hot and fast then. I wiped my eyes and blinked, trying to keep them back, but a sob bubbled up despite my efforts. And then the road dissolved before me in a watery blur, and I felt the whole of it coming together, the fear and relief and terror and gratitude and…the other thing.

I pulled the Camaro onto the grassy shoulder and rested my forehead on the wheel. I knew what had my heart clutched tight. All I had to do was look at Trey, and it sang in my head, the knowledge that I was deeply and totally and irrevocably…

I swallowed hard. Even thinking the words made me dizzy. I had to tell him, though. I owed him that much.

I took a deep breath and let it out slowly. "Trey?"

No response. I looked over. He was asleep, his notebook fallen open in his lap. For the first time I could see what he'd written clearly enough to read it. When I realized what it was, my chest went all soft and melty.

The reasons he was with me. He'd started a list.

Number five was sweet, number seven unexpected. And number thirteen? Specific. Very specific. But he'd put special emphasis on number one, which had been marked with an asterisk.

Showing up, it read.

My heart cracked all the way open then, but it kept beating. And my lungs kept pumping. And eventually my eyes cleared and the road opened before me with a bright clarity.

I reached over and double-checked his seatbelt. Smoothed his hair back from his forehead, even though I knew the wind would kick it into a mess again the second we hit cruising speed.

Then I pulled back onto the road and took us home.

Author Note

Savannah is a city full of stories—ghost stories, gossip stories, old stories, new stories. Some really happened, and some are burnished with the bright hand of invention. But they're all true, including Tai Randolph's version.

The Westin Hotel does sit on Hutchinson Island, on the banks of the Savannah River, right next to the Savannah International Convention Center. They're both lovely places, very well-maintained and security-conscious. Any nefarious activities at either place are entirely the product of my imagination and have no basis in reality. The Savannah-Chatham Metro Police Department is equally blameless for the villains I helped to infiltrate its forces.

Most of the places I mention do exist: River Street, Wassaw Island, Turner Creek, Oatland Island Educational Center, Skidaway Island State Park, The Olympia Café, the Marshall House Hotel. Café Gelatohhh in City Market really does serve the best gelato in the city. I especially recommend the buttermilk version—tell Joel I sent you and he'll probably treat you extra special.

Club One is very real also, and has great pool tables in the basement. If you're looking for The Speakeasy, however, you're going to have to look elsewhere. It does exist, but its location really is secret. If you manage to find it, remember...shhhhh.

And if after reading about German-Thai fusion, you find yourself with a craving for bratwurst curry, don't look for it in

Atlanta—head to the Schnitzel Shack in downtown Rincon, Georgia, just up the road from Savannah.

Tai's history is on the mark as well—the curse, the ghosts, and the Cornerstone Speech itself are all very real even if intangible. No copy of the speech exists, however, and finding such a thing would be a major historical coup, as would digging up the Lost Confederate Gold. There are thousands of people looking; maybe one day some intrepid explorer will find the map that will lead him—or her—to the X that marks the spot.

To receive a free catalog of Poisoned Pen Press titles, please contact us in one of the following ways:

Phone: 1-800-421-3976
Facsimile: 1-480-949-1707
Email: info@poisonedpenpress.com
Website: www.poisonedpenpress.com

Poisoned Pen Press
6962 E. First Ave. Ste 103
Scottsdale, AZ 85251